Sons and Princes

James LePore

James LePore

THE
STORY PLANT

The Story Plant
The Aronica-Miller Publishing Project, LLC
P.O. Box 4331
Stamford, CT 06907

Jacket design by Barbara Aronica Buck

ISBN-13: 978-0-9841905-2-2

Visit our website at www.thestoryplant.com

First Story Plant Paperback Printing: May 2011

Printed in the United States of America

This book is dedicated to my daughters, Erica, Adrienne and Jamie, with love, and with gratitude for choosing me to be their father.

Sons and Princes was not a secret as I was writing it, but only my editor, Lou Aronica, saw it in progress. The heart of the book is mine, but its shape and direction are the result of his patient and clear-eyed professionalism. Not to mention his loyalty. My wife Karen is the first angel to come along, Lou is the second.

Instead of thy fathers shall be thy sons, whom thou shalt make princes in all the earth.
—Psalm 46:16

Book I
Joe Black

1.

Joe Black Massi's funeral had been a singular experience. His body, or rather sufficient parts of it to make it identifiable, had been found in a suitcase in the Gawanus Canal in Brooklyn on the first day of the year 2003. The old man, sixty-six and with a long list of enemies, had been missing for a month. One arm, one leg and the torso had been consecrated by the church and buried in a crowded cemetery in Bloomfield, the blue collar town in North Jersey where Joe and his wife Rose had settled after spending thirty-five years in the same apartment on Carmine Street in Greenwich Village. There had been no wake or mass, just a ride from a local funeral home to the cemetery, where a rented but kindly priest had incongruously commended Joseph Massi Sr.'s soul to God. Under a forbidding gray sky, Joe's sons, Chris, forty-two, and Joseph Jr., thirty-two, and his wife, Rose, her hand shaking, her face white and grim, had dropped white carnations onto the casket and watched as it was lowered into the ground, three hearts burdened with Joe Black's legacy of anger and bitterness. Of the family and friends they had invited, only a handful had appeared. Joe Black was a solitary man, and his career as a Mafia assassin had created a wide gulf between him and even those who were close to him.

Now, four months later, Chris and Joseph were back on the same headstone-dotted hillside to bury Rose, felled by a heart attack on a bus ride to Atlantic City with a group of friends. For Rose, there had been a wake, modestly attended, her body surrounded by floral arrangements, prayed over; her friends and relatives chatting quietly for two days and two nights in the hushed rooms of the same funeral parlor that had dispatched her husband. It had rained heavily overnight, and the morning sun shone unfiltered onto the cemetery's newly green lawn and burgeoning shrubs. The sky overhead, scrubbed clean by the rain, was a pale, diaphanous blue. Behind the mourners, at the crest of the hill and to their right, stood an old chestnut tree, its spreading branches reaching almost to Chris and Joseph, who stood side by side watching as thirty or so people filed past the casket, each laying a red rose on it before moving on. Among these people were Chris' ex-wife, Teresa, his two children, Tess, sixteen, and Matt, about to turn fourteen, Teresa's father, Anthony "Junior Boy" DiGiglio and his wife, Mildred. Chris, the eldest son, was the last to drop his flower, the last to say goodbye to Rose.

Turning from the casket, he saw Tess and Matt standing in the bright sunlight about twenty yards away. Beyond them, Joseph and Teresa were walking away, arm in arm. Chris had grown used to seeing Tess as a young woman. In her simple black dress, lightly made up, she was a replica of her mother, her high cheek-boned Mediterranean beauty needing very little to enhance it. Matt was a different story. Tall like his father, but gangly and coltish, he was transformed by his dark blue funeral suit, white shirt and simple tie into a startling preview of the man he would be. It put Matt in a new light, and, given his son's attitude lately, that light was troublesome to Chris.

He had watched his son carefully over the last two days. In unguarded moments he was, like any thirteen-year-old boy, awkward, shy, brash, dopey and vaguely panicked about his status between boy and man. When he thought he was being watched or when approached by people, (more than one of whom commented on the remarkable resemblance between Matt and his paternal grandfather, Joe Black Massi), he was a painfully obvious caricature of gangster coolness.

Chris reached his children, kissed them, then turned and walked with them to the limousine that would take them to Vesuvius, a Southern Italian restaurant on the Newark-Bloomfield border that Joe Black and Rose had begun to frequent when they moved to Jersey. There, a post-funeral luncheon was to be held.

The owners of Vesuvius, a couple in their fifties, the man pot-bellied and balding, the woman stout and amateurishly made up, had put on their best clothes and were waiting in the bright sun on the sidewalk out front when the limousines arrived. They were at the same time proud and very nervous at the prospect of Junior Boy DiGiglio, a true Mafia don, visiting their simple trattoria. Standing beside them were two men in the employ of DiGiglio who had spent the last two hours thoroughly going through the restaurant and the apartment above it. As the limos and cars bearing the mourners arrived, a gray van pulled up to the curb across the street and two men in tan suits emerged, each carrying a camera with a zoom lens attached. The don waited in his limo as his driver and bodyguard, both killers, got out, introduced themselves to the owners and greeted their colleagues. When Chris and Joseph emerged from their limo, DiGiglio did the same and allowed himself to be introduced to the owners by

Chris before heading into the restaurant. The rest of the party had also arrived and were drifting inside in twos and threes. While this was going on, the men in the tan suits were taking pictures, concentrating on the famous Junior Boy DiGiglio, whose public schedule it was usually impossible to know in advance, but also snapping away at Chris, Joseph, Teresa, Mildred (who had arrived with her daughter) and even Tess and Matt.

Vesuvius, its facade drab and inconspicuous, in a neighborhood that had been slowly losing ground to urban blight for twenty years, was surprisingly elegant inside, with real linen and good silverware on the tables, each one of which was centered with a long-stemmed red rose in a simple glass vase. This last was a bit much for Chris, but it was Joseph's idea so he said nothing. Later, when he learned that the owners, much taken by Rose and her imperious northern Italian ways, had supplied the flowers and vases free of charge, he was glad he had kept his counsel.

At the back of the room were French doors that led to a brick-walled courtyard, where less formal tables, painted black, were set around a tall grape arbor whose vines were just beginning to climb and go green. The day was warm and beautiful, the first after almost a week of rain, and the owners had thought that al fresco might be a welcome touch. They beamed when they saw that Chris and Joseph were pleased with their arrangements. A trestle table under the arbor was loaded with food, the bar inside was open, and soon people were drinking and talking while waiters in black slacks, white shirts and black bow ties were passing around trays of hot and cold hors d'oeuvres. The restaurant was closed to the public. Joe Pace, Junior Boy's driver, stood quietly just inside the front door, while the don's bodyguard, Nick "Nicky Spags" Spagnoletti, calm and alert, placed himself a few steps behind and to the side of DiGiglio, an attitude and position he would maintain the entire day.

Joseph Massi, now thirty-two, had been strung out on heroin on and off since he was eighteen. He claimed to be clean at the moment, and Chris believed him because he had come to learn the signs. He watched as his charming and handsome younger brother chatted up the DiGiglio faction, starting with Mildred, whose facade was, as usual, sweet and indecipherable, then moving on to Nicky Spags, who nodded absently once or twice before brushing him off, settling finally into a conversation with a thick-necked capo regime named Rocco Stabile, who had taken a liking to both Massi brothers when he first met them years ago.

Chris made his way around the restaurant thanking people, kissing second and third cousins he hadn't seen in years and making small talk, some of it, as with the now dispersed faction from Carmine Street, enjoyable for the honest nostalgia it added to his otherwise confused mix of feelings. Ending up in the courtyard, he saw that Matt had joined Joseph and Rocco. He watched intently for a moment as they chatted under the far right corner of the arbor, the dappled shade cast by the grape vines overhead fluttering across their faces. Matt, his black hair slicked back, his suit hanging loosely on his reed-like body, nearly a head taller than Rocco, was making his usual transparent attempt at the studied casualness of the confident tough guy, a pose that grated on Chris even though he had seen it a dozen times in the last forty-eight hours. Then he spotted Teresa alone at a table in the far left corner, and walked over to join her.

"So," he said when he was seated, "have you thought about it?"

"It's not something I can decide in one night, Chris."

"Look at him over there," Chris said. "Who do you think he's trying to emulate, the junkie or the Mafia thug?"

"Chris..."

The night before, Chris had joined Teresa on the funeral home's wide, wrap-around porch, and, while she smoked, told her of the misgivings he had been having over their son's recent behavior, much of it centered around his naive conception of the Mafia life and his perceived position within it. Worshiping the wrong heroes was bad enough, Chris had said, but Matt's arrogance, the superior attitude he struck as the only grandson of the great Anthony DiGiglio, required immediate action, immediate intervention by both parents. His idea was for Matt, who was finishing eighth grade at a public school in North Caldwell, the bedroom community in Jersey where Teresa lived, to attend high school in Manhattan and live with Chris there starting in September. Teresa had noticed the same behavior in the boy. He was disdainful of his sister, most of his "straight" classmates and even his Mafia-related cousins, children of lesser gods, as it were. But he remained by and large respectful to her, and relatively easy for her to handle, and so she had not drawn the same dire conclusions as Chris had. And, of course, the remedy he was proposing had aroused all of her instincts to, as a mother, keep her son under her wing, and shred anyone who tried to take him from her nest.

"I didn't ask you to decide," Chris said. "I asked you to think about it."

"He'll never agree."

"We don't need his permission."

"He's fourteen. He's not a baby."

"He's a baby when you want him to be, and he's grown up when you want him to be."

"You want me to give my son up for no reason?"

Teresa raised her voice when she said this, and her large brown eyes turned slightly feral, a look, Chris knew, that usually preceded the unleashing of an anger and a stubbornness in his former wife against which there was no hope of prevailing. Shaking his head, acknowledging to himself the stupidity of an ad hominem attack, he said, "I'm sorry. That wasn't fair."

"That's okay," Teresa replied. "I know you love your son."

"I just want you to think about it."

"I will, but I'm not promising anything."

Chris shook his head but said nothing. She would not think about it, he knew. Defeat had entered Chris' life of late and stolen one of the linchpins that held his identity, or what he thought was his identity, together: his law license. The thought of another loss, this one involving his son's very future, was not a happy one. Teresa's mind had closed. These signs he knew, too. And why blame her? Why should she give up custody of her son because he was acting like a snob? Teresa excused herself and got up to join her mother at the other side of the courtyard. When she was gone, Chris sat quietly for a moment and contemplated his dilemma.

The Mafia life was open to Matt, but Chris had never considered the possibility that he would actually enter it until the last six months when the boy had started to turn a surly face to the world and carry himself like a prince. This behavior would have been only marginally worrisome in the average thirteen year old, but in Junior Boy DiGiglio's grandson, it was a cause for great concern. What Chris had not spoken of to Teresa, either the night before or today, was the bottom line reality of what the "Mafia life" meant: there was no respect, no authority, no career unless you killed people. No one knew the rules better than Junior Boy, and he never broke them. No effete young man with unbloodied manicured hands would ever be allowed to join the club. No exception would be made for Matt because he was the don's grandson. In fact, that would be the worst thing Anthony could do. Matt Massi would have to kill to make his bones, kill on command and as often as Junior Boy thought necessary to ensure that the boy was qualified and would be accepted in an organization whose bylaws spoke of violence and death as others spoke of quorums and proxies. For as long as he had known her, Teresa had been in denial about certain aspects of what her father did for a living. Even if he wanted to do such a thing, he doubted he would ever be able to break through her defenses to force the image of her son as a killer onto her brain. She was as grounded in the real world as anyone he had ever met, except when it came to her father's business and her son's innocence.

A hand placed on his shoulder broke Chris' reverie. Turning, he saw that it belonged to his daughter, Tess.

"Can I join you?" she asked.

"Of course."

"Do you want me to get you some food?"

"No, I had some."

Tess sat down next to Chris. She leaned close to her father, as if to speak in a whisper, but said nothing. Chris put his arm around her shoulder and drew her to him.

"I love you, Tess," he said.

"I love you, too, Daddy. I'm sorry about your law license."

"I am too, sweetheart."

Chris kissed Tess on the forehead, then brought his arm away from her shoulder and sat facing her. In her sorrow, her face remained composed and her bearing proud. She looked like her mother, but her grit was Massi grit, and so was her very sharp mind. She placed her hands – young and flawlessly molded – palms down on the white tablecloth before her, and Chris noticed that she was wearing Rose's engagement ring, a small but near-perfect diamond in a simple platinum setting.

"Is there anything you can do?" Tess asked.

"You mean to fight it?"

"Yes."

"Except for the most unusual circumstances, it's irreversible."

At Chris' request, Teresa had relayed the news of his disbarment to Tess and Matt, who were in school when he called three days ago. He had then become consumed by the wake and the funeral. This was the first either of the children had mentioned it.

"What were you and Mommy talking about?"

"Your brother."

"Oh, Al Pacino."

"Right."

"He gave the finger to those camera guys when we were getting out of the limousine."

Chris shook his head, and said, "You're not one to tell tales."

"When I told him he was a jerk, he told me to get fucked. Mommy's oblivious, that's why I'm telling you."

"I've been distracted lately, as you know. But I'll handle Matt now. You stay out of it."

"I wish he'd just grow up. Life would be so much easier."

"He'll be okay. You just go about your business. And don't tell me any more tales. You'll get in the middle. It's obvious, anyway."

"I can't ignore it."

"Try."

Chris didn't think that Matt would be okay, nor was he at all confident that he could handle the situation. He was not a full-time parent, and Teresa was a formidable obstacle. And then, of course, there was Junior Boy, who, for all Chris knew, was thinking of grooming Matt for a leadership position in the family business. How to thwart those plans?

"Will you be around this weekend?" Tess asked.

"Yes."

"Maybe I'll come in with a friend. We can go to some galleries downtown."

"Sure. We'll have lunch."

"I think Mommy wants me," Tess said, looking across the courtyard to where Teresa, standing next to her mother, was waving toward their table.

"Go," Chris said, kissing her on the cheek. "I'll call you tomorrow. We'll talk about the weekend."

During his conversation with Tess, Chris noticed that Joe Pace, Junior Boy's weight-lifting driver and mechanic, had been standing silently in the archway that led from the restaurant to the courtyard. Pace had been sent over from Palermo when his parents, distant DiGiglio cousins, were killed in a mysterious explosion in 1976. Now thirty-five, he had been a trusted retainer ever since. In his dark suit, with his blank face and deliberate ways, he looked every bit the Mafia killer and bodyguard that he was. When Tess rose and walked over to her mother and grandmother, Pace immediately walked over to Chris.

"The don would like to speak to you," he said quietly, when he reached Chris' table.

"Sure," Chris said, "where?"

"Upstairs."

There was more nostalgia in store for Chris in the owner's second floor flat, whose old world formality brought him swiftly back to the years he had spent on Carmine Street. The white lace doilies on the arms of chairs, the floral design cut into the green carpet, the linoleum in the halls: he would not have been surprised to see Rose crossing under the archway from the kitchen into the living room, wiping her hands on an apron that never seemed to get soiled. But it wasn't Rose who greeted him, it was Anthony DiGiglio, who, turning from a window where he had been peering out through a slit in the Venetian blinds, extended his hand to shake Chris' then pointed to easy chairs facing each other across an intricately carved mahogany coffee table.

"I'm sorry about those cameramen," Junior Boy said to Chris when they were seated. To Joe Pace, who was standing with his hands clasped in front of him, DiGiglio said, "You can go. Tell Nick to stay by the door."

Chris shrugged his shoulders slightly and remained silent, gazing with expectant interest at the man who, for five years, from 1985 to 1990, was his father-in-law. In those years, they had built a relationship based largely, though not wholly, on mutual respect. But they had only infrequently crossed paths in the years since, and even less frequently had they interacted in any meaningful way, though each knew the basic post-divorce history of the other. This included Chris' indictment in 2000 for conspiracy to commit stock fraud, his trial, acquittal and subsequent bitterly fought battle with the New York Bar Association. Junior Boy, to Chris' eye, had aged well. Though his classically Italian face had become lined and thickened, the years had done nothing to diminish its proud bearing and the force of character that stamped all of its features.

"Teresa tells me you lost your case."

"Right," Chris replied. "I've been disbarred."

"This was recently?"

"I got the letter the day my mother died."

"That wasn't a good day, I guess."

"No."

"What now?" the don asked.

"I don't know."

"What about your father?"

"My father?"

"We know who killed him."

"Who?"

"Barsonetti."

"Barsonetti? Why?"

"He heard rumors," DiGiglio said, "that Joe Black was holding two million in cash that the Boot had entrusted him with before he died. It was supposed to go to his grandsons, but since Barsonetti had killed them both, he felt it was rightfully his. He offered Joe Black a position as a capo and a share of the money if he would give it to him. Joe refused. Barsonetti took it as an insult."

"Is it true?" Chris asked. "About the money?"

"Who knows? It sounds like old man Velardo. He never trusted the banks. And you know Joe Black. He could keep a secret like Fort Knox."

"That's it?" Chris said. "Over a rumor? An insult?"

"I believe there's more to it."

"Like what?"

"Who do you think wired Paulie Raimo?"

"He wired himself."

"He wasn't smart enough. I think it was Barsonetti."

"The other defendants went down," Chris said. "They were Barsonetti's people."

"He sacrificed them."

"Why?"

"To get you, to ruin your life."

Chris remained silent. Paulie Raimo, his last client, had come to him under indictment for securities fraud. Raimo and his two co-defendants worked for Jimmy Barsonetti, a rogue Mafia don who Chris had barely heard of at the time. Raimo, a punk who thought himself clever, began wearing a wire to all of his meetings relating to the case. Chris made the mistake of joining Paulie and his two cohorts for a hastily arranged dinner meeting one night at which there was an obscure discussion of a new scam they were contemplating. Obscure but enough to get Chris indicted.

"This is what I hear." DiGiglio continued. "When the Boot died, your father's obligation to the Velardo family was over. He turned down Barson's offer without giving it a second thought. He did not mince words, as you probably know. He was done with killing, done with the life. He and Barson were from the same town in Sicily. To Barson, Joe Black was a hero, a legend. When Joe rejected him, it was – to him – the worse kind of insult. It meant that a *paisano*, a countryman from the same low social status, was contemptuous of him. He couldn't kill him, however. He had just killed the Boot's grandsons when he moved on their territory in Brooklyn. He knew the other families were angry. He was afraid of starting a war, afraid of Joe's many friends in the other families, including mine. Then Raimo gets arrested. Who referred him to you?"

"I don't remember."

"You were set up," Junior Boy said. "Barsonetti avenged Joe Black's insult by destroying his son's life."

"But you're saying he killed him anyway."

"When Joe Black found out Jimmy Barson was behind Raimo's wire – had orchestrated your disgrace – he went after him. Something went wrong. Joe Black was killed."

"A justified killing," Chris said.

"Yes. There could be no reprisals."

"Did my father actually have friends in the other families?"

"He allowed no one to get close, but he was highly respected. He was the last of his kind, Chris."

"What kind is that?"

"Honorable, loyal, tight-lipped, reliable; one hundred percent in all categories."

"A good honorable tight-lipped killer."

"When the need arose, yes."

"How did Barsonetti know about the money?"

"The Boot's grandsons probably offered it to Barson," the don replied, "to save their lives. The people who killed Joe Black tortured him to get him to talk. Of course he didn't. That kind of a story gets around. As to the rest, I'm surmising, connecting dots. For one thing, Raimo would never have worn a wire like he did – one of his co-conspirators was a made guy, a captain – without Barson's permission. It would have meant instant death."

Chris shook his head, the full import of what his ex-father-in-law was telling him beginning to sink in. His father had died trying to avenge Chris, and had withstood brutal torture in order to keep his word to his don. This was at once both a comfort and a blow to Chris, whose heart had ached at not knowing how or why Joe Black had died. But that hurt was replaced by a new one. Joe Black had been done with killing, done with looking over his shoulder, freed from the hushed prison of caution and silence that had been his professional life. Yet he had picked up his gun again to avenge his first-born son of the wreckage that had been made of his life.

"He still has the head," Junior Boy said.

"What?"

"They brought Jimmy Barson your father's head. He boiled it down. He keeps the skull on his desk."

Chris shook his head. He thought his surprises were over, but it seemed his whole life lately consisted of surprises.

"Do you know how to use a gun, Chris?"

"Yes. Joe Black taught me when I was a kid."

"I have a proposal. It's one you can refuse if you want." Chris saw, not amused, a flicker of a smile cross the don's craggy face as he said this.

"I'm listening."

"We'll set Barsonetti up for you. You look him in the eye, then kill him. We'll take care of the body. Afterward, you'll have our protection."

"This," Chris said, "is a favor you'd be doing for me?"

"Yes."

Chris did not respond immediately. He looked over toward the front windows, their blinds drawn tightly closed. He could hear an air conditioner humming somewhere in the apartment, which was, otherwise, as respectfully silent as a church. He had quit smoking ten years before, at the age of thirty-two, but would have gladly lit up now if he could. Junior Boy was appraising him across the coffee table, his arms and hands forming a steeple and resting on his chin. Such was the mundane setting for the pivotal moment of his life.

"I'm worried about my son," Chris said.

"Matt?"

"Yes. I want him to live with me in New York, go to high school there. I don't want him in your world."

"Have you spoken to Teresa?" Junior Boy asked.

"She's against it," Chris replied. "She thinks you really are in the trucking business."

"Is this a condition?"

"Yes."

"So," the don said, "you're putting conditions on a favor I'm doing for you?"

"Something tells me," Chris replied, "you'll benefit from Barsonetti's death."

Junior Boy smiled broadly, and not without warmth. "So I'll be doing you *two* favors," he said.

"You don't have to do either."

"Where can I get in touch with you?"

After the luncheon, Chris, in no hurry to get back to New York, where he was living in two small rooms above a bar owned by his old friend, Vinnie Rosamelia, returned to the cemetery. The mid-May day was still cloudless and beautiful. Rose's handsome bronze casket had been lowered into its grave, which was covered with raw, reddish-brown earth. His father's headstone stood next to it. Someone had placed a bouquet of white carnations on Joe Black's grave. Peering at it, Chris noticed a card among the flowers. He bent down to pick it up, then shaded his eyes with his right hand as he read: *To Grandpa Joe, We love you and miss you. Tess and Matt.* The card fluttered to the ground as Chris put both of his hands to his eyes and sobbed into them. It is one of the rules of life that parents give their children a lot of heartache, but when they die, it is a wrenching loss, as if that heartache was after all something we needed more than anything else in the world. Tonight, or tomorrow, Chris would think about becoming a killer, about trading his soul for his son's. At the moment, childhood images of his parents, Joseph and Rose Massi, filled his head to the exclusion of all else.

2.

"Dad?"

"Tess?"

"Yes. It's me."

"What is it?"

"Matt's been in an accident. I think he's okay. The police were here. They say he beat some kid up at a party. Mom's on her way to the hospital. She just left with grandma. I thought you should know."

"What hospital?"

"St. Barnabas."

"Are you sure he's okay?"

"The police said he was hurt but not bad."

"I'm going over there. I'll call you later."

"Dad, you don't have a car."

"I'll borrow Joseph's or I'll take a cab. I'll call you later."

Chris had had dinner the night before at La Luna, a restaurant on Hester Street owned by a family friend named Lou Falco. Falco, who had been at Rose's funeral earlier in the day, had spent much of the evening at Chris' table, reminiscing about Joe Black and the various Carmine Street characters that populated the fifty-eight-year old restaurateur's memory. To Lou, the fifties and early sixties constituted Lower Manhattan's golden age, before the Chinese swamped Little Italy, and Greenwich Village became a gay circus. Chris lingered over his espresso, only half listening but not unappreciative of Lou's obvious attempt to comfort and divert him. He was in no hurry to get home where four walls and a long night of weighing Anthony DiGiglio's surreal offer awaited him. Or was it so surreal? That was the question. As he was leaving, Lou, a devotee of Italian wine, had given Chris two bottles of a private label Chianti. "This goes down like velvet," he said. "You'll sleep like a baby."

Chris had not drunk the wine. The bottles were still on the counter in the apartment's closet-sized kitchen. Neither had he slept much. The noise from Vinnie Rosamelia's bar, The African Queen, just two floors below, although as irritating as ever, was not the problem. Laying in bed in the dark, staring mindlessly at the outline of the few objects in the cramped bedroom, the problem took on shapes of its own: Joe Black putting on his overcoat and fedora, checking the clip of his gun, his movements deliberate, heading out for one last job; his skull – eye sockets gaping – on Jimmy Barsonetti's desk; the gleam of near omnipotence in Anthony DiGiglio's eyes as he offered Chris his devil's bargain; his thirteen-year-old son's idiotic parody of a gangster *dauphin*; the tall, athletic form of Chris himself, aiming a gun very similar to Joe Black's at Barsonetti's chest, firing, then moving closer, leaning over and squeezing off another round into the barbaric don's forehead.

The ringing of the phone next to his bed at three a.m. had neither awoken nor startled Chris. Indeed, he had picked up the receiver calmly as if he had been stoically expecting more painful images to be presented to him, and there they were: Matt in a car flipping over or slamming into a tree, Matt lying bleeding on a hospital gurney, doctors and nurses and DiGiglios and their sycophants swarming around him.

At the hospital waiting room an hour later, Chris found, in addition to Teresa and her mother, Mildred, her mother's spinster sister, Carmela and Junior Boy's brother Frank. Also in attendance were a New Jersey State Police lieutenant named Jorge Corrado, who was a family friend, and Tom Stabile – a family lawyer and Teresa's boyfriend of the last five years. At the nurse's station, two uniformed West Orange police officers were talking to an Indian woman in a white smock with a stethoscope around her neck. Teresa, her face haggard, was sitting on a couch filling out a hospital form on a clipboard resting on her lap. Mildred and Carmela sat protectively on either side of her. Corrado, in full uniform, was sitting Mussolini-like in a chair to the side of the women, with Stabile and Frank DiGiglio standing behind him. Two televisions mounted high on the walls on either end of the waiting room were blaring out news from a twenty-four hour cable channel. In this din, Chris was told that Matt had indeed not been hurt badly. He had a gash on his forehead, which had been stitched, and he was resting in a nearby E.R. cubicle waiting to be admitted to a room for purposes of observation overnight as a precaution due to his head trauma.

"How did you get here?" Teresa said.

"Joseph's car. What happened?"

"Nothing," Teresa answered.

"What do you mean, 'nothing'? What are those cops doing here?"

Mildred and Carmela stiffened at the tone of Chris' voice, and Stabile went to stand behind Teresa, placing his hands on her shoulders.

"That's been taken care of," Frank said, as he came over to address Chris quietly, leading him by the elbow away from the women. Chris allowed himself to be led, but after ten paces or so, he shook DiGiglio loose.

"What happened, Frank?"

"Another kid went after Matt. Matt fought back."

"This is Matt's version?"

"Yes, of course."

"And the car accident?"

"The cops were called. Matt and his buddy panicked. They took off in the kid's parents' car. They went off the shoulder on 280 into a ditch."

"Why were the cops called?"

"The other kid was hurt pretty bad."

"How bad."

"Broken arm, broken ribs."

"How could that be?"

"Matt had a baseball bat, one of those aluminum ones."

Chris shook his head. He had known immediately that the presence of Frank DiGiglio, the calmer and more sophisticated of Junior Boy's two younger brothers, meant that Matt was in deeper trouble than what would follow from a boyish tussle and a joyride. But to hear that his son, who would turn fourteen in two weeks, would take a baseball bat to someone, for whatever reason, was a jolt. Pretension to gangsterhood was one thing, true violence was an altogether different story.

"Where's the other kid?" Chris asked.

"He's having surgery at St. Michael's."

"What's Corrado doing here?"

"He put in a word for us with the cops."

Chris looked over to the couch where Tom Stabile had pulled up a chair and was sitting facing Teresa. Corrado, who would receive an envelope with, Chris guessed, at least twenty-five hundred dollars in it for his night's work, was still sitting stiffly, staring up at the nearest television. Such was Anthony DiGiglio's power, and the enormous burden of being in debt to him, that a high ranking state police officer would allow himself to be on public display this way, the purpose of his presence obvious to anyone with half a brain. This thought led Chris to take a closer look at Frank, outwardly unprepossessing with his receding hairline and in his off-the-rack slacks and shirt. Did he know about Junior Boy's offer? Chris could see no extra interest in Frank's eyes and guessed he did not. What this meant, he would leave for another day. At the moment, there were other things on his mind.

"Which room is Matt in?" he asked.

"Down that hall on the right," Frank replied, nodding toward a corridor just before the nurse's station. "The first door."

Chris headed that way, but after only a few steps, he saw Teresa in his peripheral vision rise, and heard her call out to him, "Where are you going?"

"To talk to Matt," he said, turning to face his ex-wife.

"That's not a good idea," said Tom Stabile, who had followed Teresa to his feet.

Chris turned his full gaze on Stabile, whom he knew was proud of his position as one of Anthony DiGiglio's top lawyers and the trusted boyfriend of his daughter and only child. In the years that Chris had known him, Stabile had never displayed the least bit of insight into the high price he had paid for his "position." Though their backgrounds were similar, self-respect did not seem to be part of Tom Stabile's lexicon. It occurred to Chris that if he was ultimately to decide to put himself in DiGiglio's debt, he would do it – unlike Tom Stabile – knowing that he had sold a piece of his soul. He held Stabile's gaze for another second, his eyes neutral – to someone who did not know him well – then turned to Teresa, and said, "Come on, let's go talk to our son."

Chris knew that Teresa, who had shared his bed for five years, did not miss the meaning of the look he gave Stabile. He watched as she paused, then, taking her lawyer boyfriend by the arm as if to draw him back, or keep him in place, said, "I've talked to him. You go ahead. I'm staying here all night."

In the cubicle, Matt was lying on his back on a gurney, still in the baggy pants, loose shirt and sneakers he had worn to his party. A portion of his head had been shaved just above the hair line to expose his lacerated scalp. His lustrous black hair fell over a clean white dressing that extended across most of his forehead. Chris thought he looked handsome, lying there, the upper portion of the gurney tilted up so that he could survey his surroundings. That, he knew, was one of Matt's problems. He was too good looking for his own good. People, even adults who should know better, deferred to him for that reason alone. Add to this beauty his place in a very powerful crime family and you had a brew much too heady for a pubescent boy. His face was drained of its usual high color, but he seemed alert, although disappointed that the person who walked through the door was his father and not someone else.

"Who were you expecting?" Chris asked as he stood at the foot of the gurney.

"No one."

"Your grandfather, maybe?"

"No. Mommy, I guess."

"What happened?"

"This kid attacked me."

"Who?"

"Sean McBride."

"Why?"

"Why?"

"Yes, why did he attack you?"

Chris watched as Matt looked away, then over his father's shoulder toward the door. The boy did not know it, but these movements were part of his answer. Although this was by far the most serious of any that had preceded it, Chris had been in similar situations with his children in that past. His rule of thumb was simple: the response he received, although important and telling, was not as critical as the fact that the question had been put with authority and with an unmistakable expectation that it be answered honestly.

"Tell me what happened, Matt."

"He's a jerkoff."

"What did he do?"

"He's been bugging me for weeks."

"How?"

"He's got things to say about grandpa."

"What kind of things?"

"I don't know. Things."

"So he isn't in awe of you or your grandfather."

Silence.

"What did he do tonight?"

"He bugged me. He was drunk and wouldn't stop."

"So you hit him with a baseball bat."

"An aluminum bat."

"What difference does that make? He's having surgery right now."

"I'm glad he's having surgery. He deserved it. Maybe he'll shut up from now on."

"Tell that to the judge when you go to court."

"I'm not going to court. Tom took care of it already. And Uncle Frank."

"The other kids at the party will be questioned."

"They'll never say anything against me. And neither will Sean. He'll say he fell down some steps."

When this exchange ended, the contempt on Matt's face and in his voice made Chris want to slap him and slap him hard. It would have been the first time he had ever laid a hand on either of his children in anger. He controlled himself at the last second, his hand stayed by the realization that his anger, cold and pure, could be put to better use than striking his fool of a son. Where had this anger, an old friend, been these last two years? Why had it taken Matt's painful condescension to arouse it?

Matt must have seen the fury that appeared for just an instant in his father's eyes because Chris noticed the boy's eyes widen and thought he saw the first glimmer of contrition, or fear, in them. Good, he thought, there will be more of both to come, I promise.

As he left Matt's room, Chris almost literally bumped into Teresa, who was on her way in. She halted, and then tried to brush past him, but he took her arm and pulled her back into the corridor. They stared hard at each other for a second in the glare of the hospital's fluorescent lighting.

"What?" Teresa said.

"Why didn't you call me?"

"I know you. You would have made him into a criminal, blown it all out of proportion."

"It would be hard to blow this out of proportion, Teresa. That was a violent thing he did."

"You would have found a way."

"That's your excuse for taking the easy way."

"It's my father's way. He sent Uncle Frank."

"He's at a party drinking on the night of his grand-mother's funeral. He beats another kid with a baseball bat. He drives – probably drunk – without a license. He ruins somebody's car. And he gets off scot free. Not only does he get off scot free, but he sees how things are fixed for him, how everybody kisses his ass."

"What would you have done? Let him go to court? Let him go to jail?"

"Yes."

"He'll never come to live with you, Chris. That's my answer. You might as well know it now."

Chris knew that even though their divorce had been a blow to Teresa, she had respected him for the way he handled his role as provider and father. She had swallowed her pride for the benefit of her children, who were ages four and two at the time of the separation and loved their father very much. Looking at her face now, tired but grim and defiant, he wondered if the bad taste still lingered in her mouth, and if this was her way of spitting it out once and for all. She would ruin Matt to hurt Chris, the way Rose had ruined Joseph to hurt Joe Black, who had been helpless to resist his relentlessly protective wife. But Chris was not Joe Black. Or was he? Suddenly, assassination did not seem so surreal, not if it meant tearing his son from the grip of Teresa and her family. The harsh irony of this thought forced a bitter smile onto Chris' face.

"What are you smiling at?" Teresa asked.

"Nothing. I'm just tired."

"You played your best card when you divorced me, Chris. You're not getting Matt away from me, whatever's going through your head."

"I'll call you tomorrow," Chris replied. Then, seeing a side exit at the end of the hall they were standing in, having no desire to shake hands with or say goodbye to Frank DiGiglio *et al* in the waiting room, he turned and left the hospital.

3.

"You don't have to have anything to do with my father."

"Yes, I do. He'd be my father-in-law."

"I mean his business."

"That wouldn't matter. I'd be in the family."

"You decide. I'll still love you, either way."

Chris looked around Washington Square Park, seeing it but not seeing it. In his world – a world he had been trying to escape since he was fourteen – *family* had two meanings, equal and not separate. He felt today the way he did on the day ten years earlier when he woke up in St. Vincent's Hospital, his nose and both of his legs broken, barely remembering the split second car crash that ended his meteoric track career, but not his running from Joe Black.

"Of course I prefer marriage," Teresa continued. "I much prefer it. This is our son, or daughter, inside of me."

"There's no way you're having an abortion."

"We could elope. I don't mind."

"Why should we insult your parents when we're the ones who caused this problem? You're their only child. Your mother's probably been looking forward to your wedding since the day you were born."

"I'm sorry about this, Chris."

"There's nothing to be sorry about. It's the hand of God."

"I don't mean the baby. I mean who my father is. We could move away. I wouldn't mind that either, if you thought we should."

Number one in his high school class, Chris went from LaSalle Academy on the Lower East Side uptown to Columbia on a full academic scholarship, and then on to NYU Law School, where he was named editor of the Law Review in his last year. In the spring of 1984, in the second semester of his first year, he went to a classmate's party and there met a twenty-year-old undergraduate named Teresa DiGiglio. Drinking wine on a fire escape overlooking Washington Square Park, Chet Baker's dreamy version of "Let's Get Lost" drifting out to them from the crowded apartment, they clicked. Later, they walked in the park and sat on a bench near the arch and kissed, while nearby three black teenagers were rapping out a song about "niggah" brotherhood.

Two years later, they found themselves on the same park bench discussing a future that, to his disgust, Chris had refused to confront while having great sex and lots of fun with the cherished daughter of a Mafia overlord. That future had just landed on his head. On a trip they had taken in March to Florida, Teresa had, she said, missed a day taking her birth control pill. If she had told him the truth: that she had taken herself off the pill in January, Chris might have been angry, but he would have almost certainly respected her for taking her life in her own hands. In the face of his self-indulgence and immaturity, what were her choices? It was not this initial deceit that ultimately destroyed their marriage, it was the assumption that grew from it on Teresa's part, the assumption that Chris would fit in in New Jersey and, eventually, come to see and accept the very great advantages of being in the DiGiglio family.

Having manipulated him once – for the greater good of both of them was her rationale – she assumed she could do it again. But Chris was not controllable. His conscience had led him into marriage. His pride would lead him out of it.

That night, they broke the news to Anthony and Mildred at a casual dinner on the patio of the don's estate in Upper Montclair, a verdant redoubt in North Jersey's rolling hills. There was no gnashing of teeth. Indeed, it seemed to Chris that Junior Boy and Mildred were secretly delighted with the imminent prospect of a wedding and a grandchild in one fell swoop. They were a Mafia king and his queen, but, like virtually all Italians, they valued family – blood family – above all else. And, of course, it did not hurt that Chris' father, an official member of *la cosa nostra*, was known to and respected by the don. After the meal, Chris found himself alone with Junior Boy in his book-lined study.

"You can have the use of this library whenever you want it," the don said.

Chris, his back to the quiet, spacious room, had been looking at a shelf that contained Dante, Boccaccio and Gibbons, among others, all bound in soft and obviously worn morocco leather. Turning, he saw his father-in-law-to-be seated behind his large mahogany desk, leaning back, his elbows resting on the arms of his plush chair. The don, who had turned fifty the month before, was a roughly cut but handsome man. His graying hair and the age lines that were beginning to appear on his face served only to burnish his Imperial-Roman features with a dignity and a stark superiority that set him apart from most other men.

"Thank you," Chris replied.

"Your father and I worked together once."

"I don't think I'll ask what the job was."

"Richie the Boot's son was kidnapped in Italy by the Red Brigade," DiGiglio said, smiling. "He asked my father to negotiate his release. My father sent me to Italy, and the Boot sent Joe Black to help me out. We delivered the ransom, picked up the kid and brought him home. Half of one of his ears was cut off. He was seventeen years old, a spoiled brat who thought he was an aristocrat."

"When was this?"

"In the early seventies."

"How is he now?"

"The kid?"

"Yes."

"He's a grown man. He raises horses in Kentucky. He wears his hair long."

Chris knew that there was a reason for this meeting. In the silence that followed, he waited for it to be revealed. When it came, he was not ready for it.

"What do you think of me?" Junior Boy asked, breaking the silence.

Chris was tempted to say, *I don't know you*, and leave it at that, but there was something about DiGiglio's demeanor that made him think twice. Junior Boy, already a great and feared don, was not great and feared for no reason. Chris knew instinctively that a person would be wise to speak truthfully to him, that deceit and manipulation were games he played well and always won, making his opponent's loss a painful one at the same time.

"I'm not sure what to think," Chris finally answered.

"You're ambivalent?"

"Yes."

"That's originally a psychological term, describing the state of conflicting emotions in a person for another person, like love and hate."

"I'm aware of that."

"It's debilitating unless it's resolved."

"Have you studied psychology?"

"A little. Human nature, though, I've taken a hard look at."

"You asked me how I felt."

"And you gave an honest answer. What are your plans after your clerkship?"

"I don't know. I'd like to stay in the city. The U.S. Attorney's office interests me."

"You'd be creating another conflict."

"I know."

"Would you like a brandy?"

"Sure."

In July, Chris and Teresa were married on the estate. Three hundred people, some of whom canceled plans a lifetime in the making to be there, toasted the newlyweds with Dom Perignon, and celebrated under the stars and elegant tents into the night. When Chris told his father about Teresa, Joe Black had looked at him steadily for a moment or two, his dark Sicilian face unreadable, then said, "They'll make you choose." All night long, along with the music and the noise of the party, Joe Black's words buzzed in Chris' head.

For the next five years, the agenda of the DiGiglio family was, though subtle and not undignified, in fact, to make Chris choose. No one asked him to be a killer, or hijack trucks, but with his law degree and good mind, he could analyze businesses vulnerable to Mafia takeovers, he could speak intelligently with the family's outside lawyers, of whom there were too many and who were never wholly trusted, and he could help immensely in the intricate laundering schemes that cleaned the millions of dollars of dirty money that came into the family from its various enterprises each year.

Chris knew that everyone expected him to eventually abandon his idealism and leave the straight world behind. Everyone, that is, except Junior Boy. *You're stiff necked, like your father,* he would say, *an outlier. He'll get killed for it one day, but he'll die his own man.* Chris was grateful for Junior Boy's hands-off attitude. It might have been a strategy, but it helped at home, where his refusal to commit caused a great deal of friction between him and Teresa, who did not want her husband to be forever an outsider, but who took her father's lead in all things. The family waited, hoping for a change, but Chris continued to make the deadening commute from his home in the north Jersey suburbs to his job prosecuting securities fraud at the U.S. Attorney's office in Manhattan.

Chris' primary antagonists were Junior Boy's brother, Aldo, and Aldo's two sons Aldo, Jr. and Sal. Aldo, whose crude exterior camouflaged a keen if parochial mind, a mind that saw Chris from the beginning as a threat to his sons' position in the family. Unfortunately, the don seemed to respect Chris, and thus it would not do for Aldo to reveal his true feelings. His boys, however, were Chris' age, and a challenge coming from them would be seen as natural, even expected. Neither Aldo Jr. nor Sal was very bright. Both were spoiled and arrogant, and predisposed to resent Chris, an Ivy League lawyer who refused to get his hands dirty in the family business. Chris saw early on that they were their father's surrogates in a guerrilla war aimed at undermining the elitist son of the notorious Joe Black Massi.

Family gatherings, of which there were many, were the battlegrounds. The weapons were remarks—only half in jest, usually tinged with a crude sarcasm, sometimes openly insulting—aimed at Chris' loyalty to the hated U.S. Attorney and FBI in Manhattan, offices that had been systematically decimating the Mafia families in the five boroughs of New York through the decade of the eighties. "It's too bad your father didn't have a son" was one of Sal's favorite statements to Chris.

The war ended, along with Chris' marriage, on a Sunday in April of 1990 after a party held at Aldo Sr.'s house to celebrate the christening of Aldo III, Aldo Jr.'s first son. It appeared to Chris, at least, that Aldo Jr. viewed the fathering of a son as a feat of substantial magnitude, so puffed up was he the entire day. He referred to the child more than once as "the little don" and asked Chris with mock curiosity why he had given his son an American name like Matt. Sal also had a son, age four, who took pleasure in torturing Matt, then two. Before dinner Chris watched as Sal Jr. ripped a toy truck from Matt's hands, pushing him to the floor in the process, while out of the corner of his eye he saw Sal Sr. beaming.

Before the desert was served, Chris excused himself and quickly drove to his and Teresa's house, only ten minutes away, where he picked up the Glock .45 caliber semi-automatic pistol that had been one of Junior Boy's wedding presents, along with some rope. When he returned to Aldo's house, he saw Sal standing by himself in the driveway smoking a cigarette. He parked and got out of his car with the Glock pointing at Sal's chest. He forced Sal into the driver's seat of his car, then got into the rear seat behind him and whacked him on the head with the gun with enough force to daze him so that he could tie him up at hands and feet with no trouble. In the house, he found Aldo Jr. and told him there was something he wanted to show him in his car. Outside, he poked the Glock hard into Aldo Jr.'s ribs and told him to get in the car next to his brother, who was awake but moaning. Chris got in the back seat and placed the gun against the back of Aldo,Jr.'s head.

"I don't ever want to hear your voice again," he said, "or your brother's. I don't ever want to see a cross-eyed look from either of you. And I want Sal's jerkoff son to stay away from Matt. I would kill you both right now, but I think you should have this one warning. Do you understand?"

Aldo, who was sweating profusely and had turned white, managed to get a yes out before Chris told him to untie his brother and take him into the house.

At home, Chris called Teresa and told her to get a ride home with someone. Later, when the kids were sleeping, Chris quickly packed a bag while Teresa hovered around him in their bedroom.

"Tell me again why you're leaving," she said.

"I almost killed your two asshole cousins. I don't know what stopped me."

"So you think you're a killer like your father?"

"I don't know what I think. I know I have to leave though."

"What about the kids?"

"I'll come by and talk to them."

"My father will be heartbroken."

"I've told him the family business is not for me. He should have kept Aldo and his idiot sons off my back."

"What about me? I thought you loved me?"

Chris had finished packing and was standing by the bed looking at his wife of five years, in many ways more a stranger to him now than when they first met. Which of them had changed more? Which of them had tried harder? He didn't know.

"They forced me to choose," he said, "and I'm choosing."

"You didn't answer my question."

"I don't know if I love you. That's the truth."

"That means you don't."

"Teresa, did you think the constant fighting, the constant pressure to join the family, wouldn't have an effect on me?"

"Your father's a hit man, your brother's a junkie, so you think you have to be a saint, is that it? You can't condescend to be a part of my family. We're dirty, we're sinners. *Everyone's* dirty, Chris, *everyone's* a sinner. You refuse to grow up, to open your eyes and see that."

Chris hired a lawyer, rented a small apartment in the West Village and waited for the DiGiglios to react. But they never did. He was allowed to divorce Teresa. No mention was ever made of what he did to Aldo Jr. and Sal. After a while, he stopped looking over his shoulder. He left the U.S. Attorney's office and took a job with DeVoss and Kline, a respected and successful white collar criminal defense firm on Wall Street. In time, his visitation arrangement became more like shared custody. Tess and Matt adored the life he offered them in the city. His career soared. In 1995, he was made a partner at the firm, and in 1997, he bought a spacious three-bedroom loft in Tribeca, from which he could walk to work.

In those years, if his life was a record, this was the A side. The B side was the off-key tune played by his parents and his brother. Joe Black, getting older and sent out only

on special cases, nevertheless made his living in the same
way as he always did. Joseph, after making several non-
attempts at college, settled into a life of drug use, rehab
and street scams, living off of a series of girlfriends and
the cash that Rose slipped him from time to time behind
her husband's back. The idea that the A and B sides of his
life could ever come together in any sensible way never
occurred to Chris. Both tunes played in his head, the one
sweet, the other bitter.

●

On the drive from the hospital back to the city, as
Chris watched the sun rise behind the Manhattan skyline,
he called Joseph and asked him to find out as much as he
could about Jimmy Barsonetti: where he lived, where he
hung out, who were his friends, his enemies, did he have
a routine, what were his vices. No longer tired, after parking the car in a garage near his apartment, Chris bought
coffee at a deli and walked to Washington Square Park,
which was empty at this early hour except for the usual as-
sortment of the lost and the homeless. It occurred to him
that the park's old-fashioned green benches had become
icons of change in his life. He chose one near Stanford
White's famous arch, and sat to sip his coffee and think.
He had no doubt that his handsome and devious younger
brother, who had been roaming the city at night since he
was seventeen, would accomplish his mission. Armed with
this information, Chris would find a way to kill Barsonetti
on his own, without Anthony DiGiglio's help. Junior Boy
would keep his end of the bargain, but Chris would not
be in his debt, as he would be if the don set the killing up.

Chris would lose his soul, but not to DiGiglio. And he would have his son.

When he finished his coffee, Chris left the park and began walking up Fifth Avenue. The thought of failure had occurred to him, but did not faze him. He knew how to handle a gun and he was not afraid to die. No one took more precautions beforehand nor acted more decisively when the moment came than Joe Black Massi, and his blood ran strong in Chris' veins. Barsonetti would be over-confident, complacent in his power, and Chris would find a way to put a bullet in his head and walk away unseen.

The morning broke full and fair and clean as Chris, letting his mind wander, in no hurry to return to his tiny, airless apartment, joined the city's throng. At St. Patrick's Cathedral, he stopped for a second, recalling the spring day, only seven years ago, when he held his six-year-old son's hand and walked him into a church in Jersey for his first communion. Without thinking, Chris ascended the famous cathedral's long gray steps and entered its vaulted chamber, cool and hushed after the heat and noise of the city. He was surprised at the number of people kneeling and sitting in pews, lighting candles and genuflecting as they passed the altar. To his immediate right was a holy water font. He reflexively dipped his fingers into it, and felt the cool water penetrate his being. He did not make the sign of the cross as he had a thousand times when he was a boy. There was no prayer in the catechism in aid of murder, no patron saint of assassins.

Turning, he exited the church and began the long walk downtown.

4.

Chris had inherited his father's eyes: coal black pupils surrounded by deep brown irises embedded with tiny flecks of a mesmerizing dark green. Set in a field of clearest white, they were eyes both guarded and vigilantly watchful, the eyes of the Sicilian peasant who is by nature wary of strangers and fiercely mistrustful of official authority. Softened by long lashes, framed by a graceful brow above and planed cheekbones below, they stamped his visage with the feral pride of the hawk or the eagle. His dusky complexion also came from his Sicilian father, but the glinting color in his eyes, his straight nose – still slightly crooked twenty-seven years after his accident – full lips and square chin were his Tuscan mother's contribution to a face that was as captivating as it was darkly handsome; captivating because in a way not quite definable, it seemed both to invite and bar entry to Chris' inner being. After he recovered from his car accident, Chris' mother – one foot still in the hilltop Tuscan village where she was born, fearful since his early boyhood that her first-born son's charismatic beauty would lead inexorably to a tragic end – was secretly happy that his face had been permanently marred.

Ten days after burying Rose, Chris traveled uptown to meet his brother Joseph at the penthouse bar of the Peninsula Hotel. Facing each other across a drinks table along a plate glass wall overlooking Fifth Avenue, the most casual observer would quickly see that Chris and Joseph were brothers. With the room's muted light obscuring their age difference, they could easily be mistaken for twins. Closer scrutiny, however, would reveal subtle but distinct differences: his eyes as piercing, his features as classically handsome, his lustrous black hair falling carelessly across his brow, Joseph's was a more refined, almost feminine beauty. It was as if portraits of the same striking model had been made by artists of markedly different sensibilities, Chris by Michelangelo, perhaps; Joseph by John Singer Sargent. These differences held true in gesture and body language as well: Joseph's drink was an elegant prop, Chris' a part of his arm.

"Are you clean?" Chris asked, putting his drink – a single malt scotch over ice – down on the gleaming black table, next to a candle flickering under a filigreed cover, also black.

"You know I am," Joseph answered.

"How do I know? I haven't seen you since the funeral."

"I'm clean. What's going on with the house?"

"The closing is next week."

"When will we get our money?"

"A few days later."

After Joe Black's death, Rose had put their house on the market, and by March, a contract had been signed for its sale. Chris' share of the proceeds could not come too soon. When his indictment was announced, almost two years ago, he had immediately been let go by his law firm. In eighteen months, he went through his savings of a hundred thousand dollars, and his 401K of two hundred thousand dollars to pay for his living expenses, child support and legal fees. Three months ago, broke, in the middle of a fierce and expensive disbarment battle, he rented his condominium in Tribeca and accepted Vinnie Rosamelia's offer of the apartment above the African Queen.

"Why don't you take it all?" said Joseph. "Call it a loan."

"You're not serious."

"Sure I am. I'm rolling in dough."

"That won't last long."

"You could be in for a surprise this time."

Chris eyed Joseph across the small table, thinking it would be hard to find a spoiled five-year-old with more brazenness – and less moral compunction – than his thirty-two-year-old brother, whose current girlfriend was a forty-two-year-old artist with enough money to live on the Upper East Side and indulge Joseph's wishes regarding clothes, cars and cash. The timeline for the relationship would depend upon how quickly Joseph returned to heroin, which is when the abuse and the money drain would really start. This is how it had been with all of his other women. Why would this one be any different?

"Thanks," he said, "but I'll be okay"

"I'll spend it, Chris," Joseph said. "You know me."

Yes, I do know you, Chris thought. *A hundred grand will buy a lot of heroin.* Out loud, he said, "It's yours to do what you want with. Now what about Barsonetti? Did you come up with anything?"

"A little. He lives in Forest Hills. He was married, but his wife died. No kids. He has about a dozen captains who are also his bodyguards. They rotate, two on, two off, twenty-four/seven. Very bad guys. When they're not with him, they're breaking heads or supervising his ongoing business and one-time scams. He hires people to do his killings, Chinese, Mexicans, never Italians or Sicilians, never anybody from the city. He has a big gambling book in Queens and now owns the entire Velardo operation in Brooklyn. Just asking about him made people nervous. They say he likes to have his enemies' heads brought to him."

"What else?"

"He goes out in his car a lot. He probably does a lot of business from the car, probably with throw-away cell phones. He just made a big score ripping off and reselling those phone card things. About two million, they say. I don't think he's stupid."

"Anything else?"

"Not really. Like I said, people are afraid to talk about him."

"That's it? Does he have a favorite hangout? Does he have a routine? Does he like women? Little boys? Does he go to the track? What?"

"Nobody seems to know. Or they won't talk. I'm sorry. There *is* one more thing. Remember Nick Scarpa, from the neighborhood?"

"The fighter?"

"Yes. He's been in jail forever. He got out a few months ago. He's living in Jersey, but he hangs out in the city. I ran into him a couple of nights ago. He's working for a guy named Labrutto, running errands, getting his car washed. Nick's got a cauliflower brain, if you know what I mean. Labrutto makes porn videos. The rumor is he's backed by Anthony DiGiglio. Scarpa says he made a delivery from Labrutto's house in Jersey to a house in Forest Hills. As he's leaving, he sees Barsonetti come out the front door and get into a big Lincoln. Barsonetti wears an eye patch so he knows it was him."

"What was in the package?"

"Nick wasn't sure, probably cash. It wasn't big."

"That's it?"

"That's it."

"How can I reach Scarpa?"

"I have his number. I told him you might want to talk to him. What's going on?"

"Nothing. Stop asking around about Barsonetti. Let me talk to Nick Scarpa first."

The two brothers stared at each other across the table, the candle's small flame dancing in their beautiful eyes. Usually, it was Joseph who was telling the lies or keeping secrets, but tonight, their quiet role-reversal seemed almost natural, such had been the upheaval in their lives – especially Chris' – of late.

"Okay. Whatever you say," Joseph said. "There's something else I have to tell you, though."

"Go ahead."

"I hear they found Paulie Raimo's body."

"What's that got to do with me?" Chris asked.

"I hear Eddie Dolan thinks you were involved."

"Come on."

"This is what I hear."

"You don't think I killed him, do you? Or had a hand in it?"

"No," Joseph answered, "because I know who did. But it's not what I think, it's what Dolan thinks that matters."

"Unbelievable," said Chris, leaning back in his plush chair, and picking up his drink.

"I know," said Joe. "Joe Black fucks with us once again. Even after he's dead, he fucks with us."

"Where did you hear this?"

"Reliable people, believe me."

"Who killed Paulie?"

"You don't want to know that."

Joseph was right. Chris did not want to know who killed Paulie, because if he did, he might be forced to reveal it someday, and that would only lead to more trouble. Finishing his scotch, he caught the waitress' eye, and motioned for two more drinks. Joseph was also right that Joe Black was giving them heartache even from the grave. Ed Dolan was an Assistant United States Attorney in New York, in charge of an organized crime task force. Chris and Ed had once, long ago, been best friends, playing every street sport imaginable in tandem and running track together at LaSalle Academy, until one day, in 1977, Joe Black Massi gunned down Ed's father while on a mission for his capo, Richie "the Boot" Velardo.

When Chris was an Assistant U.S. Attorney, he worked in the securities fraud section at 7 World Trade Center, while Dolan worked at the federal complex in Foley Square. They rarely crossed paths, but when they did, no words were ever spoken and the chill was palpable. When Chris left to go into private practice, Dolan stayed and made a career as a federal prosecutor. It was Dolan who prosecuted Chris for conspiracy to commit stock fraud. At the trial in the spring of 2002, Dolan's star witness was Paulie Raimo, a low-life who had been a client of Chris' right up to the announcement of his indictment. After Chris was acquitted, it was Dolan who goaded the federal and state ethics authorities into disbarment proceedings, something they may not have done in the absence of Dolan's meticulous portfolio of Chris' undeniable Mafia connections.

"No, I don't want to know," Chris said, finally. "And I don't believe you know, either. But if you do, don't go around talking about it, even to people you think you can trust. Pop never said a word about what he did, because he knew that in his world, he couldn't trust anybody."

"Don't worry about me."

"Don't worry? I know you, Joe. You'll brag to one of your idiot friends, and he'll end up giving you up for a few dollars or to try to gain favor with some other idiot a few steps above him in the food chain. Then you'll be dead or crippled. And for what? For bragging, for being a show-off."

Joseph brushed back the lock of silky black hair that fell perpetually onto his forehead, then picked up his drink – a martini with a fancy name – and sipped from it. Putting it down, he said, "Are you finished?"

"I'm finished."

"Good. I'm trying to help, that's all. I hear something like this, you want me to tell you, don't you? So you can be prepared? I mean, if Dolan wants to pin Raimo's murder on you, then that means you're in a whole different ball game with him. It means he wants you dead or permanently locked up. It means he'll break the rules – make up shit – to get to you. It means he's lost his mind, but he's a cunning fuck, so it worries me."

Chris had already come to these conclusions. It did not take any great analytical skill to reach them; but hearing them from Joseph was surprising. Not that he was stupid, or lacked insight. To the contrary, self-serving schemers needed to know a great deal about human nature in order to successfully manipulate their victims. Chris was surprised because there was the ring of credibility in his brother's voice, as if he actually cared about something or someone other than himself. Sarcasm, irony and anger had ruled their relationship for so long that, for a moment, Chris did not know how to answer.

"I appreciate it," he said, finally. "He's probably just trying to scare me, but of course it helps to know."

"I don't know, Chris. He brings you to trial on nothing, he gets you disbarred. But he's not satisfied. He wants to put a murder charge on your head."

"You could be right, but Ed Dolan's the last of my worries right now."

"What could be worse than being falsely charged with murder?"

A real one, Chris thought, then smiled and said, "Not much, you're right. And I know how much Dolan hates me. But let it go. I can't think about him right now. How's Sharon?"

"It's Marsha."

"Marsha."

"She's fine. She wants to meet you."

"Sure."

"Speaking of girlfriends, do you remember Danielle Dimicco?"

"Of course."

"I got a call from her yesterday."

"How is she?"

"She's good. She's taking acting classes, waiting tables. She still thinks she can break through."

"What about her?"

"Her roommate's gone missing. She wants someone to check in on her."

Joseph had met Danielle in the brief time – three months – he attended NYU's film school in the fall of 1990. A beautiful aspiring actress and model, only seventeen, she fell hard for the sexy rebel that Joseph had no trouble affecting in those days. Five years later, after addicting her to heroin and ignoring her tortured attempts at rehab, he left her at the altar of her parish church in Queens. Joe Black paid the Dimiccos for the cost of the reception, and Rose paid to send Joseph to Florida to recuperate from the stress of having to make such a "courageous" decision. Most of the members of both families were relieved. They knew Joseph was poison. Soon afterwards, Chris heard that Danielle had moved to California where she was said to be working at staying clean of heroin and resurrecting her career, but she had been off of his radar ever since, until tonight.

"I didn't know you kept in touch," Chris said.

"We talk once in a while. I stop by sometimes to see her mom."

"She's sick, isn't she?"

"She's in a wheelchair."

"And the father's dead?"

"Right."

Chris said nothing.

"No, not to borrow money," Joseph said. "I feel sorry for her all alone in that crappy little house, so I've stopped in. That's all. You don't believe me."

"You're not thinking of joining the Peace Corps, are you?"

"No," said Joseph. "I'm still the same prick you've always known."

"And there's nothing in it for you? Like inheriting Mrs. Dimicco's house, or cashing in her savings bonds?"

"Will you help out Danielle or not?"

"Why can't you do it?"

"Danielle asked me to ask you. She knows I'm a fuck-up. She says she'll pay. She's worried about her friend."

"Is she still in Los Angeles?"

"Yes. The roommate moved to Manhattan a few months ago, but she hasn't been heard from in some time."

"Where in New York?"

"Not far from you," Joe answered, sliding a piece of paper across the ebony table top. "Scarpa's number's there too."

"I can walk there from my place," Chris said after reading the address.

"So you'll do it?"

"Sure. She probably took a trip to Europe."

"I doubt it. She's an orphan, and Danielle has become her only family. Danielle says she definitely would have called if she left the city for any length of time."

"How long has it been?"

"Over a month."

"Why did she come east?"

"Something about a guy, and a movie deal."

"So she's an actress too."

"Allegedly."

"'Allison McRae,'" Chris said, reading from the note in his hand. "What does she look like?"

"Blonde hair, blue eyes. She's a farm girl from Wisconsin."

"How old?"

"Danielle's age, thirty."

"I liked Danielle," Chris said. "She was a sweet kid. You did her a favor by standing her up."

"I know. I liked her too. That's why I did it."

"Tell her I said I'd be happy to do this for her. Tell her I don't want her money."

"I will."

They had finished their second drink, and the waitress had left the check.

"What's up with Jimmy Barsonetti?" Joseph asked.

"I told you, nothing."

"Nothing you care to talk about."

"Right."

"And you're not worried about Ed Dolan?"

"I am. I agree with you, he's psychotic. But what can I do? If he comes after me, I'll deal with it."

"Too bad Joe Black's not around when we need him. He killed the father, he could've killed the son, too."

Only a week or so ago, Chris would have cringed at a comment like this from his brother, who spoke of Joe Black as if they were intimate, which they were not, and who was never shy about dropping his father's name to advance one of his petty scams.

But tonight he simply gazed at Joseph evenly and then shook his head slightly. Instead of replying, he looked down at Fifth Avenue through the thick plate glass. Shooting arrow-straight uptown, cars and people ebbed and flowed on it as on a dark moonlit river, a glittering river at the bottom of a canyon of skyscrapers. When he received the letter from the Bar Association notifying him of his disbarment, Chris' hand had trembled as he opened the slender envelope and read it. His first thought was that

Ed Dolan, once his best friend in the world, had finally gotten his revenge.

It appeared now, if what Joseph was saying was true, that he had been wrong. Ed, the fair-haired companion of his youth, wanted to charge him with premeditated murder, a capital offense in New York, where they executed by lethal injection. He had responded to Joseph's concerns with a calculated casualness, but in his heart a cold wind was blowing. DiGiglio, Barsonetti, Teresa, they had been a formidable enough lineup of foes. But now here was Dolan, looking for a third and killing shot at him. They had come a long way from their days on the streets together, a long way from their grueling practices on the oval at East River Park, a long way from a boyhood that had one day been happy and carefree and the next loaded with guilt and remorse, hatred and anger.

5.

It's a mystery why boys bond. It may be as deeply rooted as the need to learn the skills needed to hunt, so that the tribe can survive. One boy spots and admires the future slayer of game in another, and a friendship begins. Hunting to survive has faded away, to be replaced in American culture by sports, which require the same skills: brute force, deftness of hand, foot and mind and bravery.

In the summer of 1976, two fifteen-year-old boys, one of Italian descent, the other Irish, were involved in such a friendship. The Italian, Chris Massi – already six-foot tall, lean and ascetically handsome, with hair almost black and a pair of dark and very arresting eyes – was a quietly confident boy, certain that he would find a way to succeed, indeed excel, in any endeavor. He loved sports and all contests, finding in them an outlet for his abundant physical energy and a competitiveness that seemed to run in his veins. The Irish boy, Ed Dolan, a compact five-nine, with a shock of blond hair and a sunny but infrequent smile, was the more somber of the two. He pursued his goals doggedly. If he lost, his face clouded over and he became angry, at himself and at the world. Chris did not like to lose either. But he was able to analyze his losses, and learn from them, whereas Ed was not. Losing was to Ed a matter of innate weakness, to be willed into submission.

The boys had just finished their freshman year at LaSalle Academy, located on the corner of Second Avenue and Second Street on Manhattan's Lower East Side. Both had run track at LaSalle: Chris, cross country and then the mile and two mile indoors and outdoors; Ed, sprints and middle distances. Chris and Ed lived within a few blocks of each other. They had their running in common, and they early on formed a friendship that each considered a blessing, awash as they were in a sea of new faces, many of them black and Hispanic, and, what was worse, that is, more alien, many of them from uptown, the land of the rich and the privileged.

A person's history consists essentially of a series of unexpected events. One of the first such surprises occurred for Chris in the spring of 1974. He had been sitting quietly at the dining room table early on a Saturday morning, reading the Daily News. He had read his horoscope, then scanned the movie ads for pictures of half clad women and was reading the News' cornucopia of a sports page when Joe Black sat down across from him, and said, without preliminaries, "You're going to LaSalle Academy."

"What?"

"You have to take the test, but you're in. I spoke to Father Nativo this morning."

Chris could hear the noise from the kitchen, where his mother had been cleaning up after breakfast, stop.

"I'm in?"

"Yes. You have to take the test. But don't worry about it, you're in."

"I'm not worried about the test, Dad. Jesus. What if I don't want to go?"

By this time, Chris knew that he had no choice in the matter. His father had never approached him on a serious issue before, and had rarely repeated himself. Chris understood with no need for thought that these two factors alone put the importance of the issue at a ten on the Richter scale of parental intention. The knitting of Joe Black's thick black eyebrows and the firm set of his mouth and jaw were scary, but superfluous.

The resumption of activity in the kitchen Chris read as a sign of his mother's lack of interest. Rose had chosen to go to war with her husband over her second son, Joseph. Chris knew that she loved him, but also that he was slowly losing her, not to Joseph but to what she had made of Joseph: the answer to her loneliness. Except for extraordinary moments like the current one, Chris had spent the years since Joseph's birth with two hands-off parents, a situation he was neither unhappy nor uncomfortable with. He knew his mother's game plan and her priorities when it came to her children. Rose he could fight, if she cared. But not Joe Black. It took a certain amount of courage to even look him in the eye. When Chris did now, he saw immediately how foolish his last question had been.

"When's the test?" Chris asked in what he thought was a cold, even biting, tone of voice. He was, in his heart, happy about the prospect of going to LaSalle, where he pictured himself competing and beating out several hundred boys in all sorts of challenging contests. But there was no advantage to be gained, he felt, in appearing to accept his father's will with grace.

"Next Saturday."

"Where?"

"At the school."

"Why LaSalle?"

"You can run there."

"Run there?" Chris thought he meant he could run to school each morning.

"You run, Chris. When your mother sends you to the store, you run; when you play football on the street, you run like a crazy man; you run down the stairs and up the stairs all day long. You're always running. When you're sitting still watching the television, you're running, like you have a motor."

"I like to run."

"I know. LaSalle is the champion of track. You can run there, with a uniform, be a champion."

Chris did so well on the city-wide entrance exam that he was admitted to Regis, the school for prodigies and geniuses run by the Jesuits on Park Avenue. He was, in fact, admitted to all of the top schools in the jurisdiction of the Archdiocese of New York. But there was no question of his going anywhere but LaSalle. It never bothered Chris that Joe Black had fixed – completely unnecessarily – his admission with the local parish priest. He took this for what it was: a crude but loving attempt by an unsophisticated man to help his son gain access to a world he himself would never know. He never felt like LaSalle was forced on him. After all, how often does one of the gods come down from Mount Olympus – or up from Hades – to deal personally with one of their mortal offspring?

The boys used East River Park that summer of 1976 – their first and last together – to train. The park, built during the depression, had long been a haven for the immigrant and home-grown poor that had been crowding into the Lower East Side's tenements for two hundred years. Once well kept, the boys knew it only as a ruin, its promenade and amphitheater vandalized and closed, its ball fields and lawns rutted and littered. It had a cross country loop, though, and a cinder oval around a soccer field near the river. They ran punishing distances one day, and then the next they timed each other in the running of their respective events, each urging the other on, each showing off their talent and grit for the other. This training tired them, but not to anything near exhaustion. Fifteen-year-old boys, they could run all day and all night if they felt like it. Often, when they finished their workout, they would join the crowd at the park's two dilapidated basketball courts near the entrance on Houston Street, looking for half-court pickup games of three-on-three or five-on-five full court if they were lucky.

On one of these days toward the end of the summer, Chris, Ed and a little black kid with a wicked jump shot took on three Puerto Rican boys in bandanas and tight jeans and beat them badly not once but four or five times running. The Puerto Ricans were game, but they were not basketball players. Chris and Ed, on the other hand, were not only good athletes, but they knew only one way to play at anything: full out and to win. They did not notice their opponents' friends getting restless as they watched on the sidelines, a group that included three dark-haired girls in shorts and skimpy tops who, as the beatings continued, began to smile behind their hands and to whisper among themselves. One in particular, whose wavy black hair fell midway down her back and whose bright yellow halter top showed off a good deal of golden skin, was intent on Chris, who was not wearing a shirt, and whose lithe, tanned body glistened with sweat in the late afternoon sun. As they continued to win, rather than let up, Chris and Ed – especially Ed – intensified their playing. Ed was not a graceful player, but he was strong and he was determined, much stronger and much more determined than the skinny teenager who was guarding him. Ed became near obsessed with taking this boy low and either muscling up a shot or, if the other two defenders collapsed on him, flipping the ball back to Chris or the black kid for an open jumper. There was a glint in his friend's eye that Chris had never seen before, as if he was angry and determined not only to win but to humiliate the Puerto Rican boys. Elbows flew all the time in these games, but today, if there had been a referee, Ed would have fouled out about midway through the second game, such was the abuse he was reining on his hapless opponent.

Ed scored the winning basket of the last game on one of his typical head-down drives, flipping the ball up and in off the backboard from his hip before crashing full force into his wispy defender. Unfortunately, this blow spun the boy around and propelled him face first into one of the steel uprights that supported the backboard. Head met steel with a clang, and the boy crumpled in a heap to the ground. He lay sprawled on the hot asphalt, unmoving, for several long seconds, while all involved – in the game and on the sidelines – gathered to stare down at him. Groggy, he was helped to his feet by a teammate, blood streaming from a cut above his right eye. Ed had grabbed the ball as it fell through the basket, and now he flipped it to Chris and said, "Next game," turning to head toward a spot above the foul circle. The third Puerto Rican boy, however, the biggest and strongest of the three, grabbed him by the shoulder and spun him around, at the same time drawing a stiletto from his back pocket and flipping it open pointed at Ed's belly.

"We will play our game now," this boy said, stepping toward Ed, holding the knife in the classic underhand position.

"It was an accident," said Ed.

"Accident? So now you will have an accident."

Before Ed could respond, Chris, holding the basketball under his arm, stepped to his side, ready to go back to back with his friend in a fight he knew – they both knew – they would lose, but hoping, and looking, for a way out. A stillness followed in which could be heard the shouts and thumping of the five-on-five game in progress on the adjacent court. Suddenly, the boy with the knife lunged at Ed, who reflexively put his hand out to ward off the knife that was coming at him. Seeing this, Chris cupped the basketball in his right hand and swung it from his heels into the side of the knife-wielder's head, sending him flying through the air about ten feet before he was stopped cold by a nearby chain link fence, where he, too, crumpled to the ground. Chris then turned to see Ed holding his left hand to his chest, the front of his white La Salle T-shirt bright red with blood. Seeing this, the crowd disbursed in all directions, leaving the knife boy on the ground and Chris holding Ed around the shoulders.

"I'll call an ambulance," said Chris.

"No," Ed replied. "It's just my hand. Let's get out of here." As he said this, Ed held out his left hand, which was bleeding heavily from a long and deep laceration along the pad of the palm. Chris grabbed his shirt from the edge of the court where he had dropped it earlier and wrapped it quickly around Ed's wound. Looking around, he saw that the court and sidelines were empty and that the game on the adjoining court was continuing seemingly without interruption.

"You were pounding that kid," he said.

"Fuck him."

"Do you know him?"

"They're swarming like rats, taking over the neighborhood. Taking jobs down on the docks."

The docks on the Hudson River, near Ed's West Village apartment, were where Ed's father worked loading and unloading cargo ships. Chris knew this, but he did not know that Ed Sr.'s job security was under threat, from Puerto Ricans or anyone else. Seeing the light of anger still in Ed's eyes, and knowing instinctively that pride and shame and teenage pain were somehow also involved, he flipped the basketball toward the knife wielder, who was now sitting against the fence holding the side of his head, and said, "Do we have a story?"

"I fell. There was glass on the track."

"That sounds good to me."

In January, two days before his sixteenth birthday, Chris ran a 4:07 mile indoors at the Millrose Games at Madison Square Garden, to this day the third fastest time recorded for any schoolboy in the world. So remarkable was this achievement for a fifteen-year-old that it made the sports pages not only in the city, but around the country as well. Soon afterward, however, his track career ended, as did his friendship with Ed Dolan, as did, indeed, boyhood for both of them. In February, Joe Black Massi killed Ed's father while trying to deliver a message for his boss – gunned him down in the back room of a bar. Two weeks later, Chris broke both of his legs in a car accident on the Grand Central Parkway, ending his running career for good.

The loss of his friend – whose hatred for the Massi family would endure for his entire life – and the loss of his ability to run, broke Chris' heart. It was the struggle with this heartache, a struggle that he eventually won, that began to shape him into the man he was to become. You would have to kill Chris Massi in order to defeat him. In that way and in other ways that he would discover at a crucial time in his life, he and his infamous father were very much alike.

6.

In the months leading to his disbarment, Chris had lain in bed countless times waiting for the noise to die down in his friend's infantile club two stories below before he could sleep. But the bar was quiet when he returned to Bedford Street from his meeting with Joseph at around ten o'clock. Chris remembered as he climbed the stairs that Vinnie had mentioned that he had switched "ladies" night from Wednesday to Thursday as a means of jump-starting the weekend, when business was at its peak. Chris' apartment had been carved out of a larger one that ran across the front of the four-story building. His matchbox living room was on the corner, and had a window that led to a fire escape that was lit from below by the glow from the neon "African Queen" sign above the club's door. The dramatically scripted sign was in hot yellow, except for the "i," which was bright green and in the shape of a thick palm tree, or, if you preferred, a fat penis.

Chris brought three cold Coronas outside and sat above the palm tree/penis, which alone among its fellow letters flicked on and off at regular intervals. New York is never actually quiet, but only relatively so, and tonight was a relatively quiet night, especially with the club being slow. There were the usual sirens and horns in the distance, and the steady buzz of the city that no one really hears unless they choose to.

Chris' post-divorce run of good fortune ended – though he did not know it at the time – on the March day in 2001, when Paulie Raimo walked into his office carrying federal indictment papers in his pocket. Chris' age, Raimo, who lived in Hempstead on Long Island, had grown up in Brooklyn where he began his criminal career at the age of fifteen selling marijuana in his high school cafeteria. Twenty-five years later, he had graduated to stock fraud and was now charged as a co-conspirator in a classic pump-and-dump scheme. He and two other mob types – all linked to Jimmy Barsonetti, the recently ensconced don of Brooklyn – were alleged to have muscled their way into control of a small brokerage in Great Neck. Once established, they began making substantial purchases of selected stocks on margin via straw men, pumping the price of these stocks up by lying to the firm's clients about the issuing company's performance, then selling at large profits before the stocks fell back to their real values. Over five million dollars had been made before the NASDAQ and NYSE computers flagged the brokerage and arrests were made.

Chris had handled enough pump-and-dump cases, both as a prosecuting and a defense attorney, to know that each had the same basic storyboard, although there were several things about Raimo's that heightened his interest. First and foremost was the name of the lead trial attorney for the government, Ed Dolan. Dolan, fifteen years an Assistant U.S. Attorney, was the head of the same task force started in the mid-eighties by then United States Attorney and now Mayor, Rudolph Guiliani, a task force that had put large-scale Italian-American organized crime virtually out of business in New York by the early nineties. *U.S. v Raimo* involved three low level thugs who did not even know enough to include an occasional loss among their illegal trades so as to at least keep the stock exchanges' computers confused. The real target was almost certainly Barsonetti, a newcomer who rumor had it had carved out his Brooklyn fiefdom by killing off the last remnants of the once mighty Velardo family. The plan – a typical prosecutor's tactic – would be to get Raimo or one of his co-conspirators to turn on Barsonetti. Not until Barsonetti was indicted would a lawyer of Dolan's stature appear as lead counsel. But here he was handling a nickel-and-dime case that would normally be in the hands of an assistant a year or two out of law school.

Second, the lawyers representing Raimo's co-defendants refused to enter into a joint defense agreement with Chris. These agreements, which provide for the sharing of information among defense counsel, are common in cases where co-conspirators have the same basic defenses, and are not likely to turn on each other. What was it that these lawyers, or Barsonetti, who was surely paying the legal fees and pulling all of the important strings, knew that Chris did not? Third was Raimo's attitude. A loser with two short prison terms under his belt, Paulie seemed to Chris almost from the beginning more to be feigning worry than actually feeling it. Even when Dolan made it clear that the government would not plea bargain – that Raimo would either have to plead guilty to the entire fifteen count indictment or go to trial – the former teenage marijuana dealer turned stock hustler did not really seem fazed.

These were not signs that Chris missed. It was just that he could not fathom their meaning at the time. When he himself was indicted, in the fall of 2001, on the strength of evidence surreptitiously taped by Raimo, their hidden meaning took a back seat to Chris' active – not to say manic – cooperation with his lawyer in his own defense. His acquittal, a year later, brought tears of relief to his eyes, but his joy was short-lived. Less than a month later, he was notified that the Bar Association had begun disbarment proceedings. It was Ed Dolan who had made himself lead counsel in *U.S v. Raimo*, Ed Dolan who tried, and lost, *U.S. v. Massi*, and Ed Dolan who filed the formal complaint with the Bar Association that led, after another bitter, year-long struggle, to Chris' disbarment. And now Dolan was trying to pin the murder of Paulie Raimo on him, to send Chris to the gas chamber. Farfetched? Not if you knew the players and their histories. Not if you saw Ed Dolan's fifteen year old face, as Chris did, a few hours after he returned from identifying his father's body at the Bellevue Hospital morgue on a cold and bitter morning in February of 1977.

"Your fucking father! Your fucking father!" Ed had screamed. "Your fucking father!"

"What?" Chris had replied. "My father what?"

"He killed my dad. Shot him dead. Your fucking grease ball wop fucking father!"

Ed's face was white, and his lips were blue from waiting under the Sixth Avenue el in the cold for Chris to walk by on his way home from school. It was not a sight Chris was ever likely to forget, and he hadn't. He remembered it, and the bloody fight that followed, as he finished his last beer. Joe Black brought death home with him that day, and now Chris wondered if it ever really left. Maybe, he thought, he would have to exorcise it with a killing of his own.

No one knew why Ed Dolan Sr. interfered in the business between Joe Black Massi and Johnny Logan at Valerio's Tavern on that February night in 1977, least of all Joe Black. There was talk afterward that Logan and Dolan were partners in the renegade numbers, drug and loan shark operation that Logan was known to be running in the recently opened and crime-plagued Two Bridges Houses where Logan lived and whose twelve thousand residents were a dream market for his rackets.

In those days, the entire Lower East Side, from Houston Street down to the Manhattan Bridge, was controlled by Richie Velardo, who was then in his early sixties, and in command of a gang of some two hundred soldiers of various rank, all of them violent men. Logan had been somehow deluded into thinking that he did not have to turn over a percentage of his profits to Velardo, or even ask his permission to operate in the don's territory. Perhaps the warnings he had been given had not been forceful enough, or perhaps Logan, seeing opportunity in the upheaval and turmoil taking place throughout the city at the time, wanted to start a war, to wrest control of the Two Bridges area from the Boot. What better way to do it than to poke his finger directly into Velardo's eye? One thing was certain: Logan had no idea his impulse – either to be an outlaw among outlaws, or to carve out a kingdom of his own – would resonate far into the future and affect the lives of people completely unknown and unconnected to him at the time.

In 1977, the ten-block-by-thirty-block strip of Manhattan along the East River between the Williamsburg and Manhattan bridges was a no man's land of grime-coated tenements, facing each other, row upon row, across streets that baked under the summer sun and turned heartlessly cold in winter. Except for a handful of ill-conceived federally financed public housing projects – which only served to ghettoize the area even more – this part of the Lower East Side was little changed physically from the first part of the century when it was a cauldron of dirt poor immigrants from all over the world.

It was into this unhappy landscape that Joe Black Massi drove from his apartment on Carmine Street, across Lower Manhattan, to confront Logan. He had received a late call from Andy O'Brien, the owner of Valerio's and on the Boot's payroll for years, informing him that Johnny Logan, the would-be *capo*, was having a drink in the back room with an unknown companion.

Joe Black's car, a five-year-old, nondescript Ford, had barely had time to warm up by the time he parked it on Madison Street across from the fortress-like footings of the Manhattan Bridge. The cold bit at him as he walked the two unlit, windblown blocks to the bar, where, entering, he was happy to feel the flush of heat in the front room, and also to note that the place was empty. O'Brien, behind the bar, nodded toward the back, and, without bothering to shake hands or say hello, Joe took off his heavy wool overcoat and scarf, and pushed open the door to O'Brien's "club," a twenty-by-twenty, windowless room with a worn out hardwood floor and three or four wooden tables and chairs, where regulars could have a private conversation or an all night card game.

Inside, at a table in the far right corner, he found Logan and Dolan, who he knew by sight and of whom he had heard stories of his days in the late forties and early fifties as an enforcer – for what side Joe did not know – in the series of wildcat strikes that broke the once iron grip of Joseph Patrick Ryan on the then thriving International Longshoremen's Association on Manhattan's Hudson River waterfront. The yellowed lamp hanging over their table cast a deceivingly mellow glow over the two Irishmen, whose dark eyes revealed little, except for a gleam of displeasure at the appearance of Joe Black in the room.

"I need to talk to you alone," Joe said, directing his gaze at Logan, who was sitting on the right side of the table.

"What about?" Logan answered. He and Dolan looked at each other, and then back at Joe, who was standing just inside the door, about ten feet away, in partial darkness.

Joe did not reply. He rarely said anything twice, or made any effort to press his opinions on others. On the table between Logan and Dolan was a bottle of Canadian Club, about two-thirds full, and two glasses.

"This is my friend, Ed," said Logan. "I know what you're here for. You can talk to both of us. Have a seat."

Joe walked over and put his coat and scarf neatly over the back of a chair to his left, then returned to his position near the door. At five-nine, a hundred and eighty pounds, wearing a navy blue turtleneck sweater and black slacks, there was nothing spectacular about Joe physically, except for his dark eyes, perhaps – the way they seemed to see you and not see you, as if you were already dead.

"The don has accountants," said Joe. "Did you know that?"

It was Logan's turn to remain silent. Dolan had not yet said a word, but he seemed restless, and this Joe Black noticed.

"They have made a study of your business," Joe continued. "They believe – with caution – that you have made a profit of two million dollars in the last year. Don Velardo wants one million dollars, in one week. Also, you must stop doing business until he permits you to resume." He spoke in the formal, stilted, slightly hesitant English of the European peasant who, driven by shame and ambition, had worked with great intensity not to master it so much as to keep its complexities and maddening contradictions at bay.

"And what if I refuse?" Logan said.

"Then I will cripple you. And if you continue to refuse, I will kill you."

"Who is this fucking goombah?" Dolan said, putting his hands – massive, powerful hands – on the table in front of him.

Joe lifted his sweater at the waist, and put his hand on the barrel of his gun, a .44 Magnum, in 1977, one of the most powerful handguns you could buy, legally or illegally. At ten feet, it would take off Dolan's arm at the shoulder, or his head at the neck for that matter. Joe had not had to use it as often as people thought. Displaying it was usually all that was usually necessary, his reputation being the most effective weapon in his arsenal. But tonight it was not enough, as Dolan – six-two and all muscle – in one motion, rose, lifted the table in his hands, and hurled it at Joe like a discus. Its leading edge slammed into Joe's chest, knocking him violently backward against the door and pinning him there for a split second that seemed like an eternity to the three men in the room. Joe Black's sternum was broken, but he did not know it at the time. He flung the table back toward Dolan and crumpled to the floor, spinning quickly as he did behind the table where he had laid his coat. Dolan picked up a chair, lifted it over his head and advanced toward Joe, who rose to one knee and drew his gun. When Dolan was three feet away and the chair was at the top of its arc, Joe fired, the bullet taking Dolan in the chest and stopping him dead in his tracks, literally. As Dolan's body slumped to the floor, Joe turned the gun on Logan, who had not moved from his now almost comically exposed seat at the vanished table.

"Do you have a gun?" Joe asked.

Logan nodded.

"Put it on the floor, slowly."

Logan did as he was told, his limited imagination never having offered up a scene such as the one he had just witnessed. Joe picked up the gun, a cheap, .22 caliber revolver – a throwaway – and checked the cylinder, which was full. He then shot Logan once in the stomach with it. Joe wiped his Magnum clean with his sweater, then bent over and placed it firmly in Logan's right hand, placing his free hand gently, almost, it seemed, respectfully, on Logan's chest as he did, to prevent him from toppling over. Placing his hand over Logan's hand, his trigger finger over Logan's, he fired the gun into the opposite wall, ensuring a positive paraffin test, if the police were inclined to do one. He let the Magnum fall to the floor. Dolan was lying on his side, the blood from his chest wound soaking into his flannel shirt and thick wool sweater.

Joe wiped Logan's revolver clean, and, kneeling beside Dolan, placed it firmly into a grip he formed with the former longshoreman's right thumb and fingers and fired it past Logan's left shoulder. Hoping that both Dolan and young Logan were in fact right-handed, Joe rose and surveyed the carnage. Logan was still sitting in his chair, blood oozing through his fingers where he clutched his stomach, his face drained of its color, his eyes fast losing their connection to the world. He was still breathing. Ed Dolan was not. As Joe was putting on his coat, the door creaked open about twelve inches and Andy O'Brien first looked, then sidled into the room, closing the door quietly behind him.

"Is anybody out there?" Joe asked.

"No."

"Call the police," Joe said, quietly, looking around the room one last time. "Leave everything as it is. I wasn't here."

O'Brien was staring at the two bodies, his eyes grimly accepting the heavy price of Richie The Boot's protective services.

"Did you hear me?" said Joe. "I wasn't here."

"Yes. I heard you."

"The kid's still alive. Give me a minute, then call. He might get lucky."

●

There were fifty thousand longshoremen on the New York and New Jersey waterfronts in 1950, and fifteen thousand in 1970. By the end of the century, there would be only a few thousand. Containerization, not corruption, killed the union – and the trade – that Ed Dolan had, as a strapping and courageous young man newly arrived from County Armagh, fought so hard and so long to save. This he might have been able to accept, since it applied across the board, but the post-Ryan, government-run daily shape-ups, where work was not necessarily or automatically based on seniority, were a bitter blow. The very fairness he fought to impose on the system operated to exclude him from the steady work he needed to maintain his dignity and feed his family.

By the early seventies, he was working one or two days a week, at most, unloading ships. The rest of the time, he was mostly idle, unable to find work in a city whose economy was in a free fall, and where almost any job he could do was controlled by unions who would be loathe to admit a middle-aged newcomer even in good times. When his young cousin, Johnny Logan, called, in late 1976, to offer him a piece of his business at the Two Bridges Houses, in return for Dolan's "muscle" as Logan had absurdly put it, Ed, angry and disillusioned, decided to give it a try. He was afraid of no man, and anything, he felt, would be better than hanging out in saloons or watching his son go off to school while he stayed home with nothing to do.

Dolan's wife Margaret was off on a five-day tour of Jersey City's saloons when he was killed. The police had no choice but to take Ed Jr. out of school and bring him up to Bellevue to identify his father's body. When he returned, Johnny Logan's girlfriend Moira, a darkly beautiful young woman in pointy boots, a red leather jacket and a striped scarf, was waiting for him in front of his apartment building on Washington Street in the West Village. Johnny was alive. She had been allowed in to see him for a second before his surgery. *Joe Black Massi killed his dad, then gut shot Johnny, then made it look like a shootout between the two cousins. It was no shootout. Don't believe anything else. Andy O'Brien worked for Richie Velardo. He'll lie to save his own life. It was Joe Black. He's the murderer.*

Moira, tears, makeup and strands of wet brown hair streaking her face, hugged Ed Jr. and cried on his shoulder as they stood in the small tiled foyer of his tenement. There was a vulnerability, a nakedness, in Moira's eyes that had caught at Ed's stomach. Now, breathing in her perfume, he felt an intense stab of desire, and was immediately shamed by it. Then he watched the building's tired old wooden door swing quickly open and shut as she left to return to Beth Israel Hospital. He had not cried. That would have to wait. He had to figure out how to find his mom. But before that, there was something else. He had to find Chris Massi. Chris had to know how much he hated him. He had to know.

7.

The day after his drink with Joseph at the Peninsula, Chris borrowed Joseph's car, a Saab convertible leased for him by Marsha, and drove to Joe Black and Rose's house in Jersey. Earlier in the week, he had rented a small truck and moved the things that had sentimental value to a storage facility he rented just off the Garden State Parkway in Clifton. These included photo albums, a leather-bound set of the Harvard Classics, a few pieces of solid old world furniture and a collection of curio-sized dragons – in ceramic, blown-glass, bronze and various semi-precious stones, that had surrounded Rose on Carmine Street and then in the small house in Bloomfield. The rest of his parents' things, including all of their clothes and the remaining furniture, he gave to the Salvation Army. On Friday, he went to clean the place up in anticipation of the closing that was to be held the following week. The evening before, he had called Teresa to see if the kids were willing to help, but Tess had promised to tutor a friend for a math exam, and Matt had been invited to help inaugurate a new pool on the grounds of a mini-mansion owned by one of his friend's parents. It seemed, incredibly, that his bat-wielding son had escaped all punishment for his conduct on the prior weekend, an outcome that Chris chose not to discuss with his ex-wife on the phone but that nevertheless brought his blood to a boil. The mindless work at his parents' house was a welcome diversion.

Primarily in the living room, but also scattered in the rooms throughout the now empty house, there were groups of cardboard boxes containing things that Chris was too busy to make decisions about prior to the Salvation Army truck's arrival earlier in the week. His work today was to go through these boxes, sort out the few things of value, and put the rest at the curb. There was a garage that needed to be looked at, but he saved that for last. In two hours, he had about twenty boxes of various sizes neatly stacked out front. The few things worth saving, including his parents' immigration and citizenship papers, their marriage license, Rose's recipe books and a bundle of aging greeting cards tied in a faded red ribbon, he put in a small box, which he placed in the back seat of the Saab.

The house needed to be swept clean, but he decided to first attend to the garage. There he found a neatly organized workbench and much more in the way of tools, including the typical power tools found in men's workshops all over America, than he expected. On Carmine Street, there was a hammer, a couple of screwdrivers and a pliers in a kitchen drawer, and that was it. Joe Black had apparently needed something to do in his retirement. Chris took a hammer from a hook on a peg board. The weight of it in his hand pulled at his heart.

After the gunning down of Ed Dolan, Sr., Chris put the professional Joe Black outside the pale, and, thereafter, never fully admitted the father Joe Black into his life. He survived by suppressing both his love and his hatred for the man whose blood flowed in his veins. The hammer reminded him of the father he never knew. He decided to box up and keep all the tools, and while doing this, he came across an old cake tin with something heavy in it. Inside, he found a 44. Ruger in an oiled pouch, a box of full clips, and an envelope with fifty-five hundred dollars in cash in it.

Joe Black did not speak about what he did for a living. He had dinner with his family most nights, took them occasionally to Coney Island or Jones Beach, and even went to Chris' track meets. On the days he killed people, he acted no different than on the days he didn't. Hefting the Lugar, Chris thought of Jimmy Barsonetti, a man who, if there ever was one, deserved to die. He knew in his bones not only that he deserved to die, but that the truest justice comes at the hand of the victim, or his family. Had this been Joe Black's code? On the one chance he had had to ask that question, Chris had been too young, and too paralyzed by the weight of Joe Black's persona to speak up. He "followed orders" his father had said, but what happened when the orders he received were evil? What did Joe Black do then? That was the question Chris had never asked, afraid of what the answer would be. He had never given his father the benefit of the doubt, and now he wished he had. He might be looking for that benefit himself soon from his own children. He replaced the gun and carried the tin out to the Saab, where he put it under the front seat. As he was doing this, he heard a car pull up. Turning, he saw Teresa in the driver's seat of her Mercedes SUV, which she had double-parked next to the Saab. Tess was in the passenger seat next to her.

"Hi," Chris said, looking into the car through the passenger window, acknowledging first his daughter and then his ex-wife. "What's up?"

"She wanted to help you," Teresa answered.

Tess got out, approached Chris and kissed him on the cheek, then turned to say goodbye to her mom.

"What about dinner?" Teresa asked.

"We'll go out someplace after we finish here," Chris replied.

"Not too late. It's a school night."

Chris and Tess watched as Teresa pulled into the driveway, then backed out and drove off.

"What happened to your tutoring?" Chris asked when she was gone.

"I cut it short."

"Who was it with?"

"Rory Peterson."

"Was that a good idea?"

"All she wanted to do was talk about boys anyway."

"I guess there's no chance she'll be tested on that subject."

"At my high school, you never know."

They worked for the next two hours, Tess sweeping down the entire house and cleaning the kitchen and both bathrooms, while Chris finished in the garage, and then cleaned out the basement. He was finished before Tess, and decided to go out for pizza, stopping on the way back to pick up a bottle of red wine. The tiny Cape Cod-style house had a wide and handsome front porch – its best feature – and there they sat cross-legged to eat their dinner, drinking the wine out of paper cups.

Tess had tied her long hair back to work and scrubbed down in the kitchen sink while Chris went out for the food. She rarely wore makeup, and now, her face glowing from the hard work, she looked lovely as she sat facing Chris in the slanting late afternoon sunlight. Watching her eat and sip her wine, Chris saw both the child and the woman in her, and felt the mix of loss and pride that is familiar to all parents who watch their children become young adults before their eyes. He knew that he was the star of his daughter's life, and had thanked God many times that he had remained so despite all of his troubles.

"Speaking of boys," he said, "what's going on with you and Phil Martell?"

"We broke up."

"Oh? What happened?"

"The summer's coming. He's going to California to see his dad."

"That didn't last long."

"No, a few months."

"But you liked him."

"I thought he was really cool at first."

"Any residuals?"

"You mean am I heartbroken?"

"Yes."

"No. He was pretty happy when I ended it, which was annoying, but I'm fine." Tess smiled as she said this and now there was more woman in her face than girl.

"Speaking of relationships," she said, "what's going on with you and mom?"

"Why?" Chris asked. "Did she say something?"

"No, but she's acting weird. Is it Matt?"

"It must be. I've told her I want him to live with me in New York."

"Oh. Well..."

"I know. She'll never agree to it."

"Never in a million years. Matt's replaced you in a way."

This statement took Chris by surprise. There was too much insight in it, too poignant a reminder that his own mother had replaced her husband with her youngest son, and the havoc that had wrought. He had seen the parallel between Joseph and Matt, but not until now the one between him and Tess. He did not respond.

"Tell me about Grampa Joe," Tess said. "You never talk about him."

"Joseph talks about him enough for both of us."

"He makes him sound like a cartoon character. I want to hear it from you."

"Why?"

"Did you love him?"

"Yes."

"Matt says he was a hit man."

Chris stared hard at his sixteen-year-old daughter, but she did not flinch or look away. At the same time, he was thinking about the rapid yes he had given in response to her last question.

"I hated him, too," he said.

"Why?"

"I'll tell you what. We're finished here. Let's go down to that Applegate Farm place and get some ice cream. I have lots of memories of your grandfather, good and bad. I'll tell you a story or two, but I can't promise more than that."

"Are you worried I won't be able to handle it?" Tess said. She had, Chris realized, seen the introspection in his eyes. "Because I can."

"No," he replied. "I believe you can. I wouldn't be telling you otherwise." *It's not you I'm worried about*, he thought, and then, rising, he held out his hand and helped her to her feet and they headed to the car.

8.

Chris tracked the winter of 1977 daily through the window in his room at St. Vincent's Hospital. Cold and gray, and occasionally stormy, it reflected perfectly the state of his heart. For four weeks, with his right leg hanging from a counterweighted pulley, there was nothing to do but look out at Seventh Avenue and contend with the numbing reality that he would never run competitively again. Occasionally, a storm of anger would rise and howl in his head and then abate, matching the winter storms outside that blew snow and grit sometimes horizontally across his window, temporary distractions from the bleakness. Toward the end, his cast was shortened and he was allowed to hobble around his room using a walker. His left leg had been set and casted as well, but it could bear some weight. He had been told that the cast on the left leg would come off in a few weeks, but that the one on the right leg, where a steel plate and screws had been used to bring his shattered tibia together, would have to stay on until the spring or early summer. One or both of his parents came every day to see him. He was bitterly angry at his father, but out of a misguided sense of fairness, he did his best to shun them both.

It was snowing on the day of his discharge. Joe Black, his face red and his dark overcoat and fedora still wet, appeared early in Chris' room to take him home. His roommate of the last few days, a basketball player at NYU who had had knee surgery, had gone home the day before and his bed had not been filled. Chris, pushing his breakfast aside, had spent the fifteen minutes before his father arrived practicing with the walker, dragging himself from door to window and back again until he broke into a sweat and had to stop. He had just settled back into bed when Joe Black entered the room with his usual quiet step.

"You have some color," the senior Massi said, after drawing a chair near the bed and seating himself. "Your face looks good." Chris' broken nose, resulting when his face bounced off of the windshield on impact, had healed on its own, and the bruises around his eyes had subsided and disappeared after a couple of weeks.

"You're early," Chris replied. "They told me nine sharp."

"I know. I wanted to talk."

Chris did not answer. In his moments of high fury over the past four weeks, he had assembled a series of diatribes against his father, some cold and deliberate, some hot and emotionally-charged, all meant to deliver stinging blows. But now that the moment of truth had come, these searing indictments faded from his head.

"Talk?"

"Yes, talk."

"About what?"

"About me."

"I don't want to."

"Yes, but the time has come."

"What about me," Chris said, suddenly finding his voice. "Why can't we talk about me? I'm the one who's crippled."

"You're not crippled. Your legs will mend."

"Go ahead, then, talk."

"I'm sorry I couldn't come to your track meet. I could have taken you home."

"You were working."

"Yes."

Eying his father across the short distance between them, Chris knew with the instinctive certainty of the young, but nevertheless with a mix of despair and apprehension in his heart, that the revelations made by father and son this day would in all likelihood have to suffice for a lifetime.

"You have heard that I killed your friend's father," Joe Black said, and then, gesturing toward his son's legs, "you think that's what's brought this on your head."

"No, I don't. It's just bad fucking luck."

"You weren't meant to run."

"I guess not."

"You were meant for other things."

"That's for sure."

"Do you know what I do, Chris?"

"No."

"Do you want to know?"

Chris had been hoping for a month for a collision with his father, but not on this very issue. *You asked for this,* he said to himself. If he could, he would have run from the room, run from Joe Black's soft voice and calm, implacable manner, run from the precipice beyond which gaped the rest of his life.

"No," he answered.

"I will tell you. I kill people."

Chris gazed at Joe Black now as if seeing him for the first time in his life, and for a second, he thought he saw in his father's coal-black eyes what it was that made him a killer. What he saw wasn't frightening or repulsive. It was a coldness. He could kill. He had crossed a boundary that most people never come close to.

"Why?"

"If I told you of my life, Chris," Joe Black said, "I would feel that I was begging for your approval. I will tell you this much. I first killed when I was seventeen, in order to eat. When I came to this country, I made a contract for life to follow the orders of don Velardo, which I have done and will continue to do."

"What happened with Ed's father?"

"He attacked me without cause."

"Did he have a gun?"

"No, but Logan did, and I could not take the chance that together they would kill me. I am sorry you have lost your friend."

"He hates my guts."

"Openly?"

"Yes."

"Then you are forewarned."

"Of what?"

"If he is like his father, he will brood, and not forget."

"I'm not afraid of Ed Dolan."

"That's good," the senior Massi said, "because, one day, you will be tested, by him or someone like him. When that day comes, remember what I said here today. Do not beg for any man's approval, even if he is your son, or your father. And once you give your word, you must keep it, or die trying." Joe paused to look at Chris, then said, "If you have a last question, I will try to answer. Otherwise, I will help you to dress, and pack your things."

Chris turned from his father, and looked out the window, where he saw the snow swirling on the wind. The fear and anger that had welled up in him when Joe Black walked into the room, saying he wanted to talk, had subsided. He would never run track again. His father was a hitman for the Mafia. His mother was pummeling his father with his five-year-old brother. There was enough to contend with in these simple facts. More than enough. Turning back to Joe Black, he shook his head. "No," he said. "I can't think of anything."

"Good," Joe replied. "Then let's get you home."

9.

On the day after cleaning out Rose and Joe Black's house – a Saturday – Chris headed back to Jersey to pick up Matt and Tess for an outing in New York. They lived in the same house in North Caldwell that Junior Boy had bought Chris and Teresa as a wedding present in 1985. As he was parking in front, he had a glimpse of Matt washing Teresa's car at the bottom of their long driveway. Tess was sitting on the front steps talking on her cell phone. Chris bent over and kissed her on the top of her head, then rang the bell. Teresa, her dark, naturally wavy hair long, like Tess,' was wearing cream-colored linen slacks and a pale blue short-sleeved cashmere sweater. Her face was made up and she was wearing understated but very good jewelry.

"Come in," she said, motioning him through the wide entrance foyer into her spacious kitchen. "I don't have anything to offer you. I'm going out."

"That's okay. I'm fine," Chris' said.

"We have to talk," Teresa said.

"What's up?"

"First, my father wants to know what time you're bringing the kids back. They're coming over for dinner and he wants to stay and talk to you."

Chris did not answer immediately. Junior Boy could have used any number of intermediaries to arrange a meeting. Doing it through Teresa meant that he wanted her to know about his new relationship with Chris.

"Tell him around nine o'clock. What else?"

They were standing in the kitchen, Chris leaning against a counter near the refrigerator and Teresa opposite him near the open doorway, through which they could both see Tess still chatting on her cell phone. It was obvious to Chris that his ex-wife's dark eyes were glittering with something much more than curiosity over his meeting with Junior Boy, however unusual that might be.

"He mentioned Matt going to LaSalle in the fall."

"Good."

"Good? What's going on Chris? Did you make some kind of a deal with him behind my back?"

"Is washing your car your idea of punishing Matt for what he did?"

"What did he do? He got into a fight. Didn't you get into fights when you were his age?"

"I never broke anybody's arm and ribs with a baseball bat. What he did was ugly. If he does it a few more times he'll be an ugly human being. Doesn't that bother you, Teresa?"

"Are you going to work for my father, Chris? Because if you are, you'll really be a hypocrite. I don't know what you're cooking up, but whatever it is, don't think you're getting Matt from me. I'll fight you both."

Chris knew this to be a hollow threat. Junior Boy's power over his daughter was complete. It extended to all areas of her life. The fact that it was rarely exercised made it more effective, not less. Teresa had traded her independence if not her soul for the high and safe and very comfortable ground on which her father kept all those whom he loved. Chris could take no satisfaction from this knowledge, however. He was about to make a similar bargain with the don. The only difference he could see was that while he would keep his independence, he would lose his soul. The more Teresa clung to Matt, though, the more Chris was convinced that he was doing the right thing in taking him from her for a few years. A few very important years. Looking now at his ex-wife, he could see fear and something close to hatred in her eyes. But he did not care. He would return Matt to her a man, not a thug or a mama's boy like Joseph or, what seemed more likely, a Caligula in the making. That's all he cared about. Teresa could get in line with the others who had turned on him: his former law partners, the bar association, Paulie Raimo, Ed Dolan. One more adversary wouldn't matter.

●

The track event was the Nike Outdoor Classic high school meet, held at Columbia's Baker Field. Chris had purchased tickets weeks in advance – unnecessarily, since the seventeen-thousand-seat stadium was only about a third full – hoping he would be able to bring Tess and Matt, to show them something of what he had done, once, in his life. The day was beautiful, and there was a full schedule of both boys and girls events, involving individual runners and relay teams from all over the country. With Chris' help, Tess was able to follow the girls pentathlon, in which identical seventeen-year-old twins from Texas vied for the lead all day. The one Tess was rooting for won the championship when she beat her sister by a fraction of a second in the eight hundred meters, a race that had the entire crowd on its feet.

Chris caught his breath at the staging of the boys mile, wondering if his record would be challenged or broken, but no one came close. The winner, a tall, angular boy from Maryland, ran the race in 4:28, with a Haitian boy from LaSalle Academy coming in second at 4:29.5. After this race, Tess went off to the ladies' room, handing Matt her program. Chris watched him as he studied, at first casually and then with increasing interest. Chris knew that his name, with the numbers 4:07 after it, appeared in the *world high school records section*, under the names of Jim Ryun and Marty Liquori. Matt had been told about Chris' running career, and the car accident that ended it, but had never spoken of it. He had seen the top six school boy milers in the country – twenty-five years after his father set his record – run their hearts out with the winner twenty-one seconds off his father's pace.

"Dad," he said, showing Chris the program, "did you see this?"

"Yes," Chris answered, "that's me, or was me. Did you see the kid from LaSalle? He's only sixteen. He can be really good."

"How old were you?"

"Two days short of sixteen."

"That's unbelievable."

"What would you think about going to LaSalle, Matt," Chris said, "living with me in the city? You could run track, break all my records."

Chris could see that Matt was about to say something, but checked himself. They locked gazes for a second, and in that second, Chris had his first glimpse in months of his son.

"The exam is in July," Chris continued. "I can pick up an application for you."

"That's an impossible record to break."

"I wasn't finished. I wanted to beat Ryun and Liquouri. It was all I thought about. Until my accident."

Matt had made an effort today to suppress the gangster pose he had been affecting. He did not realize that the sullenness that had taken its place was just as wearing on his Chris's nerves. Chris now saw what looked like thoughtfulness in his son's eyes, and he was grateful. After twenty-five years, his few moments of glory as a track star had finally done him some good. "Think about it," he said, and then Tess returned, and all three turned their attention back to the stadium floor.

After the meet, Chris drove downtown to Carmine Street, where they browsed in the Unoppressive Nonimperialist Bargain Bookstore. Tess, a voracious reader and nascent political junkie, bought five books. They had dinner at Cent'Anni, the only Italian restaurant left from Chris' boyhood days on the three blocks that make up the whole of Carmine Street in its diagonal span from Seventh to Sixth Avenue. Chris had left a message on Joseph's answering machine inviting him and Marsha to meet them, and to his surprise, they did.

Chris had never met Marsha, and she surprised him as well by turning out to be very far from the newly, and richly divorced, fashion-obsessed, desperately fading beauty he had pictured in his mind. She was a petite blonde with a British accent and freckles, looking more like thirty-two – Joseph's age – than forty-two. An illustrator who had crossed over into the fine art world, and whose work was selling at a fancy Soho gallery, Marsha certainly had money, but she had earned it, and, if talking to her for one evening was any guide, she seemed to really like Joseph, and why not? Chris had never seen his charm and gentlemanly attentiveness, not to mention his luxurious beauty, more on display than they were that night.

Marsha noticed Tess' bag of books, and they began discussing politics, while Matt told Joseph about the track meet, emphasizing the twenty-one second difference between Chris' record-setting race in 1977 and the time run today by the "best high school miler in the country." Their conversation shifted to major league baseball. They were both avid Yankee fans and they began to plan their first outing of the year to Yankee Stadium. Chris had always had misgivings about their relationship. Not because he was afraid that Joseph would be a bad influence on his impressionable son – the only time that Joseph acted like half a man was when he was around Matt – but because he was certain that sooner or later Matt's heart would be broken when the real Joseph – the sweating, trembling, pasty white, morally weak heroin addict – was revealed to him. Tonight, he was grateful for their bond, for their talk of track and baseball. Tonight, Matt was just a boy talking to the uncle he idolized. Soon, Chris would take a step that would put him beyond redemption. But tonight, he would try to enjoy what was left of his small family, putting aside for an hour or two the thoughts of skulls on desks, body parts in suitcases, childhood daemons and revenge that had been swirling in his head for the last ten days.

10.

"I spoke to Teresa," Junior Boy said.

"She told me," Chris replied.

"What did she say?"

"She thinks we're in collusion."

"She's a smart girl."

"She'll fight you."

"I know," the don answered, "but most battles are won before anyone takes the field."

They were in the sunroom of Teresa's house. The room, added after Chris left, with its sky lights and removable glass walls, was a screened porch in the summer and a solarium in the winter. The weather had been hot for late May, in the nineties, and the walls had been taken down. A ceiling fan spun some ten feet above them. The wicker chairs with floral print cushions that they sat in were tasteful and comfortable. On their return from the city, Tess and Matt had gone off to their rooms, and Teresa and Mildred were sitting in another part of the house. Outside, the night's stillness was punctuated occasionally by the sound of an airplane overhead or the rustling of the tall trees that surrounded the property.

"What about the Velardo family?" Chris asked.

"You mean why aren't they interested in avenging your father?"

"Right."

On the wicker table between them was a tray containing a pitcher of lemonade, two tall glasses, a bottle of grappa and two short glasses. After pouring himself a half glass of lemonade, Chris gestured with the pitcher toward the other tall glass, an offer the don declined with a wave of his hand.

"The Velardos are no more," DiGiglio said.

"What happened?"

"When the old man died, there was a lot of turmoil. His sons were old and sick. The grandsons fought each other for sole ownership. The nephews tried to form their own family. A small war started. Barsonetti helped the nephews kill the grandsons, then wiped out the nephews and took all the business."

"Barsonetti again."

"When the Boot was dying," Junior Boy said, "I went to see him. He was from the old school. He lived quietly up on his hill. My father respected him, but he knew the sons were fools and the grandsons were greedy. He knew there would be trouble. He told me to do what I could for the old man. Velardo was ninety at the time. Barsonetti had been trying to ingratiate himself, especially with the grandsons, but the old don saw through him. He asked me to be watchful after he died, to use my judgment if I saw trouble for his family. When he died, it was Barsonetti who stirred things up."

"Did you try to stop him?"

"No. There was nothing worth saving in the Velardo family. The grandsons and nephews were predisposed to kill each other, anyway. There wasn't a man among them. But a promise is a promise, so Barsonetti will die."

"When did all this happen?"

"Six months ago. I've been waiting for things to calm down."

"Have they?"

"Yes. Jimmy Barson thinks he pulled a fast one."

"And Joe Black's death brings me into it."

"Yes. Have you thought about it?"

"It's only been a week."

"Ten days."

"How long do I have?"

"Another week, no more."

"I'll let you know."

Junior Boy leaned forward and poured grappa into the two short glasses.

"Have you read any history, Chris?" he asked.

"You can't get through Columbia without reading some history."

"Do you know why some nations thrive, and others don't?"

"Why?"

"The sword. They're not afraid to kill, not afraid of the consequences of killing."

"Indiscriminately?"

"Of course not. But deciding who's an enemy and who's not is not difficult. The effete and the fat and the cowardly claim that it is. Everything's relative to them. They'll eventually be killed by people – nations – who smell their weakness."

"Enemies are to be killed."

"Yes. Before they kill you."

"And this applies," Chris said, "to Mafia families, as well as nations?"

"To all groups of humans that band together," the don replied. "Tribes, nations, Mafia families."

"Weakness always sets in, doesn't it?" Chris said. "Rome declined and fell."

"The Romans believed that Romulus and Remus were born of a she-wolf. Six hundred years later, they lost their feral nature and were destroyed."

"Six hundred years is a good run."

"There was no United Nations then, or academic elite, or New York Times. In a democracy, people can choose a policy of appeasement and cowardice. They can commit national suicide. But my family is not a democracy, and I won't let it be destroyed."

"Do Aldo and Frank know about your proposal to me?"

"No, but if you accept, I'll tell them."

"Why not tell them now?"

The don, his face in the shadows of the dimly lit room, drank down his grappa and poured himself another glassful. As he did, he leaned forward, into the cone of light cast by a nearby lamp. Chris had asked his last question with some trepidation. It came close to being an insult, challenging DiGiglio's judgment as it did for no apparent reason. But the don's face was unreadable. If he were playing poker, he could be holding a royal flush or a bunch of garbage.

"Are you asking that question," his former father-in-law said, "because you don't trust me?"

"I'm trying to understand your motivation here."

"I told you my motive. I'm giving you a chance to avenge your father's death, personally."

"And then I go back to being a disbarred lawyer?"

"You'll find something to do, I have no doubt."

I will, Chris thought. *I don't know what it will be, but it won't be a hitman for the Mafia, if that's what you're thinking.*

"To your decision," the don said, raising his glass.

Chris picked up his glass, and, saying nothing, clinked it against Junior Boy's. Then they both drank down the fiery liquid that the Italians have been making from the dregs of the grapevine since the days of empire.

11.

The next day, Sunday, Chris walked the thirty-odd blocks east to Allison McRae's apartment on Suffolk Street. On the way, he passed LaSalle Academy, still in business, the Christian Brothers still plugging away at their largely unnoticed mission of educating the country's urban poor. In 2001, Chris had donated ten thousand dollars to the school. Passing its grime-darkened, yellow brick building, unchanged from the years he was there in the mid-seventies – and probably since it was built in 1838 – he contemplated the pledge of another ten thousand he had made for 2002, which would have to come out of his share of the money from the sale of his parents' house. Luckily, he had made no pledges beyond that. He also passed the section of elevated railway on Sixth Avenue, long abandoned even when he was a boy, under which he and Ed Dolan had battered each other on that grim winter afternoon in 1977.

On the Lower East Side in the summer, people are out in droves on the streets, their give and take generating an edgy, in-your-face energy that Chris knew from years of walking the city demanded a certain amount of respectful attention. As he approached Delancey Street, he turned his mind to the present and altered his gait from the steady, easy striding of the last thirty minutes to a sort of alert gliding as he drifted on the surface as it were of the crowds, the better to negotiate their various eddies and crosscurrents. These crowds, speaking many languages and in a wide range of decibels, thinned as he approached Suffolk Street near the entrance to the Williamsburg Bridge, where the traffic on the inbound side appeared to be backed up all the way to Brooklyn. The day was sunny and the air freshened by an early morning shower, giving the neighborhood a patina of pleasantness, which, looking around, Chris knew was an illusion. This was not the New York of postcards or even of romanticized starving artists. Starving artists may live here, among the drug addicts and prostitutes and the dirt poor – the rents were cheap for all – but they would not deceive themselves about the character of the neighborhood. It was seedy and dangerous and not even remotely romantic.

At the corner of Delancey and Suffolk, three black men, looking to be in their mid-thirties, were standing with their backs against a temporary construction wall passing around a bottle wrapped in a brown paper bag. Chris kept them in his peripheral field of vision as he turned the corner and headed down Suffolk Street to number one-twelve in the middle of the block. At the top of the building's front steps, he saw a young woman, in her mid-twenties, searching through a large, woven bag that was slung over her shoulder. As he approached, she drew out a pack of cigarettes, extracted one and lit it with a plastic lighter. She sucked it down like it was marijuana, then turned her gaze to Chris, smoke streaming from her nostrils. They assessed each other for a second, aliens making random contact, Chris in his khakis, walking shoes and polo shirt, his attitude open but careful; the woman in low-cut jeans, a tight fitting, long-sleeved black cotton shirt with a pink lightning bolt on the front, darting between her small breasts, a leather cuff bracelet on one wrist and a look of challenge in her heavily made-up eyes.

"You can't be a narc," she said.

"No."

"Or vice."

"No."

"Or a john."

"No."

"Then what?"

"I'm looking for Allison McRae."

The woman did not answer immediately. Instead, she took another drag on her Marlboro Light, then ran her free hand through her short, platinum blonde hair, exposing a quarter inch of brown roots, her demeanor and body language changing from confrontational to something else, something Chris could not quite read. She wasn't hiding her drug habit or her prostitution, but she was no longer flaunting it.

"Are you a movie guy?" she asked.

"Movie guy?"

"Allison's an actress."

"No. I'm her cousin. Her mom asked me to stop by. She hasn't heard from her in a while."

"What's your name?"

"Chris Massi. And you are?"

"Michele. I live across the hall from Allison."

"What floor? I'd like to go up and see her."

"The fourth, but she's not home. She's doing a movie in Los Angeles."

"When did she leave?"

"About a month ago."

"Why wouldn't she tell her mother?"

"She never mentioned a mother. I've been putting her mail in her apartment."

"Have you heard from her?"

"She called last week. She said she'd be back soon to pick up some things and close down the apartment. She's staying out there."

"Do you have her number?"

"No. Sorry."

"Are you an actress?"

If Michele was an actress, then Chris was an astronaut, but his instincts told him that he should look around Allison's apartment, and Michele was his easiest way in.

"No," Michele answered.

"Would you like to be?"

"You want me to let you in? Is that it?"

"I'd appreciate it."

"You want sex?"

"No," Chris answered, taking out his wallet, "but I can loan you fifty bucks. You can pay me back when you're working."

"Fine," she said, snatching the bill from his hand. Chris could see by the surprise and avarice that flashed in quick succession in Michele's eyes that the fifty dollars was a godsend. It meant an easy score of dope and a few less hours of dealing with the perverts and desperados on the street.

Allison's apartment consisted of a small living room with a kitchen alcove, a bathroom and a tiny windowless bedroom. There was a dirty plate and a glass coated with the remains of some dark liquid, probably soda, on the coffee table in the living room. The rest of the place was fairly neat, with a tired cotton rug under the coffee table, a rocking chair, a bookshelf and a hardwood floor worn thin but swept clean.

On the wall next to the kitchen alcove was a telephone, which emitted no dial tone when Chris picked it up. Next to the phone was a small cork bulletin board with two photographs pinned to it. One of them was of an attractive young blonde woman, presumably Allison, and a heavy set, swarthy man in his forties. They were standing in front of a palm tree in bright sunlight holding tropical drinks – the kind with parasols sticking out of them – smiling at the camera. They were in bathing suits and the man had his arm around the woman's waist, his hand resting possessively on her hip. The other was of Allison and a dark-haired, pretty woman of the same age, both in bikinis, apparently taken at the same vacation spot.

As Chris was looking at these pictures, Michele's cell phone rang, and she stepped into the hall to have her conversation. Chris unpinned both photographs, and turned them over. On the back of the one of the two women was written, in bright red ink, "Allie, What a great trip!!! I have lots more pictures. Call me when you get back. Heather XXXOOO." Chris put both pictures in his shirt pocket, then sat on the sofa to go through Allison's mail, which Michele had piled neatly between two faded corduroy cushions. It was a hundred percent bills and junk mail. Looking around, he saw that the only drawers in the apartment were in the kitchen alcove. These he went through but found nothing of any moment. The bookcase did not contain books but rather neat rows of photocopied screenplays with blue and red covers, the kind you can buy on the street in Soho and the East Village for ten dollars. He pulled one out at random and saw that it was Robert Towne's *Chinatown*, heavily dog-eared and highlighted in the portions where Evelyn Mulray appears, played by Faye Dunaway in the movie, with scribbled notes covering the margins so densely that, at first, it looked like intricate art work.

He replaced the script and turned to see Michele standing in the doorway, leaning against the jamb with her right shoulder and hip.

"I told you there was nothing here," she said.

"Where did she keep her clothes?"

"In cardboard boxes on the floor, but she took all her clothes with her."

"Who are these people?" Chris asked, taking the pictures out of his pocket and walking over to hand them to her.

Michele took them and glanced quickly at them before replying: "This is Allison with a producer she was seeing. I never got his name. The girl is a friend from L.A."

"Heather."

"Right."

"What's her last name?"

"Johnson, Jansen, I'm not sure."

"Do you know where she lives?"

"No, just L.A."

"When did Allison move in here?"

"In the winter, January, February."

"Why did she leave these pictures behind?"

"She didn't. I found them in the sofa cushions when I started putting the mail there. She had a dozen like them up there, which she took. So I just stuck these back."

Chris reached out and took the photographs back. He looked at both images, then said, "When did she take this trip?"

"A few weeks after she moved in. It was snowing like a bitch here."

"Where is this place?"

"In Mexico. A place called Palmilla. Allison said it was beautiful."

"Where did she go the second time?"

"The second time?"

"Heather says, 'call me when you get back.'"

"Oh, right. She went with this guy again. I think to Florida for a week."

"Was she doing heroin?"

Michele did not answer. She looked at Chris and held his gaze for the first time since they'd met. Behind her eyes, he saw, very briefly, another Michele, lost and almost forgotten, the one whose life heroin was trying to destroy. "You'd know," he said.

"She thought it was cool at first."

It was Chris' turn to be silent.

"I didn't turn her on, if that's what you're thinking."

"Who did?"

"Her producer boyfriend. He even gave her some to give to me. It was great smack, not like the shit on the street. Where do you think she is?"

"She's probably getting high with him right now. I don't think she's making a movie. If you see her, will you tell her to call me?"

Chris handed her one of the last of his DeVoss & Kline cards, with their number crossed out and his apartment number written in.

"So you're a lawyer," Michele said looking up after reading the card.

"I used to be."

"I'll bet you were a good one. Did you do any custody cases?"

"Child custody?"

"Yes."

"No. Nothing like that. Why?"

"No reason."

"Get off the street, Michele, get clean. Go to Legal Aid. They'll help you to see your kids."

"My kids are dead."

And soon you will be, too, Chris thought. Then he turned and left.

12.

"Tell me about Labrutto?" Chris asked Nick Scarpa.

"He's a bad guy," Scarpa answered. "There's a couple of things I have to do for him, then I'm quitting."

"Is that why you're willing to take me to his house unannounced?"

"That and for your old man."

"What do you mean by *bad guy*? The porn movies?"

"The porn movies, the drugs. He's got a sidekick that gives me the creeps. He keeps girls like slaves."

"You mean in chains, locked up?"

"No, but the kid he's got there now is doped up all the time. She's his current porn star. I feel sorry for her. I'd like to get her out of there if I can."

"How long have you been working for him."

"Since I got out of the can, six months."

Chris gazed out the passenger window. They were in Nick Scarpa's Pontiac, Nick driving, his crooked fingers gripping the steering wheel at ten and two, crossing the Hudson River on the upper deck of the George Washington Bridge. The day was for the moment warm and sunny, the sky a dome of blue, the thunder clouds massing up river at the northern horizon only a distant threat.

"How long were you in."

"In the last twenty-seven years, twenty-three."

"For what?"

"Armed robbery. Two of them."

"How old are you?"

"Fifty-two."

"Are you done now?"

"Yeah, I'm rehabilitated."

Nick Scarpa smiled when he said this, and, as he did, his face was transformed. A happy twinkle replaced the slightly confused look in his eyes, and his broad grin, revealing a full set of white but crooked teeth, softened the fierceness of his mashed nose and blurred the scar that ran along his jaw line from ear to chin. For a second, Chris could see the handsome teenager who lived in the tenement next to his on Carmine Street in the sixties, who occasionally walked over to the playground of Our Lady of Pompeii school to shoot baskets with him and his friends.

"Armed robbery's a young man's game, Nick."

"I'm done," Scarpa said. "The next time I go up, it's for good. I got two grandkids I can't do that to."

"I appreciate what you're doing."

"It's no big deal. Like I said, I'm quitting anyway."

"Have you been to Barsonetti's house other than the one time?"

"No. I think the albino usually makes those runs. He was sick or something the day I went."

"Who's the albino?"

"The sidekick. He lives in a cottage on the property."

Nick had not asked Chris what his interest was in Jimmy Barsonetti, nor why exactly he wanted to talk to Labrutto. He had simply agreed to bring him along the next time he went to Labrutto's house in Alpine, a small, mansion-dotted town situated on the cliffs on the Jersey side of the Hudson. That day turned out to be the day after his Sunday visit to Allison McRae's apartment on Suffolk Street.

"Did you box in prison?"

"A little in the beginning. To let people know I could take care of myself."

Nick, Chris knew, had won the Golden Gloves middleweight title at age seventeen. A wild man in the ring, when he turned pro two years later, he was already being compared to LaMotta and Basilio. Even now, Chris knew, glancing at Nick's big-knuckled hands as they clenched the steering wheel, a blow from the ex-fighter-ex-con would do a lot of damage. A few, delivered in sequence and with the bitterness of a wasted life behind them, could easily be fatal.

"Have you killed anyone?" Chris asked.

"Sure, two people."

"Who were they?"

"One was a Puerto Rican who came at me with a knife one night in the Bronx. I shot him in the heart. The other was a black guy who tried to rape me in Chino. I cracked his head against a sink. His two buddies had shivs. I got stabbed a few times, but they both ended up in the prison hospital."

"What about Joe Black?" Chris asked.

"Joe Black?"

"Yes. Who did he kill?"

"People who deserved to be killed, mostly."

"Like who?'

"Bad guys from other families, guys who tried to put the Boot out of business. He killed a guy once who raped two women over by the old West Street, by the docks."

"Who told him to do that?"

"No one, he just did it."

"How do you know this?"

"I talked to one of the guys he was with."

"Jesus."

"Joe Black was the toughest guy in the five boroughs," Nick said, "but that wasn't all there was to him. When your brother first came up to me, I thought it was thirty years ago, and I was looking at your old man."

The Joe Black Chris remembered was old, his face a grim, expressionless mask, his once jet black hair turning grayer with each passing year. But there was another Joe Black: the young man in the photographs culled recently from the house in Bloomfield, standing in the sun next to his new car on Carmine Street, toweling himself off after emerging from the sea at Coney Island, holding his son Chris by the hand on the day of his First Communion. That Joe Black looked remarkably like Joseph, even to the hint of the I've-got-a-secret smile that Joseph seemed to have patented in his teens. The picture on the beach Chris had had to look twice at to make sure it was Joe Black and not Joseph.

"He was a good guy, Joe Black," said Nick.

"He was?"

"When I did my first stickup, he hunted me down. I was holed up in a basement apartment in Brooklyn, out in Green Point. Joe Black comes in through the window one night. He's got that look in his eyes. Very quiet, very scary, that was your old man. He wants me to turn myself in, do my time, come out to fight again. I was entitled to one free crime, he said, but no more. Antoinette was pregnant at the time. She was eighteen – she lost the kid – what kind of a man was I? he said. I bluffed him, then I ran. Of course, I was caught, but I thought I was a tough guy. I was nineteen. And here I am today."

"How did you know him?"

"Your father?"

"Yes."

"Back then, Carmine Street was more Italian than Little Italy. Everybody knew each other. Joe Black came to all my fights."

"How old was he?"

"Twenty-nine, thirty."

"What brought that on?"

"What?"

"That first stickup. You won the Golden Gloves. Everyone said you had a career."

It was Nick's turn to look out the window. They were heading north on the Palisades Interstate Parkway, a low volume, scenic road that runs along the edge of the famous cliffs that for twenty miles drop straight down in vertical columns to meet the Hudson River five hundred feet below.

"I threw my last fight. Did you know that?"

"No. I was just a kid, then you went away."

"The Boot, did you ever meet him?"

"A couple of times. He was at my wedding."

"He told me I'd never fight again. He mentioned how pretty my sister was. I took a dive. A week later, I pulled my first job. Six months later, I was in Attica, doing three-to-five."

"Joe Black worked for the Boot."

"That's common knowledge. Are you saying I should be holding a grudge?"

"Why not? It was because he had muscle like Joe Black that Velardo was so feared. He might have sent him to cut your sister if you didn't throw that fight."

"Life is hard, Chris. I thought you figured that out by now."

They had turned off the highway onto a leafy street that ascended into the hills, thick with tall and ancient evergreens, that gave Alpine its name. Glimpses of stone turrets, glass solariums, gated entries, long winding driveways and beautiful lawns and gardens were to be seen as they glided along, with an occasional full-blown mansion appearing and slipping quickly by, like the mirage of a giant ship at sea. At number 516 they were stopped by a thick wrought iron gate, ten feet high by twenty feet across, anchored by stone pillars topped with what looked to Chris like security cameras. Through the gate they saw, about a hundred feet away, a man walking toward them along the gravel driveway, moving in and out of the shafts of morning sunlight finding their way through the over-hanging branches of the tall trees that lined the drive.

"I'll tell you what," said Nick. "Madison Square Garden has those Friday night fights. We'll go Friday. We'll have dinner. I'll tell you what I know about your father. He wrote me when I was in Attica, my first bid. I still have the letters. I'll bring them."

Chris shook his head. It was unbelievable to him that Joe Black Massi had ever written a letter. The image of his father taking up pen and paper, with the thoughtfulness that that act implies, stopped Chris cold. For years, Chris had clung to the belief that his father was not quite human, not entirely like everyone else, who lived and breathed and made mistakes and felt all sorts of things, like anger, jealousy, hate, sadness, annoyance, all the things that human beings felt all the time. Did such a man write letters to a nineteen-year-old in prison? Did such a man avenge the rape of women who were strangers to him?

Did such a man try to point out the road to redemption to a hard-headed young fighter turned armed robber?

Chris had built a wall around his heart after his car accident and the killing of Ed Dolan Sr., a wall that he would not let Joe Black breach while he was alive. Now that Joe was dead, here comes cockeyed Nick Scarpa trying to vaporize it with a word or two. There was nothing new age about Chris Massi. He did not believe that the dead communicated with the living. But he did believe that certain things were meant to be. He had never thought to look for sources of information concerning the reclusive and solitary Joe Black Massi. Why would he want to learn things that would cause him pain? But here the universe had handed him a primary source who had good things to say. Considering that he was about to follow in his father's footsteps, it would certainly be worth hearing that those footsteps led occasionally down paths of righteousness and honor, qualities that at the moment Chris sorely needed to associate with the Massi name.

13.

Before Chris could answer, his attention was drawn to the man in the driveway, who had reached the gate and was swinging it open. He could be seen clearly now: tall and thin, in his late twenties, platinum blonde hair swept back from his forehead and kept in place with some kind of gel, his complexion milky white – if he wasn't albino, he was the closest thing to it – his eyes hidden by very dark sunglasses, his black slacks and black pullover shirt making him look even thinner than he probably really was: an eerie stick figure gesturing them to drive onto the property, which Nick did, and to stop, which Nick also did, once he was inside the gate.

"Who's this?" the man said to Nick, nodding toward Chris as he leaned into the driver's side window. "A friend of mine," Nick answered.

"Does Guy know he's with you?"

"No, but it'll be okay."

"Who is he?"

"Chris Massi. He used to be Junior Boy's son-in-law."

The albino stepped around to the back of the car and pulled his cell phone from the clip on his belt. As he dialed, he swung the heavy gate shut. Chris and Nick watched through the chrome-trimmed mirrors on the sides of the old Pontiac as he talked on the phone.

"I met Labrutto when I got out of Chino in 1987," Nick said. "At the time, he was living in a rented bungalow in West L.A."

"Was he doing porn then?"

"He was just starting."

"Does Junior Boy know about his connection to Barsonetti?"

"I doubt it."

"What's that all about?"

"I think it's something pretty nasty."

"You mean nastier than the usual nasty?"

"Yes."

"Like what?"

"The girl has said some wild things."

"The one who's stoned all the time?"

"Yeah, Stacey. You'll probably meet her."

Chris was about to ask another question when the albino reappeared at Nick's window.

"Go ahead," he said. "You know where to park."

As the car rounded a curve in the driveway, they passed a small caretaker's cottage with a black BMW sedan parked next to it. A quarter mile farther on, they came to the house, a low-slung, modernistic affair set on a small rise, with a gravel circular driveway in front, in the center of which was a metal sculpture, about ten feet high, painted red, that looked like a bird with a broken neck. At the front door, Guy Labrutto himself greeted them, and Chris immediately recognized him as the fat, swarthy man in the photograph he had taken from Allison McRae's apartment the day before. He was wearing a freshly manicured goatee, and he was now dressed all in black, but it was clearly the same man in tropical wear with his hand on Allison's hip on the beach in Mexico.

Nick introduced Chris. Labrutto, eying his surprise visitor but showing no sign of unease, led them into a sunken living room where a trio of oddly shaped chairs were set around a large glass coffee table. Labrutto, remaining standing, gestured toward the chairs and Chris and Nick sat. They were facing, about twenty feet across the room, a full glass wall through which they could see a woman, apparently naked, sunning herself – a cell phone resting on her stomach – on a lounge chair beside a kidney-shaped swimming pool, its surface a shimmering pale blue as it caught the late morning sun. The woman, who on closer inspection was actually wearing a string-like thong bikini, with no top, was Allison McRae.

"The son of the famous Joe Black Massi," said Labrutto. "I hear you've had some trouble. Do you need work? I can use you."

Chris was not insulted by these remarks. No serious Mafioso – no serious businessman for that matter – would be so impulsively condescending. It was obvious that Labrutto, a lowlife, was puffed up by what he believed was his new found stature in the world of organized crime. He did not know that he was being used and that it would take only one or two false moves for him to end up at the bottom of a lake in the Adirondacks. The people who would be happy to take his place making porn videos and giving half the profits to Anthony DiGiglio were legion. Even if he had felt some sting from Labrutto's comment and question, Chris would not show it as he was not about to lose the opportunity to get to Barsonetti that the effete and beady-eyed film-maker presented.

"No," he replied, his voice neutral. "I'd like you to introduce me to somebody."

"Who would that be?"

Chris glanced at Nick. He did not want to implicate the ex-fighter any more than he already had. Jimmy Barsonetti would soon be dead, and people would be wondering how he had been reached.

"I see," said Labrutto, noting Chris' glance. "Why don't I get us something to drink? Nick has to run some errands. Then we can talk. What would you like?"

"Water would be fine."

"Come with me, Nick," said Labrutto

While Labrutto and Scarpa were out of the room, Allison pulled her long blonde hair back into a pony tail, rose from her lounge, and, her back to the glass wall, slowly stepped into a pair of form-fitting midriff jeans. Then, turning sideways, her slender body in profile, she slipped into sandals and pulled on a pink half tee shirt with puffy sleeves and silver sequins sprinkled across the front. Chris watched, a captive audience of one, as she crossed the pool's concrete apron and entered the room through its sliding glass door. Inside, she seemed startled to see him, then, regaining her composure, putting a bright smile on her face as if it were a prop or makeup, she approached him with her right hand extended.

"You must be a friend of Guy's," she said. "I didn't know he was having company. I'm Stacey."

Chris rose to introduce himself and, while shaking Allison's hand, he took the opportunity to look directly into her once pretty blue eyes, which had a hard bright sheen to them, to feel the clamminess of her palm, and to note the fresh track marks on the inside of her left forearm .

"Do I know you?" Chris asked. "Your last name is...?"

"It's Electra, but that's a stage name."

"I see. And your real name?"

"Oh, that's long forgotten."

"Do you know a woman named Danielle Dimicco?"

"Danielle Dimicco?"

"Yes. She wants you to call her."

The confusion in Allison's eyes, emerging briefly from her drug-induced miasma, was all Chris needed for an answer. Something else appeared for a half second in those glazed-over eyes, something that may have been fear or panic or just junkie paranoia. Chris was pondering this flash of emotion when her fake smile returned and it was his turn to be confused. But then he saw she was looking over his shoulder at Labrutto, who had reappeared, followed by Nick carrying a tray containing a bottle of designer water and a glass filled with ice, which he placed on the coffee table.

"I see you've met Stacey," Labrutto said.

"Yes."

"She and Nick are just about to go out."

"Oh," Allison said, "I thought Mickey..." "I need Mickey here," Labrutto said. Then, to Nick, he said, "The work on my car is done. Run Stacey down to the Mercedes dealer on Route 9. Follow her back here."

"Let me get my purse," Allison said, and then she gave Chris a short wave and said, "Nice meeting you," before heading off into the interior of the house.

"Nick won't be long," Labrutto said to Chris. "I'll meet Stacey outside," Nick said, as he nodded to Chris and headed toward the front door. Labrutto watched Nick go and then excused himself to "make a quick call." When he returned a few minutes later, he and Chris took seats facing each other across the glass coffee table. Chris said nothing. Labrutto shifted his considerable weight in his chair, crossing one leg over the other, arranging his flowing silk shirt over his basketball-sized belly and smoothing out his beautifully tailored black slacks as he did.

"So," said Labrutto. "Who do you want to meet?"

"Jimmy Barsonetti," Chris replied.

"Jimmy Barsonetti? Are you crazy?"

"No, I'm serious."

"I can't help you. I never met the man."

"I heard you guys hung out together in California. I must have heard wrong."

"You did. Like I said, I don't know him."

"That's too bad. Do you know anybody who can vouch for me?"

"I might. What would you want to talk to him about?"

"A business proposition."

"What kind of a business proposition?"

"It involves two million dollars in untraceable cash."

"To be stolen?"

"When you mention it, he'll know what I'm talking about."

"I told you, I don't know him."

"You never know," Chris said, "you might meet him in the next day or two."

The eyes are the window to the soul, but Labrutto, a drug dealer, a pornographer, an abuser of women, did not have one as far as Chris could see. Instead, a series of calculations appeared to be taking place in the stocky little producer's head, a spinning of wheels and symbols that he was fairly certain would come up *yes*.

"I would have to go to a lot of trouble," Labrutto said, finally, "to get an audience with Barsonetti."

"I could pay you for your trouble," Chris said. "How much would you want?"

"A hundred grand."

"I'll give you fifty when the meeting is set up and fifty when it's finished."

Labrutto nodded and stroked his goatee.

"What's to stop me," he said, "from going to Junior Boy with this. I assume you know he and I are in business together?"

"Nothing," Chris answered, "except he'd wonder why I came to you to get to Barsonetti."

"Why would I bring Barsonetti into it?"

"You could lie to him, but I think he knows me better than he knows you."

Labrutto's eyes narrowed at this suggestion that he had no credibility with Junior Boy. "You know it would be on Barson's terms completely," he said. "You'd be searched. You'd be isolated."

"I don't want to kill the guy. I want to make him an offer he can't refuse."

"You could end up like your old man."

Chris had smiled wryly when he used the famous line from *The Godfather*, but now his face went blank as he took a breath and stared quietly into Labrutto's eyes. He had no choice but to let this insult to his dead father pass.

"One last thing," he said.

"What's that?"

"I can't get the money without some help. If I were to die, I've left a trail that leads right to you and Jimmy Barson."

"I'll be sure to tell him that."

"Good. I want him to know who he's dealing with."

"How can I reach you?"

"I'll call you tomorrow."

"Then we're done," Labrutto said. "You can wait for Nick here. I have some work to do."

When the porn producer went off, Chris poured himself some water and took a long drink. There had been no need for Labrutto to insult Joe Black, except as a show of power, which was absurdly unnecessary. Placing his half-full glass gently on the glass table, he assessed his feelings. He was angry, not so much at the reference to his father's degrading death, but at the fact that an idiot like Labrutto could feel so free to make it.

Shaking his head, he turned his thoughts to Barsonetti, who, Chris was certain, would not be able to resist the temptation of Richie the Boot's legendary two million dollars. In his mind, stealing it from Joe Black's son and killing him in the process – for no doubt that's what he would want to do – would have a beauty and symmetry that would eventually lull him – somehow, somewhere along the line – into letting down his guard. Like the music that charms the snake.

Glancing around the room, Chris decided he had had enough of Labrutto and his pretentious house. He rose to leave, and as he did, he spotted Allison's cell phone on a small table next to the sliding glass doors. He walked over to it and picked it up. Reflexively, he turned it on and pushed the redial button. After three rings, a female voice – a voice he thought he vaguely recognized – said, "Leave a message, I'll call you back." He clicked the phone to off and put it back down on the table. Then he let himself out and headed down the long driveway toward the massive front gate, where he would meet Nick for the ride back to the city.

As he was approaching the caretaker's cottage, thunder boomed and boomed again and the storm clouds, accumulating all morning over the river valley, released their torrents. The small overhang above the cottage's front door provided no protection against the driving wind and rain, and so Chris, knocking first, entered and was immediately in a sparsely furnished room that was half kitchen and half office. The BMW was missing, so he did not expect anyone to be in the cottage, but he called out anyway and received no answer. Outside, the storm was increasing in intensity, and the sky had turned almost black.

The back screen door, torn open by the wind, was swinging violently on its hinges. Chris crossed the room, pulled it shut and set the eye-hook. On his way back, on the kitchen table, he saw several porn magazines – anal teens, men on men, girls on beasts – in that vein. One of them was opened to the classified section where an ad in the lower part of the page was highlighted in yellow. It read: *Will pay top $$ for home videos. Box 2194, NY 10001.* Next to the magazines was a stack of DVDs, about six in all, each tightly wrapped in cellophane, each neatly labeled, "Candy Meets Ron." He picked one of them up. As he was idly turning it over, the front door swung open, and Mickey, the gatekeeper, entered the cottage, pointing a nickel-plated, nine millimeter Beretta at Chris.

"Put that down," Mickey said, his voice surprisingly deep for all his thinness, easily heard above the howling wind, which was battering the one-room cottage, and knocking tree branches down along the driveway.

"Take it easy," Chris said, glancing at the pistol, then meeting Mickey's pale brown eyes for a second, a brief second, before they started rolling around in their sockets and then darting around the room, looking, it seemed, for additional signs of Chris's intrusion. "I just came in out of the rain."

With his free hand, Mickey took a cell phone out of his jacket pocket, flipped it open, pushed one button and held it to his ear. His hair was plastered to his head from the rain, which, with his opaque eyes below brows now knitted in concentration, made him look scrawny and a bit stunned, like a newly hatched bird. Drops of water were running from his temple down his jaw line, and there was a gash on his forehead, oozing blood.

"I'm at the cottage," he said into the phone. "Massi was here nosing around when I walked in...He's not going anyplace...Yes, it's done...Okay. First, I need to take care of the car."

Mickey closed the phone and put it in his pocket. He was still pointing the Beretta at Chris' stomach. Chris was still holding the DVD.

"Guy wants to see you."

"Sure," Chris said. "But don't you want to wipe your face first? Here, use this."

In the motion of an abbreviated tennis backhand, he flipped the DVD at Mickey, spinning it like a Frisbee, aiming for his head. Mickey raised his free hand, but not in time to prevent the DVD, with its sharp, hard edges, from hitting him just below his left eye. Chris closed the ten feet between them in one leap, knocking his thin but wiry and surprisingly strong adversary to the floor, and tumbling on top of him. He then quickly found Mickey's gun hand – the gun was still in it – and slammed it twice against the floor, breaking the albino's wrist and jarring the gun loose. They both scrambled for the gun, but Mickey stopped, crying out in pain as he put pressure on his shattered wrist, giving Chris the chance to grab the gun and swing its barrel into the gatekeeper's face. Chris then flattened the pistol into his palm and smacked Mickey on the side of the head with it, knocking him out cold.

Silence. And then Chris' ears began working again, and he heard the hard patter of rain on the roof, and the wind blowing, though with less force, around the cottage. Still holding the Beretta, Chris went through Mickey's pockets, finding a wad of hundred dollar bills in a money clip, and a wallet. Inside the wallet were a few scraps of paper, and a driver's license in the name of Michael Rodriguez of 40909 Topanga Canyon Drive, Los Angeles. The picture on the front was definitely Mickey. The scraps of paper were empty, except for one, which had "Michele 212-534-8977" written on it in blue ink. This Chris put in his pocket, along with one of the "Candy Meets Ron" DVDs.

When he got outside, he pitched the Beretta into the woods, then made his way, inside the tree line and out of sight of the security cameras, to the front of the property, hopping over the low stone wall that ran along the street. The wind had died, leaving in its wake what promised to be a long steady rain. Chris' khakis and cotton sweater were soaked through, but he was barely aware of them. What had so alarmed Rodriguez that he thought he needed to point a gun at Chris' chest and march him up to see Labrutto? Why had Mickey left the grounds if Labrutto needed him around, as he had told Allison?

When he left the cottage, Chris noticed what looked like fresh damage to the grill of the BMW. Had Mickey, his forehead oozing blood, been in an accident? What had Chris walked into the middle of? And most important, what affect would it have on his plans to get Labrutto to set up a meeting with Barsonetti? The answers to these questions were unsettling, to say the least. He did not need to be embroiled in Labrutto's sleazy world, and, having decided to commit premeditated murder, and having acted on that decision, he did not need distractions. He needed good luck, not bad. Up ahead, he saw a car's headlights coming toward him. Sticking out his thumb, willing the driver to stop, he realized there wasn't much he could do: get home, get dry, deal with the awful pain in his rib cage, sort the rest out tonight, or tomorrow.

14.

"So how did you get back?"

"I hitched a ride into the little town there and got a cab."

"Are you sure it was Allison?"

"Yes, I'm sure."

"And she's using?"

"She's using and she's starring in porn flicks."

"I'll have to call Danielle."

They were sitting, Joseph and Chris, in the living room of Chris' apartment. Chris, on the sofa, was holding a bar-towel ice pack to his left side, where Mickey Rodriguez had clubbed him twice with his gun while they were struggling on the floor of the cottage. He had probably broken a rib or two, and the discoloration was pretty ugly – eggplant purple streaked with a lurid yellow. Chris had tried to reach Joseph immediately on his return to the city. When Joseph did not answer, he left a message, and then drank off a double scotch. Needing something more – the pain in his side was peaking – he went down to the African Queen to ask Vinnie Rosamelia for some kind of prescription narcotic, which he knew Vinnie always had on hand. Vinnie, wide eyed but asking no questions, had put Chris to bed with a nicely calibrated dose of codeine, Valium and butazolodin – the last an anti-inflammatory used on race horses—and applied a homemade ice pack, which he changed every hour or so for the four hours that Chris was out cold. As a result, though Chris' rib cage area was stiff and sore and remained darkly discolored, the swelling had subsided and the pain was tolerable.

"Are you positive it was her?" Joseph asked, eying the photographs Chris had handed him.

Chris looked at his brother and shook his head slightly.

You learn, when you are closely connected to a heroin addict, to recognize their states of being, of which there are only a basic few: clean, edging toward getting off, edging toward withdrawal, and what addicts call "correct" or "right," the non-euphoric high in which they believe they are functioning normally. Being correct is pretty much all a true junkie lives for. In this state, which lasts some eight to twelve hours after a fix, he can eat and drink a little, smoke cigarettes by the dozens, drive a car, and even, in his mind though no one else's, work. Chris knew, when he sat down for a drink with him on the Thursday evening just past that his brother was clean. He had pressed him on the issue out of an ancient anger – and cruelty – that welled up in him whenever Joseph, like a peacock, presented himself in all his striking beauty to the world, as if his cares had always been trifling and his harrowing heroin habit was the foolish but charming detour of a rich dilettante. Tonight, Chris could see that Joseph, overwrought, manic, was on the verge of scoring some dope, but he was in no mood to baby him. He was thinking about the cesspool he had stepped into in Alpine, and the unearthly look in Mickey Rodriguez's rolling eyes as he talked on his cell phone to Labrutto and pointed his gun at Chris' chest.

"It was her," he said, "bad breath, fresh track marks on her arms and hands, her pupils dilated, totally stoned, totally fucked up."

Chris watched Joseph take his time before responding. What was he thinking? He knows what junkies look like and smell like. He was one.

"At least I can tell her Allison's alive," his bother finally replied.

"Let's watch the movie first."

Chris rose carefully from the couch, put his cell phone in his pocket, and followed Joseph downstairs to Vinnie's office at the back of the African Queen, which, at six p.m. was empty except for the beautiful black bartender who gave each Massi brother a long look as they filed past.

Vinnie's office, like Vinnie, was cool and spartan: a chrome and leather couch with matching chairs faced a functional desk; on one wall was an entertainment unit, on the other a bar. Vinnie wore a goatee and kept his thick black hair fashionably clipped, like a Roman senator's. He stood gracefully erect, as he always did, appearing much taller than his actual five feet,eight inches. His liquid brown eyes were his one feminine feature. They softened what was otherwise a chiseled, imperial face. It was his haughty bearing as much as the girl in him that had marginalized him as a boy on Carmine Street. Chris Massi, respected in the neighborhood because of his father, fell into a natural friendship with his exotic neighbor, and thus, without either of them knowing it, was Vinnie shielded from much of the nastiness that was increasingly on offer in their swiftly changing part of the city.

Inside, Chris handed Vinnie "Candy Meets Ron,", which Vinnie slid into his DVD player, and the three of them settled down to watch. The film went from a simple title card directly into the action, in which a young woman, whom Chris immediately recognized as Allison's California friend, Heather, arrives at the hotel room of a traveling businessman played by Mickey Rodriguez. Heather, in a short skirt, halter top and spiked heels, is playing a faux blind date arranged by an escort service, a role within a role, which she handles fairly well. Mickey is supposed to be a closet pervert hiding behind a mask of nerdiness and inexperience. The dialogue is forced, the sound uneven. The lighting, first too harsh and then too dark, settles in to a shadowy gray pierced across the bed by a hot and glaring band of sunlight probably coming in from a window off camera. Mickey makes drinks, and within a few minutes, he and Heather have their clothes off and are going through the typical sex acts on the bed, moving in and out of the shaft of sunlight that gives the film, shot in color, a noir feel, its only professional touch, probably unintentional.

Mickey suggests bondage, which Heather agrees to, but there is for a moment a look of genuine puzzlement on her face. They resume, Heather on her back, handcuffed to the spokes of the headboard, her mouth duct-taped shut. There is cunnilingus, and there is the missionary position, and then, after several boring minutes, Mickey pulls away and ejaculates on Heather's stomach and breasts; his face – glistening with sweat, eyeballs even more rolled up into his head than usual – is a truly frightening sight.

The camera then moves to a head shot of Heather, who is staring up at Mickey, a look of real wonder – and revulsion – in her eyes, as if she had seen a statue of Medusa come suddenly alive. She then turns to her right to follow something happening off camera. A nickel-plated handgun, identical to the one Mickey pulled earlier on Chris, enters the frame, held by a stubby, hairy hand. The gun circles Heather's face for a long second, as if drawing a bead, and then, quickly, it is placed against her right temple and fired, jerking her head to the left and spilling blood, brains and bone shards onto the pillow. The hairy hand pulls the gun away, and the film ends with a very tight shot of Heather's face – contorted, bloody, eyes wide open in terror – dead.

The three men sat silently until the screen went blank, then they looked at each other, their faces grim. "It looked real to me," Vinnie said.

"You mean she was killed?" Chris asked.

"Fuck," Joseph said.

"I think so," Vinnie said. "I really do."

"I do, too," Joseph said, turning to his brother. "That's why the albino was ready to kill you. I take it he's the male lead?"

"Right, and the girl is a friend of Allison's," Chris said. "The one in the picture. Heather." Joseph and Vinnie stared at Chris.

"This is getting worse and worse," Vinnie said.

"Chris," Joseph said, "you need to move from here, right now. If Junior Boy's behind this, or worse, Barsonetti, you're a dead man. If it's Labrutto acting on his own, he'll want you dead, too, and he'll want this film. It's fucking radioactive. Labruttto will be slower finding you. He doesn't have the Mafia's resources. But he will come after you – you can't commit a worse murder than what's on that DVD."

"I'll destroy it," said Chris, who had taken the disk out of the DVD player, and was holding it between thumb and forefinger, knowing he could easily snap it in two and preparing to do just that.

"Are you crazy?" Joseph said, snatching the disk from Chris. "That's your only bargaining chip."

"You're definitely in trouble," said Vinni. "I agree the disk shouldn't be destroyed. You can keep it in my safe, if you want."

"Thanks, but I'll hold onto it," Joseph said, slipping the disk into its case, and putting it in his jacket pocket.

"I'll pack a bag," Chris said, eying his brother, surprised to see how aggressively he took possession of the DVD. Possibly, he was thinking of a way to profit from it, without a doubt something Joseph was capable of. Giving credit where it was due, however, his junkie brother had responded swiftly to his call for help. His advice had been sound. His motives could, for once, have more to do with love and loyalty than personal gain.

"Be careful," Chris said. "The gun looked like the one Mickey pulled on me, and that looked like Guy Labrutto's fat little hand holding it."

"Get ready," Joseph said, nodding. "I'll call Louie Falco at La Luna. He's got that room in the back."

"Here," said Vinni, handing Chris vials of Valium and codeine. "You'll need them."

"One last thing," Joseph said to Chris.

"What?"

"What's up with you and Barsonetti?"

"You don't need to know."

"Yes, I do. You're in deep shit, Chris. Anybody who's seen this flick who wasn't supposed to will be killed. I might be able to help you, but I need to know what's going on."

Chris looked at Joseph across the few feet that separated them. *I might be able to help you.* The irony of this statement was inescapable, but it occurred to him that they were beyond irony. In times of crisis, junkies, Chris knew from bitter experience, get high. Why hold back?

If he had a brother, Chris would find out in the next few days.

"He killed Pop," Chris said. "I thought I'd have a talk with him."

Joseph said nothing at first, just stared at Chris as if he had never seen him before.

"I think that will have to wait," he said, finally.

Chris nodded, and put the vials Vinnie had handed him in his pocket. He then turned toward the office door, thinking to go upstairs to quickly pack an overnight bag. Before he could reach it, the door swung open and two men in blue suits entered Vinnie's office.

"FBI," said he first one in, holding up a badge and an I.D. card in a two-sided leather case. "We're looking for a Chris Massi."

Book II
Joseph

1.

While Chris was in his drug-induced sleep, Ed Dolan was very much awake in his office overlooking Foley Square. His chief investigator, Rick Magnuson, had just called to tell him that, according to Antoinette Scarpa, her husband left their house early that morning to pick up Chris Massi in Manhattan for a meeting "somewhere in Jersey." It seemed more and more certain to Dolan, alone for the moment, gazing down at the cluster of famous buildings – City Hall, the Tombs, the hexagonal County Court House – that comprise the legal and administrative nerve center of the city, that it had been pre-ordained that Massi pay for his father's sins. How else to account for the fact that the New Jersey State Police, having found Scarpa's body in navigable United States' waters, had immediately notified the FBI in Manhattan; and that the FBI, having run Scarpa's name through their computers and seen "Organized Crime" stamped across the first page of his long rap sheet, had immediately notified Ed?

Dolan had endured some bad years during his tenure as head of the U.S. Attorney's Organized Crime Task Force in Manhattan, frustrating years in which organized crime as a synonym for the Mafia had faded from the public eye, and his main quarry, Joe Black Massi, had eluded him, only to be killed by another enemy, not worthy of the name. There would be no trial and public disgrace, no death sentence to hang for years over the elder Massi's head, but the next best thing had happened: Dolan had, in the last eighteen months, sent Massi's son, Chris, reeling, just missing putting him jail by the whims of a federal jury. Now, miraculously, effortlessly this time, Chris was in his sights again. What else to attribute this to but the rightness of his lifetime cause?

At six o'clock, over a beer and a sandwich with Magnuson at a local pub, Dolan was filled in on the rest of his longtime investigator's findings regarding the two dead bodies dragged that afternoon out of the river. As they were paying the check, the night clerk at his office called on his cell phone to tell him that Massi had been located and was on his way in. Prosecutors come in all stripes, and do a lot of things, but it is rare for them to actively participate, except to give legal advice to the police, in the investigation of crimes. Investigators ultimately become trial witnesses, a role that, if played by a prosecutor, could force him off the case.

Dolan, the head of a major task force, was able to break this rule from time to time without serious repercussions. He liked to go to the occasional crime scene, to ride out on a bust, and to sit in on the interrogation of a suspect or a witness that held a certain interest for him. He therefore did not expect Magnuson to be surprised when he told him, on the walk back to the office, that he would be interviewing Massi and did not need any help. Magnussen wasn't. He had had a long day – murder scenes, and the first several hours of investigation after discovering dead bodies, have to be handled with great care – and was happy to have an early night.

As he approached the third floor interview room, Dolan could see Chris through the one-way plate glass window used by agents and prosecutors to observe interviews taking place inside. Massi, in a dark blue, long-sleeved polo shirt and jeans, was sitting squarely on a metal chair, his arms at his sides, his eyes closed. He opened them with a start, as if he had sensed Dolan's presence on the other side of the glass only a few feet away. Then he settled down, and looked around the room, putting his hands on the edge of the table in front of him and pushing himself into even more of an upright position. *Still proud*, Dolan said to himself, *but not for too much longer.*

●

Ed Dolan, in his rumpled summer-weight tan suit, white shirt and knit tie, entered the room and sat down at the table across from Chris. He took his cigarettes out of his jacket pocket, lit one, then put it on the ashtray in front of him.

"You want one?" he said, nodding toward the pack of Camel Lights he had also placed on the table.

"No."

"You don't smoke."

"No."

"How's everything?"

Chris ignored this. It was too weird.

"Your people," Chris said, "told me I could come in here voluntarily, or be arrested as a material witness. A material witness to what?"

"A woman in Yonkers saw a car go over the Palisades today. She was washing dishes. Do you know anything about that?"

"No."

"There were two people in the car. An ex-con named Nick Scarpa and a junkie named Allison McRae. They're both dead. They took a nine millimeter round from Scarpa's brain. Allison was naked from the waist down. She was also loaded with heroin. Is this ringing any bells?"

"Am I under arrest?" Chris said. "Because if I'm not, I'm leaving, and if I am, I'm calling a lawyer."

"Scarpa's wife told us he picked you up this morning for a meeting in Jersey. She said he saw you in the city last week, and that he spoke with you on the phone on Sunday."

"What about Paulie Raimo?"

"Paulie Raimo?"

"I thought you wanted to pin his murder on me?"

"That's taken a back seat at the moment."

Chris assessed his old friend impassively. During his conspiracy trial a little over a year ago, he and Dolan had seen each other every day for two weeks, but had not spoken. These words on this early summer evening in May of 2003 were the first they had exchanged in twenty-five years. Chris could see the weight of those years on Dolan's shoulders, hunched and locked into a lifelong tenseness; in the contours of his once trim but now thickening body; and on his face, pale and slightly bloated, his once thick blond hair wispy and lusterless. But it was in his former friend's eyes, flat and hard, that his soul was visible. Who better than Chris to mark the stark contrast between the cautious but happy boy and the impulsive, bitter man Dolan had become?

"You saw Junior Boy on Saturday night," Dolan said. "Did he order Scarpa killed?"

Chris had seen a white van parked across the street from Junior Boy's house when he brought his kids home on Saturday night, and, during their talk, DiGiglio had mentioned that he had been under surveillance for the past five or six months.

"Are you out of your mind?" was his reply.

"You need work," the prosecutor said. "Your father was a killer. Junior Boy pays well, I'm sure. What was Scarpa's crime?"

Chris remained calm, but not without effort. He had no doubt that Mickey Rodriguez had bumped Nick Scarpa's twenty-year-old Pontiac off the Palisades, no doubt that Labrutto, alone or with others, was behind it, no doubt that he, Chris, was indeed a material witness to murder, and no doubt that Ed Dolan's bitterness had corroded his soul, had cast him adrift among the psychotics of the world. The malice in Ed Dolan's eyes was not put there by Joe Black Massi, it was put there by Dolan himself. This sudden thought was a relief to Chris, who had struggled for years with his father's role in the devastation of Ed Dolan's life, a relief he could not savor, replaced as it was, almost immediately, by the realization that Dolan's enmity was mortal in nature, and would not be restrained by such things as morality or the niceties of the law.

"Do you know a Guy Labrutto?" Dolan asked. "We found his address in Scarpa's wallet."

"I'm leaving," Chris said, getting slowly to his feet, wincing involuntarily at the sharp pain in his side even this careful movement caused.

"Go ahead. We're tracking down Allison McRae's relatives. I'm sure they'll be helpful. Don't leave the city, I may want to arrest you as a material witness – at least."

●

Chris walked the eight blocks to La Luna, which was crowded and bustling as ever. Peering over the group at the hostess' station waiting to be seated, he saw Lou Falco talking to a foursome at a table near the back. Lou spotted Chris and quickly weaved through the close packed, noisy tables to greet him.

"You don't want to walk through here," Lou said, shaking Chris' hand, and leading him by the arm back toward the front door. "Go around back, down the alley, it's the green door. Joseph said he'd be by tomorrow morning. Here's a key. What time do you want coffee?"

"I'll go out for it."

"No. You better stay in until we can find out what's up."

"Nick Scarpa's been killed," Chris said. "That's what's up, and a girl named Allison McRae, the one I was supposed to be looking for."

"Christ."

"Where did Joseph go?"

"I don't know."

"Probably to get high."

Lou, at five-eight and a rotund two hundred pounds, going bald, pushing fifty, had remained single and content since his second divorce, eating his own southern Italian food, living above La Luna. His current marriage – to his restaurant – had worked out fine. He knew Chris' family history, in particular Joseph's; had, in fact, "lent" the younger Massi countless twenty dollar bills over the last fifteen years. Like almost everyone else from Carmine Street, except Chris, Lou had a warm spot in his heart for Joseph, who was usually too charming or too genuinely desperate to resist. He also recognized that if it was *his* brother who was the junkie, he would probably feel the same anger – and despair – that he knew Chris struggled with. Joseph had caused the Massis a lot of trouble. To a stranger, he would defend Joseph. With Chris, he just changed the subject.

"What happened?" he asked. "To Nick and the girl?"

They were out on the street by now. Chris, seeing the stream of tourists walking by, headed into the alley before answering. "They were in Nick's car," he said, once in the alley's shadows, "which someone pushed off the Palisades."

"Who?"

"Do you know a Guy Labrutto?'

"No."

"He works for Junior Boy."

"Joseph mentioned an albino."

"He works for Labrutto," Chris said. "His name is Mickey. They might send him."

"Let's hope nobody recognized you in the restaurant just now."

They were standing at the back of the building, the green metal door to Chris' new home – partially blocked by a brimming Dempsey dumpster – only a few feet away. Chris was beyond tired, and his side hurt badly; otherwise, he would not have put Lou at risk by staying in his back room. With an effort, he picked his stocky friend's sleepy brown eyes out of the darkness of the restaurant's airless "backyard," no more than ten feet by ten feet square.

"Use that alley to come and go," Lou said, pointing to a narrow street to their right. "It comes in from Elizabeth Street. They pick up the dumpster tomorrow morning at six."

"Great."

"Joseph said to tell you to make sure you take your drugs. He got a kick out of that."

"I'm sure he did."

"There's food inside, and wine, and a bottle of scotch."

"Thanks."

"Chris."

"Yes."

"Don't go out tomorrow until Joseph comes. Junior Boy could be thinking about this place. He knows we go back."

"I'll leave tomorrow, Lou."

"That's not what I'm saying. Don't insult me. You can stay as long as you want. I'm saying this is very serious. Your brother's been on the street all his life. Listen to what he has to say. Get some sleep. You look half dead."

2.

After Chris Massi left, Ed Dolan went to his office and turned on his computer. As it booted up, he unlocked a metal cabinet directly behind him and pulled out some fifty sequentially numbered CDs in plastic cases and two thick black loose-leaf binders. He had been investigating Junior Boy DiGiglio and his family for the past six months with zero results. Just yesterday, the court order authorizing the wire taps on the three DiGiglio brothers' phone lines had expired. The CDs contained the actual sound recordings of the taps, burned each night directly from the audiotape in the surveillance vans and delivered the following morning to Dolan. The first binder contained the Call Log, a brief description of each call along with its date, time, the caller's address and telephone number and the corresponding CD number. In the second were over two hundred eight-by-ten color photographs taken by the surveillance team of people arriving at and/or leaving the DiGiglio brothers' homes and hangouts, cross-indexed by date and name if the subject was known.

In the top drawer of Dolan's desk was a phony affidavit in which was described links between the DiGiglio crime organization and Mideast terrorist cells operating in the United States. This document, personally drafted, printed and signed by Dolan this morning, would no doubt induce the court to extend its order. Now he might not have to file it.

When he was first told by Magnussen of the link between the murdered Nick Scarpa and one Guy Labrutto, no bells had rung. But the more he thought about it, the more he was certain he remembered a series of calls to Aldo DiGiglio's house from a "cousin Guy" at a North Jersey address. The Call Log index easily led the prosecutor to the fifteen calls from Labrutto to Aldo and one that jumped off the page from Labrutto to Anthony in Montclair dated May 13. The calls to Aldo contained the usual nonsense about "meeting at the diner" or the making of mundane plans for lunch or weekends at Aldo's house at the shore. Dolan saved the call to Junior Boy for last, hoping – praying might be a better word – that it was Junior Boy who Labrutto spoke to and not someone else in the family. His prayer was answered:

"Mildred?"

"Yes."

"Hi, this is cousin Guy Labrutto."

"Cousin Guy?"

"Yes. Can I speak to Junior Boy, please?"

Pause.

"June, it's Marie's nephew, Guy."

Pause.

"I'll take it in my study."

Pause.

"Hello."

"Junior Boy?"

"Yes."

"It's Guy Labrutto. I just wanted to thank you for inviting me to your home on Sunday. I was very honored."

"You're welcome."

Pause.

"Did you enjoy the wine I brought over?"

"I have to run, Guy."

"Sure."

Click.

Dolan then opened the Photo Log and located ten pictures taken on Sunday, May 11. Among the eleven people depicted, there were only two unknowns, a ghostly pale, skinny platinum blond man in his twenties standing next to a black BMW and a short, portly man in his late thirties dressed in black and wearing a severely cut goatee. This man was looking over his shoulder toward the FBI van when the picture was snapped, his dark eyes narrowed to slits in the bright sunlight. Magnussen had interviewed Labrutto late today and described him to Dolan. This was no doubt him, generously offering a full-faced picture of himself to the United States government.

Dolan had been hoping merely to establish that Anthony DiGiglio and Labrutto knew each other, no matter how slightly. The recorded conversation and the photograph put Labrutto in the don's home one week before the double murder, which Junior Boy might have ordered and might not have, might have known about and might not have. It didn't matter. Labrutto was a cousin to Anthony and to Aldo, with whom he spoke frequently and often met. The DiGiglios were now connected to a double homicide. And so was Chris Massi, who not only had been with Nick Scarpa on the day he was killed but had also been snooping around the apartment of the second victim, one Allison McRae, the day before. Thank God for the thoroughness of Rick Magnussen, who had promptly visited McRae's last known address and spoken to her neighbors, including a scrofulous heroin addict who actually had Massi's card.

Ed Dolan lived alone on the Upper East Side. He could have had an NYPD cop especially assigned for the purpose, drive him back and forth to work, and sometimes, he did. He often took the subway, though, not as a display of his regular-guy cred, but because these walks above ground and rides underground were the only times he was with people other than at work. They were his social life. As he made his way north on Broadway after locking up his office, he marveled at his luck.

In the spring of 2001, one of his assistants indicted Paulie Raimo, a Mafia parasite, on pump-and-dump conspiracy charges. Paulie, who hired Chris Massi to defend him, was stunned when Dolan arranged a clandestine meeting, at which he offered to dismiss Raimo's case if he would wear a wire to his meetings with Massi. Dolan's only condition was that the wire had to be Raimo's idea, conceived and executed on his own as a means of winning favor with his prosecutors in the hope of avoiding a long prison sentence. As it turned out, the only taped conversation that came close to incriminating Massi was the one that involved Raimo's co-defendants at dinner. It never bothered Ed that what he did was illegal, only that Massi was ultimately acquitted.

A few months later, the country was stunned by the attacks on the World Trade Center and the Pentagon. But, while everyone else was riveted by the war on terror that ensued, Ed Dolan was riveted on getting Chris Massi disbarred, taking advantage of the Justice Department's huge shift in priorities that left him virtually on his own in pursuit of his personal agenda. The false affidavits he submitted to the Bar Association linking Chris to organized crime were not even noticed by his superiors in New York and Washington. To him, the devastation of September 11 was a stroke of luck.

After Paulie's case was dismissed, his co-conspirators, who had been convicted and smelled a rat, arranged for his death from their jail cells. Dolan had never been worried about Raimo turning on him. Who would take the word of a scumbag like Raimo against that of a respected federal prosecutor? Still, it was nice to know that Paulie was dead, his secret buried with him, and that, thanks to a newcomer named Guy Labrutto, Dolan's luck was still running good.

Labrutto had denied knowing either Scarpa or the girl, but his address in Scarpa's wallet, and the proximity of what Dolan was convinced was a botched "accident" scene, to that address, pointed directly to the chubby porn producer, and, through him, to Junior Boy. Scarpa and Massi must have been at Labrutto's house that morning; that would eventually be easy to prove, thereby making Massi, Labrutto and DiGiglio legitimate persons of interest in a double murder investigation. This was, Dolan knew, the chance he had been waiting a lifetime for. His mind jumped at the possibilities, including the heart-stopping idea of giving Labrutto immunity from prosecution in return for his testimony against Massi and DiGiglio.

To make things even sweeter, Massi had spent part of Sunday – yesterday – going through Allison McRae's apartment on Suffolk Street, having sweet-talked her hooker neighbor into letting him in. This Rick Magnuson had learned when he went to check out Allison's last known address. Was McRae used to set Scarpa up and then herself killed? Was she an innocent victim? These questions would be answered in due course, along with the question of motive, but they weren't important. The important thing was that Massi was in the thick of it all, and, whether he was guilty of anything or not, would soon be having the worst nightmare of his life: suspected, investigated and charged with a Mafia-induced contract murder, punishable by death, a sentence he, Ed Dolan, would spend a lifetime, if necessary, making sure was carried out.

On the expansive mezzanine of the Union Square subway station, a blind woman stood against a railing – a wicker basket at her feet – singing a bluesy version of *At Last*. Dolan had heard the first long drawn out notes of the classic tune as he was entering the station from the southeast corner of Union Square Park. A cult of one, he believed in signs, and here, certainly, was one. *Yes, at last*, he thought, placing a five dollar bill in the basket and smiling, staring directly into the singer's oversized sunglasses. He was taken aback for a second when she took the glasses off and seemed to stare back at him through her opague and lifeless eyes, her head tilted as if she could actually see him, but only for a second. She was blind, like justice, a double sign. He moved on, humming, oblivious to any other interpretation of what he had just encountered.

3.

If human existence is a dream that God is having, then the hip hotel bars that materialized across Manhattan in the last decade of the last century are the imaginings of His subconscious' "A" design team, brought to us so we can enter an illusion inside an illusion, feel like celebrities while we drink fifteen dollar martinis, and watch kindred souls watching us in the mirrors and polished surfaces that invariably abound. If you were willing to pay the prices, and assume the appropriate attitudes, who would know if, at The Mercer or The Tribeca Grand, you were a hot new model or fashion designer, or a Connecticut college student home for the weekend?

When he could afford them, Joseph Massi – better looking than most movie stars, his smile an invitation to a chic and very exclusive party – loved these bars. In their subdued light, he was not the junkie who never held a job and lied his way through life. He was anything he wanted to be, or, even easier, anything a beautiful and wealthy woman wanted him to be. On Monday night at around one o'clock, while his brother was in a dead sleep on a cot in the storeroom at La Luna, Joseph was with one such woman in the lobby lounge at the Royalton on Forty-fourth Street. Her name was Jodi Flippen. Thirty years old, tall and gracefully beautiful, Jodi was the owner of an extremely successful escort service that she operated out of her apartment on Sutton Place.

"Thanks for coming out," Joseph said, lighting Jodi's cigarette. "I appreciate it."

"I was just about to curl up with a good book."

"You want some wine?"

"Sure."

Joseph poured out cold Meursault for Jodi from the bottle on ice next to the table, then freshened his own glass.

"I need your help," he said after they had both taken sips and put their glasses down on the plush white table cloth that covered their small cocktail table.

"You sound serious."

"I am," Joseph replied. "I was talking to Patrice. She said Woody Smith was here earlier. Two of your girls joined him for a drink, then they left."

Patrice was the bartender, a stunning, *cafe au lait*-colored young woman, whom Joseph had gotten to know over the past year or so.

"What is it you need, Joe?" Jodi asked.

"Did you speak to Woody?"

"He came over and paid me in person."

"How much?"

"Five thousand. Do you want a cut?"

Joseph and Jodi had never been lovers. They were, in their separate ways, equally hardened entrepreneurs, and neither could see any advantage to be gained by a bedding. Joseph had been sending Jodi clients – one or two a month – for the past five years or so, his ten percent commission one of his few sources of steady income.

"I didn't send him," he answered.

"Repeat business."

"That's not our deal," Joseph said, smiling, "but maybe it should be."

"Then what?"

"Where are they?"

"Where are they? Are you crazy?"

"I need to talk to Woody before he gets too fucked up."

"What's going on Joseph?"

Woody Smith, also *cafe au lait* colored, with a pencil mustache and pretensions to sophistication, was a sly, forty-year-old hustler, who started his street life in the eighties running a shooting gallery on Houston Street in the days before hypodermic needles were available for three dollars a ten-pack at your local drug store. It was from Woody that Joseph, then seventeen, learned how to freebase cocaine and cook heroin.

"Woody told Patrice he made a big score today," Joseph answered. "He flashed a wad of hundreds. He mentioned something about a job in Jersey."

"So? Good for him," Jodi said. "And me."

"I need to talk to him for ten minutes, Jodi, that's all."

"Why?"

"For your own good, I can't tell you."

"Always with the dramatic bullshit."

"It's not cops you'd have to worry about."

"What did he do, the little cocksucker?"

Joseph didn't answer. Earlier, when he was getting ready to go out, Lou Falco had called, and told him about Nick Scarpa and Allison McRae. The FBI suspected Chris, which was absurd, but he *had* been in Jersey with Nick, at around the time that Nick's car, with Allison in it, went over the Palisades. Labrutto had stayed behind, Chris had said, so maybe his assistant, the albino, had had an assistant of his own. Could that have been Woody Smith, who, whenever he made a sizable score, liked nothing better than to spend it on an eight ball and two high-priced whores? He had never known murder to be Woody's game, but then again he had never known a petty thief like Woody who didn't sooner or later overplay the crappy cards he had drawn at birth.

"Can you reach the girls?" he said, finally.

"Of course."

"Call them. Tell them I'm coming by. They'd freak out if I just showed up. Tell them not to tell Woody. I'll only be with him for a few minutes."

"I've never seen you like this, Joseph. So serious. You're interesting this way."

"Will you help me or not?"

As an answer, Jodi took her cell phone from her small purse, flipped it open, pushed two buttons, then, after a moment of silence, and an exchange of hellos, told the person at the other end to expect Joseph Massi to be stopping by shortly, but not to tell the client.

"They're in a suite at that new 'W' in Times Square," she said after clicking off, "Room 1707."

"Thank you."

"De rien."

"What's that?"

"I'm taking French at the New School."

"Why?"

"I have an idea of moving to Paris. Change my life. I can't do this forever. You want to come with me?"

Joseph smiled at this, and Jodi smiled back. Their table was in shadows in the far corner on the lower level of the long, three-tiered room. The candle between them cast a steady, golden glow on their beautiful faces. Jodi had been taking French and moving to Paris for the past ten years, since the night Joseph first met her at a club downtown called The Mist. A few years later, Joe Black Massi, at Joseph's request, had persuaded her pimp that it would be a good thing – for his health – if he let Jodi go, and even better if he didn't try to interfere with the new business she was thinking of starting.

"I'll come over for a visit," he said.

"You can stay clean there."

This was new ground. The only people who had ever broached the subject of Joseph's drug addiction had been his mother and his brother. Joe Black had lost it a couple of times in the beginning, once throwing Joseph over the kitchen table and into the refrigerator, but after Rose entered the fray, he pretty much gave up. His one rule: *don't do your drugs in this house.* Other junkies, the people he got high with, brought it up all the time. Their common issues – scoring drugs, getting the money to score drugs, the fear of AIDS, hepatitis and bone crushers, treatment programs and facilities, the law, getting clean, mixing drugs – were endless topics of conversation, but they didn't count.

He was about to say something nasty, then suddenly changed his mind. What the fuck? He was a junkie. The image of Woody Smith, laying up with two beautiful hookers, fucking and getting high all night, had been on his mind. Maybe Jodi was clairvoyant, sensed his need to get off; maybe she actually cared about him – a risky proposition for her, or any normal human being, for that matter. He certainly would like to get stoned. But first, he would talk to Woody Smith. If Woody pushed Nick and Allison to their deaths, it would almost certainly mean that neither the DiGiglio nor the Barsonetti family was involved. They would never use an unconnected punk like Woody to help them in a hit, and if they did, he would never live to tell about it. If Labrutto was acting alone, maybe Chris could live through the shitstorm that was about to hit him.

"What would I do, Jodi?" he finally said. "With my life, I mean, if I stayed clean."

"How long has it been?"

"Six months."

"Something's different this time. What is it?"

I can't do it. I can't stay clean. In the past, I fooled everybody: my parents, my brother, myself. If I failed, there would always be another day. That day has come and gone. I'll always be a junkie. I'll die a junkie.

"Nothing," he said, smiling. "Everything's the same."

"Come over after you see Woody," Jodi said. "We haven't had a heart-to-heart talk in a long time."

"We've never had a heart-to-heart talk."

"We'll start tonight."

"I can't. I have to make a few stops. Thanks for the offer, though."

"It's on the table."

Joseph caught the waitress' eye, and, making a scribbling motion with his hand, called for the check. Jodi slipped out of her banquette seat and headed to the ladies room. Watching her long legs and beautiful, high rear-end sway as she made her way, swan-like, across the room, regret, desire, a burning itch to be high, and fear for his brother made a potent brew in Joseph's heart.

●

At the "W" suite, Joseph found Woody Smith, in the silk robe that came with the room, stretched out on an overstuffed chair, watching Bladerunner on a large, flat-screen television. Two small candles on the coffee table, and the TV screen, gave off the only light in the other-wise completely darkened room. Joseph sat on the sofa and watched Harrison Ford chase bad androids through the streets of a very *noir* future Los Angeles. An empty bottle of Dom Perignon in an ice bucket and three cham-pagne glasses were on the table as well. "I think he might be done for the night," Nicole, the NYU graduate student who moonlighted for Jodi, had said when she let Joseph in, before retiring to the bedroom. The other girl was not in sight. Joseph had greeted Woody before sitting down, but received no answer. Now he got up, took the remote from the mulatto's hand, found the mute button, and pushed it. The sudden silence brought Woody back to the world. He had not been sleeping, just drifting in heroin land.

"Fuck," he said. "Who's that?"

"It's me, Wood, Joe Massi."

"My man. How you doin'?"

"I'm good. How're you doing? You look pretty hammered."

"Hammered. You wanna get high?"

"Not right now. I need a favor."

"Favor? Fuck."

Joseph did not reply immediately. On the television screen, Ford was meeting for the first time the android he would later fall in love with – a sultry and beautiful woman who never learns she is not human. Woody also gazed at the screen.

"I ran into your albino friend," Joseph said, taking a flyer, but unconcerned. Nothing would backfire with Smith in this condition.

"Mickey?"

"Yeah."

"He's a freak, but he pays good."

"It was on the news: two bodies fished out of the river."

"Big fucker, that river."

"The mighty Hudson."

"He shot the guinea in the head, man. Bam! Then he jumps out, and I gun that motherfucker. Bam! Almost went over myself."

"I need your help, Wood. I need to meet Mickey. I need you to set it up for me."

Woody's emergence from the land of nod, slurred and half-witted at first, reached a sudden and eerily animated crescendo with his description of the events earlier today at the top of the Palisades. Immediately afterward, as if the memory and recitation of that heart-stopping experience were utterly exhausting, his chin fell to his chest.

"Woody."

Joseph went over, lifted Smith's eyelids and checked his pulse, which was slow, but not too slow. He was out cold. Looking around the room, his eyes adjusted to the darkness, he saw a foot dangling over the arm of a small sofa facing a picture window at the far end of the room. It was probably the other hooker. He found the bedroom door and knocked. After a few seconds, Nicole, in pink panties and a tee shirt, opened it and peered at him.

"I'm leaving."

"How's Woody?"

"Nodding in and out."

"We expected him to be prancing around the room all night. The high roller."

"Superfly."

"Right."

"What happened?"

"He went right for the smack."

"Something's on his mind."

"That's fine with me."

"He'll be himself again in the morning."

"I can't wait."

"When's quitting time?"

"Ten a.m. we're out of here. I have an exam I'm trying to get ready for."

Through the half open door, Joseph could see into the over-designed bedroom. A halogen lamp, extending from the darkness on a long black arm, cast a cone of white light on books and notebooks spread open on the king-sized bed.

"Otherwise, I'd ask you in," Nicole continued, smiling for the first time since Joseph arrived.

Five hours later, Joseph was driving over the Williamsburg Bridge into the rising sun heading for the Bedford-Stuyvesant section of Brooklyn, "Bed-Stuy," as it has come to be known, with unhappy connotations. Though it is crime-ridden and filled with decrepit housing, it has its share of quiet streets lined with old but well-kept brownstones and brickfront houses, once one-family affairs now divided into as many apartments as various physical and metaphysical laws would allow. Woody Smith – half Jamaican, half a polyglot of lighter-skinned races – lived in one of these, in the basement apartment, with his mother. Joseph and Woody had never been friends, but drugs, much more than politics, make strange bedfellows, and he easily located Smith's Pulaski Street building, having been there several times to buy drugs or get high.

Joseph stopped for coffee and a bagel at a deli on Lafayette Avenue, then found a parking space on Pulaski Street with an unobstructed view of the steps leading to

Woody's subterranean apartment. While eating his breakfast, he thought over the events of the previous evening.
He and Nicole had snorted Woody's coke and made love
in his fancy hotel room. When he was leaving, she gave
him a few of the amphetamine tablets she had been taking as a study aid. Joseph didn't usually need speed; he was
wired all the time, getting three or four hours of sleep on
his good nights. But last night he had not slept at all, and
there was no telling when Woody would arrive home, so
he pulled one of the gel-caps from his shirt pocket and
swallowed it with the last of his coffee. Nicole was interesting, but a type well known to Joseph. On a career
path, with a boyfriend in Westchester County, while at the
same time addicted to the thrill of illicit sex and drugs and
the call girl's heady power, she was blithely unaware that,
life being what it is, she would not be turning too many
more corners before she ran into a buzz saw of one sort or
another.

The rest of the night Joseph had spent in two private
clubs, one in Queens, the other in the Bronx, both Mafia hangouts, trying to find out if DiGiglio or Barsonetti were looking for Chris. Joseph's drug problems were
widely known, and loathed, by the men who frequented
these places, but he was tolerated because of his father.
Joe Black's reputation as the consummate professional assassin, deeply loyal, willing to kill the Pope for his don,
had assumed near legendary status since his grizzly death.
Even the Mafia needs its mythology, and so there was a
tacit agreement not to disrespect the flawed son of one of
their lesser gods. Joseph was let in on a petty scam from
time to time, in which he acquitted himself fairly well, and,
not without his charms, as the years passed, he developed

a series of friendships among his contemporaries in and on the margins of the Mafia world that stood him in good stead for various purposes. In this group, no one had heard anything about Chris Massi being the subject of a hunt. From the rest – the "made" men, the official members of crews and of families, the occasional capo regime, the ones he never spoke to directly unless requested to do so – he received no weird looks and picked up no snatches of conversation that referred to the Scarpa/McRae murders or Chris Massi.

Joseph had called Lou Falco twice, the second time from Marsha's apartment, where he had stopped to shower and change his clothes, at six-thirty. No Mafia types had stopped in at La Luna the night before, and, as of seven o'clock – Joseph had asked Lou to check and call him back – Chris was sleeping soundly. He had also called Vinnie Rosamelia, who told him that at around midnight, the albino co-star of the snuff film, now with a cast on his left wrist, had forced him at gunpoint to let him into Chris' apartment, which he ransacked, obviously looking for the DVD Joseph had so accurately described as radioactive.

Watching the morning sunlight fill Pulaski Street, Joseph was beginning to think with increasing confidence that Labrutto had acted alone in killing Scarpa and Allison, which was an immense relief. Although Labrutto had a business relationship with Junior Boy, and was his distant cousin, he was not made, not a member of the family, by close blood or ritual, which meant he could be dealt with, that is, killed, without fear of serious repercussions. Junior Boy might not give his blessing, but he of all people would understand that the Massis' only logical answer to Labrutto's attempts to take Chris' life would be to kill Labrutto. And if Labrutto were to be eliminated, why couldn't Joseph take over his porn video enterprise and become Junior Boy's partner?

The first step would be to persuade Woody Smith, who would do anything for cash, to lure Mickey and Labrutto to a meeting where they could both be killed. The more Joseph thought about it, the more certain he felt that the universe had lined things up so that his last and best chance at redemption was at hand. His father had despised him, his brother loved him but had no respect for him. No one had to tell Joseph Massi how fucked up his life had been. Killing Labrutto would save Chris' life, and earn his respect. It might even earn the respect of Anthony DiGiglio, and, thereby, give Joseph an opportunity to make real money in the grownup world. But more than all of this, it would show that world that Joseph's days as a lackey and a drug addict were over, that Joe Black Massi's blood ran in his younger son's veins after all.

Two hours later, Joseph watched as a figure turned the corner and walked slowly down the block. There was one tree on Pulaski Street, a tall, spindly thing a few doors distant from Woody's building. Five or six crows had been raucously quarreling in its highest branches for the last half hour. As the figure approached, the crows became silent, and, one at a time at what seemed like precisely the same intervals, flew off. The figure – Woody – was almost directly under the tree when the last crow took flight. Joseph, watching intently, was about to get out of his car when another figure, a slender, balding man, wearing a dark shirt and slacks, emerged from a nearby shadow, and, coming abreast of Woody, placed a silencer-tipped pistol to his temple, and pulled the trigger. Woody crumpled immediately to the sidewalk, where the thin man, who Joseph recognized as a DiGiglio soldier named Phil Purcell, bent down and shot him twice in the forehead. A car, large and dark, pulled up. Purcell got in the front, and the car drove off. Joseph's hand was still on the door handle, his body arrested in mid-movement, as he watched the car disappear.

4.

The next day, Anthony DiGiglio was sitting at his desk in his book-lined study, reading an account of the Scarpa/McRae killings in the New York Times when Joe Pace handed him the cards of two FBI agents and told him they were waiting in the driveway. The don put the paper down and told Pace to find Nicky Spags. Then, despite the extra fifty pounds he had begun to carry in the past few years, and the arthritis beginning to announce itself in his knees, he rose gracefully from his tooled-leather swivel chair and walked to the tall, leaded-glass window facing the driveway. His study, built over the house's four-car garage, had views of three sides of the manicured five-acre property. The agents, both middle-aged, one in a tan, the other in light gray suit, were leaning against their car, which was parked facing the heavy wrought-iron front gate. Their arms folded across their chests, they were gazing silently at the small pond on the front lawn, on which a pair of swans glided gracefully, the morning sun dancing on the water around them. Junior Boy took this scene in. Before turning away, he took a moment to assess the face – creased and fleshy, not so proudly handsome at sixty-six as it was even five years ago – reflected in the window, and to dwell on the premonition of trouble that crossed his mind, not at the presence of the agents, but at the presumptions they seemed to be making as they looked over his property, his home.

That premonition became a certainty an hour later at the start of his interrogation by Ed Dolan.

"I know more about you and your family than anyone alive," Dolan said, without preliminaries or the usual cop posturing. The prosecutor was sitting at one end of a long conference table, lounging in a tilting chair, facing Junior Boy at the other end, who was sitting upright, gazing over his interlocked hands at Dolan. He did not answer.

"Your great grandfather, the first Anthony DiGiglio," Dolan continued, "ran liquor from Canada into Rochester in the twenties. He was betrayed by a lieutenant named Toretti. He had Toretti and his entire family killed – his wife, four kids, his two brothers and their entire families in Sicily. They called it the Castellamare War. There hasn't been a betrayal in the DiGiglio family since. Your father, the second Anthony DiGiglio, was at that meeting in Appalachia. He was one of the five who weren't rounded up in the cow pastures. He refused to allow his people to deal in drugs. You made your bones by killing a rogue family drug dealer. Your father died in his sleep in 1981. You moved your operations to Jersey to get under the radar of my task force. You don't deal drugs, but you do everything else: gun trafficking, counterfeit money, gambling, loan sharking. How am I doing?"

Junior Boy allowed a half smile to appear briefly on his face. "It sounds like a pulp fiction novel to me."

"You dropped out of school at sixteen. You lived in Palermo for two years. Your brothers are your top generals. Your people never talk business on the phone. They don't make scenes at restaurants. Everyone who asks to see you is searched. Am I ringing any bells?"

By talking about me, you're revealing yourself, DiGiglio thought. Out loud he said, "My brothers and I are in the trucking business."

"Yes, Blue Jay Tricking. A front."

The IRS had audited Blue Jay three times and Anthony and his brothers twice in the past ten years, with no adverse findings of any kind. But surely Dolan knew this and was building up to what he thought would be a knockout punch. "Your people," Anthony said, "said something about a material witness warrant."

"There is no warrant, but I can get one quickly. That would permit me to hold you for a while."

"On what?"

"Two murders."

"Of whom?"

"I think you know."

"You better get the warrant. My lawyer will deal with it when he gets here."

Anthony had not known that he would be questioned about the Scarpa/McRae murders. If he had, he would have had a lawyer or two meet him at the house and they would never have let him talk to Dolan. But now he was glad that he had decided to come to this "interview" voluntarily, as it gave him a chance to personally assess the dangerously unbalanced Dolan, who loomed suddenly and forcefully as an adversary.

"Who's coming?" Dolan asked. "Tom Stabile?"

"Yes."

"Too bad you can't use Chris Massi, your ex-son-in-law. I suppose you know he's been disbarred."

Junior Boy shook his head slightly and remained silent, taking note of the slight tremor in the hand Dolan was resting on the table.

"Scarpa's wife," Dolan said, "says that Massi was with her husband the morning he was killed. He was also at the McRae girl's apartment the day before. They were all at Guy Labrutto's house in Alpine yesterday morning. Your cousin Guy. The one who was over to your house last week."

Junior Boy was surprised to hear this, although his face remained expressionless. He knew that Joe Black Massi had killed Dolan's father, but not, until now, that young Dolan was mad with the need for revenge. "It looks like you're not getting that warrant," he said. "In which case, I'll wait for Stabile outside."

As he was saying this, a phone, located on the credenza behind Dolan, began to ring. The prosecutor swung abruptly, picked up the receiver, listened for a second or two, then said into the mouthpiece, "I'm bringing him out." "It's Stabile," he said, swinging back to face DeGiglio. "One more thing before you go," he continued, getting to his feet. A pause ensued, during which the slightly mad theatricality of the moment was inescapable to Junior Boy. Dolan was savoring a moment he had waited years – a lifetime – to arrive.

"I'm listening," the don said, his face deadpan.

"I'm putting this Palisades thing on your head," Dolan said, "and Chris Massi's. *He's disbarred. He needs work. His father was a hit man. You hired him to kill Scarpa and the girl.* That's my theory. Whatever I have to do to prove it, I'll do. In the federal system, we execute by lethal injection. I'll be there looking you and Massi in the eye as you take your last fucking guinea breath."

Later that day, in a quiet and comfortable back room of Benevento, a busy restaurant on Forty-fourth Street in mid-town Manhattan, Junior Boy sat sipping Pellegrino water at a round table covered with a snowy white tablecloth and set for three. He was waiting patiently for Frank and Aldo DiGiglio to arrive.

The night before, Rocco Stabile had met Guy Labrutto at a diner in Clifton to discuss the double murder that had come as a total surprise to the family. According to Labrutto, Scarpa and the girl had been caught stealing over fifty thousand dollars in cash, along with videotapes worth another fifty thousand on the resale market. The two thieves were supposed to be having sex at a secluded overlook when the car shifted accidentally and went over the cliff. Scarpa had gone wild, however, and Mickey had had to shoot him. This panicked Mickey's helper, who, when he saw Mickey get out of Scarpa's car, immediately gunned the BMW and rammed the Buick over the cliff.

No mention had been made of Chris Massi. Mickey had broken his wrist in the fight with Scarpa inside the car. The gun had been disposed of. All this Rocco had relayed to Aldo, who related it to Junior Boy at just before midnight. The don, very unhappy, but not worried, had told Rocco to track down Mickey's helper and kill him without delay. Today, he was still unhappy, but now he was also worried, and angry. The helper had not been found. Labrutto had lied to him. The FBI thought he – Junior Boy – was involved, and, incredibly, his ex-son-in-law was somehow in the picture.

Aldo and Frank arrived, greeted the don with kisses on both cheeks at his chair, then joined him at the table. Of the three of them, only Aldo looked like a gangster. Squat, swarthy, his black hair slicked back with some kind of men's grooming cream, wearing a diamond pinky ring and expensive, custom-made clothes, there was nothing understated about Aldo, who at sixty-five, had the same fire in his eyes that he had at twenty-five. A throwback to the fifties, he disdained the Wall Street look – and pretensions – that were beginning to be adopted by certain gangster elements. To Aldo, the difference between a firm of investment bankers and a Mafia family was that the bankers stole legally but without honor, while the Mafia family stole illegally but with honor. He had no wish to be seen as a member of the dishonorable group. Frank's style could not be categorized, largely because he wished to make no statement about himself by the way he dressed. Of the three of them, he alone remained slender, although under his nondescript suit, his body was wiry and strong. At sixty, he could, if called upon, still use the garrote to lethal purpose. His face unlined by age, his light brown hair kept short, he looked, if anything, like a mid-level bureaucrat, or a high school science teacher, comfortable with his monotonous existence.

"So?" Aldo said, once they were seated. "What?"

"The FBI just questioned me about Scarpa and the girl," Anthony replied.

"You're kidding."

"No, I'm not kidding," he said, softly, "and they claim Chris Massi was involved."

"Your son-in-law?" said Aldo.

"Ex-son-in-law," said Frank.

"Yes," said Junior Boy. "Scarpa's wife said Nick picked Chris up yesterday morning for a meeting in Jersey."

"Maybe he dropped him off somewhere."

"Maybe. Tell Labrutto to come to my house on Sunday. It's Matt's birthday. Make sure he doesn't leave without talking to me. I want to know why he thought he could kill Scarpa – or anybody – without my permission, and whether Massi was involved. Tell him what will happen if he lies to me."

This was addressed to Aldo, who was Guy Labrutto's uncle via his wife's sister. The tone of Junior Boy's voice – soft, matter of fact, precise – raised the hackles on Aldo's neck. He would hate to see his wife's nephew killed, but there would be no stopping it, once ordered by the don.

"Why you?" Frank asked Junior Boy.

"It's the surveillance. I was at Teresa's Saturday night when Chris dropped off the kids. He stayed a few minutes. They found Labrutto's address in Scarpa's wallet. They know Labrutto and I talk."

"Have they talked to Labrutto?"

"They didn't say, but if they did, he didn't mention it to Rocco."

"Why hold that back?" Aldo said.

"Why not tell us about Massi? Why the hit in the first place?" Junior Boy replied.

"You don't believe his story?"

"Do you?"

"The only thing I can say is that it's such an incredibly stupid thing to do that maybe it's true."

"Maybe. But Aldo, make sure you tell him how close he is to being dead. Just for fun, I'll have Nicky Spags throw him and that freak sidekick of his off the same cliff. Make sure you mention that."

"If it's the helper you're worried about, he'll be dead soon. You know Rocco."

"As soon as he's dead, I want to know."

"What about Massi?" Aldo asked.

"Find him," Junior Boy replied. "I want to talk to him. He's living in the Village someplace."

"There's nothing to worry about here," Frank said.

"Unless there's something we don't know."

Both men looked at the don.

"Ed Dolan interviewed me. By himself. Before Tom Stabile got there."

"So?" Aldo said. "You gave him nothing, right?"

"Right, but here's what he said: 'I'm putting this double murder on your head, Junior Boy, yours and Chris Massi's. Whatever I have to do to prove the two of you did it, I'll do. In the federal system, we execute by lethal injection. I'll be there looking you in the eye as you take your last fucking guinea breath."

"The fucking Irish cocksucker," said Aldo.

Frank just shook his head.

All three knew the story of Dolan Sr., Johnny Logan and Joe Black Massi; of Dolan Jr.'s vengeful prosecution of Chris Massi and the role he played in Chris' disbarment. Frank and Aldo especially had watched with keen interest as this drama played itself out. Chris' refusal to officially join the family and his divorce of Teresa were insults that still rankled ten years later. Junior Boy's attitude was different. At the time of the divorce, it grieved him to see his daughter's heart broken, but, although he was hurt as well, he was never angry at Chris. Joe Black Massi's son had acted honorably both during and after the marriage. Junior boy was a busy man, and not one to dwell on what might have been, but recently, Chris had been much on his mind. He had asked for time to consider the offer concerning Jimmy Barson, and that was sensible. There was no re-crossing that Rubicon. It had certainly occurred to DiGiglio that his only grandson might one day succeed him as don. He considered Chris' attempt at intervention a masterful stroke, motivated simply by love of his son.

As to the problem at hand, it was extremely unlikely that Chris was involved in the killing of Nick Scarpa and the girl, but whether he was or was not was irrelevant, given Ed Dolan's blood lust. Of the two links between the don and the double murder – Labrutto and Massi – Labrutto was by far the weakest. But that did not mean that Chris could be ignored, or left to his own devices. He would have to be talked to, and warned. Implicit in this line of thinking were the consequences to Chris, the very harsh consequences, should he turn out for some reason to pose a threat to Junior Boy. The don stopped short at this thought, unwilling to envision either the scenario or its aftermath, in which a young man who he at one time had loved like a son – the father of his grandchildren – was killed or hurt badly on his orders. That he would leave for another day.

The rest of the game board lent itself to an easy analysis. Labrutto's attempt at an "accident," in which two people associated with him died, had failed. A coward, but a fairly intelligent one, he would never have made such an attempt without the don's permission unless there was a countervailing force, which most likely was a betrayal to another family. He would keep Labrutto alive until he discovered who this other family was and what precisely was the nature of the betrayal. Then Labrutto would be killed and the family that had seduced him dealt with.

Then there was the execution of Jimmy Barsonetti to consider. It could not be put off indefinitely. Barson, as he was sometimes called, had taken recently to visiting a woman in Queens in the early morning hours before her husband, a cop, got home from his midnight to eight a.m. shift. The row house next door was empty. Its elderly owner had died and left it to the wife of a young DiGiglio soldier. It made for easy access to the cop's back door, which, with no access from the street, was never guarded by Barsonetti's people. But this situation would not last long. Barsonetti would tire of cuckolding the cop, or the woman would leave her husband. Frank and Aldo knew of Junior Boy's plans, but they had not been told that Chris Massi had been offered the chance to pull the trigger. The don had made more than a few such important decisions without consulting his brothers, and he fully expected them, as they had in the past, to accept this one when it was revealed to them. He had given Chris a week to make a decision. The don would use that week to determine if his former son-in-law was really a threat to the family. If he was, then, of course, things would change dramatically. Lunch consisted of a garden salad, penne with marinara sauce, fresh baked semolina bread, and a two hundred dollar bottle of Chianti. As the waiter was clearing the table, there was a knock on the door, and Rocco Stabile entered the room.

"Clean up later," Junior Boy said to the waiter, who immediately placed the dishes he had in his hands on a side table and left the room.

"Sit," the don said to Rocco, who, nodding, sat heavily in the empty chair, facing Junior Boy.

The three DiGiglios looked at Rocco, who had placed his thick, hairy forearms on the table and was waiting to be spoken to. In his middle forties, a "made man," Rocco, with his mashed nose, retro eyeglasses and earnestly knitted brow, had the look of a middle linebacker who had waited a year or two too long to retire. It would be a mistake, however, to take him lightly, as many had learned to their dismay.

"Talk," Aldo said, impatient.

"The Brooklyn thing is done."

"What took you so long?"

"He was out all night. He came home this morning."

"And the car?"

"It's in Queens being fixed."

Aldo was doing the questioning. Rocco reported directly to him.

"Anything else?"

"I stopped by the house in Alpine. The FBI was there, dusting for fingerprints, going through Guy's records."

"Did they take anything?"

"They wanted copies of all of the videos Guy made. He didn't have any, but he did have production records, which they took."

"So they'll eventually see the girl."

Rocco remained silent.

"Anything else?" Aldo asked.

"They took a water bottle and a glass that were on the coffee table. For prints."

"Whose prints were on them?"

"Guy didn't say. I didn't ask."

"Go get Guy, Rocco. Bring him to the Tick-Tock. I'll meet you there. Tell the freak to stay put. If he so much as makes a phone call, he's dead."

"He wasn't there."

"Where'd he go?"

"Guy said he sent him into the city for something."

"I told him not to make a move until I spoke to him."

This was not a question, so Rocco did not answer. His deceivingly innocent face was blank, but in his heart, he was glad that Aldo's tongue had slipped. He hated Guy Labrutto, whose pornography business, lucrative or not, was a blot on the family's honor. An order to execute Labrutto, and his albino "assistant," would be music to Rocco's battered ears. He looked over at Junior Boy, who had remained silent, waiting for a question, or his cue to leave.

"Who did the Brooklyn job?" the don asked.

"Phil Purcell."

"Who was this guy?"

"A junkie, I think. A street punk."

"Where was he all night?"

"I don't know. Philly waited outside his house. You want me to see if Philly talked to him at all?"

"I want you to find out where he spent the night. Who he talked to."

"Okay," Rocco answered, nodding once.

"You can go, Rocco," Junior Boy said. "You did good."

5.

On Tuesday morning, Chris shaved and showered in Lou's apartment. Over breakfast, Lou told him of Joseph's calls earlier and of Mickey Rodriguez' ransacking of his apartment. Chris kept his thoughts to himself, not wanting to endanger Lou by giving him information that could get him killed. While changing after his shower, Chris had come across the slip of paper he had taken from Rodriguez' wallet with "Michele" scrawled on it along with a Manhattan telephone number. He promised Lou he would not wander, but instead of returning to La Luna's back room after breakfast, he headed for Suffolk Street.

He took the same route he had taken Sunday. The weather was again good, but there was no way he could enjoy it, not with the words *double murder, snuff film and federal prosecution* mixing in his head with the images of Mickey Rodriguez' sickening orgasm, Heather Jansen's puzzled, then terrified, face as a gun was placed against the side of her head and Ed Dolan's revenge-mad eyes. As if this were not enough, the idea of killing Jimmy Barsonetti, solidifying slowly in his mind over the past ten days, kept forcing itself into this turbulent mix.

As he approached LaSalle Academy, he noticed a man dressed in black, wearing a clerical collar, directing a group of boys as they unloaded cardboard boxes from a truck parked at the curb on Second Street. Drawing nearer, he saw that the cleric was Brother John Farrell, the driver of the car that had, in February of 1977, gone off of the Grand Central Parkway into a tree, putting Chris in the hospital for a month and changing the course of his life. Seeing Brother Farrell, whose shock of wavy, once chestnut brown hair had turned pure white, and who must by now be seventy-five or more, snapped Chris back to that winter night, and to the memory of the boy who definitely had other plans, other dreams. John Farrell's face, red and etched with age and sadness, reminded him of Hemingway's famous line about the world breaking all of us, and he wondered if either he or Farrell were among the lucky ones who were stronger in the broken parts.

"Mr. Massi."

"Brother Farrell."

"It's been a long time."

Chris did not answer. John Farrell, a drinker at the time, had visited him in the hospital once and then been transferred to a high school in Chicago, his home town. He and Chris had not laid eyes on each other since.

"I've kept tabs on you," Farrell said. "I don't suppose you can say the same."

"No."

"Are you holding a grudge?"

"You weren't drunk. I thought we cleared that up?"

"A fifteen-year-old boy," Farrell replied, "will say anything to a superior in a black robe and a collar."

Chris had set a two-mile New York state high school record that night at the Nassau Coliseum. It had rained that day and then turned very cold, but the roads did not seem bad as they headed back to the city, Chris the only boy on the team that night who did not have a ride home from his parents or someone else he knew in attendance.

One moment they were going along at speed, the next they were flying, literally, off the road.

"You had your usual two or three shooters," Chris said.

"Did I tell you that?"

"You didn't have to."

John Farrell, no athlete, and not a sports groupie – the boys called them jock sucks – offered his assistance to every LaSalle coach, running team members to and from games and meets, tending to the movement of equipment and other logistics; giving him, on road trips, an excuse to be out of the Brothers' dorm, to have a few quiet beers until he was needed at the end of whatever game was being played. His routine was known to Chris and most of the the boys on the various teams but held no special interest for them. To them, he was a decent guy who taught Latin and geometry with an uncondescending wryness, and who was not keen on the infamous paddle used by some other teachers a little too quickly and with a little too much relish.

"I'm sorry," the cleric said, "nevertheless."

Farrell, not especially big, but exuding a casual strength and a charming cockiness as a young man, seemed to Chris to have shrunk with the years, in spirit as well as in body. He stood as tall as he could now, as if he were seizing some chance the universe had offered him. He had been driving carefully that winter night, at, or a little over, the speed limit. He had had his usual two or three beers, but he was not drunk. He had probably hit a patch of ice. Looking at him, blinking in the morning sun, Chris realized that the lives of two people had been bent to fate's white heat that night twenty-seven years ago. Nodding slightly, he said, "It was just bad luck, Brother, for both of us, but I accept your apology. What have you been up to?"

"I got sober – I actually *was* a drunk. Then I taught school on the south side of Chicago for twenty years. I worked at a drug rehab clinic part time."

"It took seven years to get sober?"

"I can't remember most of them, thank God. How about you? I hear you've had some trouble lately."

"Don't tell me I made the Chicago papers."

"I've followed your career via one source and another."

"Are you back at LaSalle?"

"They've made me an assistant principal. I'll teach a class or two. I can't stand the thought of retiring, and we're very short of brothers. You haven't answered my question."

"I'm fine."

"Are you living in the city?"

"I'm back in the old neighborhood, actually."

"The legs?"

"They're okay."

"Can you still conjugate the verb, cambio?"

"Is there a message in there someplace?" Chris said, smiling for the first time in forty-eight hours.

"Maybe. It's the first verb that came to mind."

"Cambio, cambias, cambiat, cambiamus, cambiatus, cambiant."

"I'm a hell of a teacher."

The boys, three of them, had finished carrying Brother Farrell's things inside, and were now sitting against the wrought iron fence of the small cemetery next door, talking and striking the various awkward poses of early teenage males everywhere.

"It looks like they're anxious to be free," Farrell said, noticing them.

"I'll leave you," Chris said, extending his hand.

"I'm an old man," Farrell replied, gripping Chris' hand with surprising strength, "but I still have my legs under me. Call me if you need anything in the way of help."

The oddness of meeting Brother Farrell at this moment in his life did not escape Chris, nor did the look in the old man's pale eyes. They were smiling and sad at the same time, and there was something else in them that Chris could not place. Thoughts of Farrell receded quickly, however, as Chris turned from Delancey onto Suffolk Street, where he saw Mickey Rodriguez standing at the top of the steps of number one-twelve, looking up and down the block through a pair of near-black sunglasses. The shadow cast by the fire escape directly above him could not obscure the rest of the albino's face, which shone translucently with its own strange, inner light.

Spotting Chris, Rodriguez reached inside his black sport coat. Chris slowed to see if the killer of Nick Scarpa and Allison McRae was going to draw a gun. Their eyes locked for a long second, during which, as if on a separate screen in his mind, Chris saw himself killing Rodriguez, executing him in the unadorned, point-blank way in which he always imagined Joe Black dispatched his victims. He had, without thinking, picked up his pace, but this thought slowed him down, as he realized he would need a gun to do this, and a better venue.

The albino, keeping his right hand inside his jacket, used his free hand to tilt his dark glasses forward, to get a better look at Chris, who came to a stop no more than fifty feet away. Before either could make a move or say anything, a silver Mercedes, coming from the next street over, pulled up and double parked in front of the building. Rodriguez quickly descended the worn brownstone steps and got into the front passenger seat. As the car drove by,

Chris mouthed the words "fuck you" to Rodriguez, who, through the car's tinted glass window, looked like a rare species of deep water fish deprived of light for millions of years. Chris watched until the Mercedes turned right at Delancey Street, and was swallowed up by the city.

The door to Michele's apartment was off its hinges, the jamb splintered, and she lay on the floor in the middle of the tiny living room in the fetal position. An outsized old kitchen knife was stuck in the hardwood floor about six inches from her head. *Please don't be dead*, Chris said out loud, as he knelt down and turned her onto her back. Her right eye was swollen shut, her left eye open, but glazed, her face raw with ragged bruises, but she was breathing – softly hissing – through her mouth. Her denim mini-skirt was hiked up above her waist. Chris pulled it down and straightened her torn blouse and bra before picking her up and laying her on the sofa, propping her head up with a cushion. He could see the fear in her good eye as it began to focus on him, and feel her body stiffen then release. She was awake and frightened, but there was no fight left in her.

"Who're you?" she whispered.

"I'm Chris, Allison's friend. I was here on Sunday."

"Allison's dead."

"I know."

"Do you know who killed her?"

"The guy who just beat you up."

"How do you know?"

"It doesn't matter. I'm calling an ambulance."

"No. No ambulance, no hospital."

"You could have broken bones in your face, around that eye."

"I'm okay."

"You're not okay."

"They'll arrest me, or try to clean me up. I'm high. I'm always fucking high..."

Michele's open eye was a regulation, farm girl blue, incongruous beneath an arched, severely plucked dark brown eyebrow and a head of spiked, harshly bleached, nearly white hair. Chris could see that under her bruises and her heavy make-up her face was a sickly green. Her street toughness had not stood up well to a dose of Mickey Rodriguez' unfiltered evil.

"I'll clean you up," he said, "then we'll talk some more. Don't move."

He poked around in the small, shabby kitchen and bathroom – the only other rooms in the apartment – and returned with peroxide, paper towels, ice in a dish and a clean washcloth soaked in cold water. Michele closed her good eye as Chris wiped off her make-up, cleaned the open wounds on her cheeks, nose and mouth with peroxide and then used the wash cloth to make an ice pack, which he placed against her swollen eye, picking up her hand – surprisingly delicate and pretty – and guiding it to her head so that she could hold it in place herself.

"Any other injuries?" he asked.

Michele shook her head.

"When did you get high?"

"This morning."

"Do you have more?"

"I bought two dime bags last night. There's one left. Why? You want some?"

"No. I was thinking you'd need it later."

For an answer, she closed her eye and turned her face to the back of the couch.

"What did Mickey want?"

No answer.

"Michele," Chris said. "I need to know what happened. If you won't talk to me, I'll call an ambulance. I'll make sure you're here when they get here. They'll fuck you up with methadone. You won't get high for a week, maybe two. You'll go through withdrawal. I can't play games with you. There's too much at stake."

No answer. Chris took his cell phone out of his pocket and dialed three random numbers. Michele turned and reached for the phone, but Chris pulled it away.

"Turn it off," she said, her voice raspy, tired. "Turn it off."

Chris clicked the phone off, his eyes locked on Michele's open eye.

"They killed Heather," Michele said.

"Who did?"

"Labrutto and the freak. They filmed it."

"How do you know?"

"Allison told me. She saw the video. She had given Labrutto my name, to be in a porn film. She called to warn me not to do it. She told me about Heather."

"You knew this when I came here?"

"Yes, but who the fuck are you? Another killer for all I know."

"What did Mickey want?"

"He told me the cops would want to talk to me, since I lived right across from Allison. He said if I told them anything, he'd kill me. I tried to stab him, but he laughed and beat the shit out of me. He said Labrutto still wants me to do a movie for him, with him – the freak – as my male lead."

"Were the cops here?"

"A cop was here yesterday afternoon, interviewing the people in the building. He caught me in the hallway. He wanted to know if Allison had visitors over the weekend. I told him about you. Then early this morning, about seven, they came back and went through Allison's apartment. I could hear the super letting them in. They knocked on my door, but I didn't answer. They slipped a card under the door. It's in the kitchen. A guy named Magnuson from the U.S. Attorney's office."

"Did Allison set Heather up to be killed?"

"Not on purpose. She thought it would just be a porn movie. When she saw the video, she freaked out."

"Did she tell anyone else about the film?"

"She said she told the cockeyed guy, Nick. He was supposed to help her escape. She figured if she couldn't get them another girl to kill, she'd be next."

"So Labrutto doesn't know that you know about the snuff film?"

"No."

"And he still wants you to be in one of his movies?"

"Right."

"So he can have another snuff film to sell, and at the same time, get rid of a key witness against him: you."

"Why am I a witness?'

"You're the only person who knows that Allison was living at Labrutto's house for the last two months. He has to kill you. He's greedy though: he figures he might as well make money off of your murder. Am I getting through to you?"

"I'm a junkie, but I'm not stupid."

"Do you have someplace you can go?"

Michele was fading, her speech slurred, her voice barely audible, but she came semi-alive at this question.

"Someplace I could go?" she said, trying to smile.

"Yes."

"If I had someplace I could go, I'd have gone there a long time ago. It's time for me to die."

"You can't die. You have to help me kill Labrutto, and Mickey."

"What's your name?"

"Chris."

"Then we'll die together, Chris."

"No, we won't. We'll live. I will, anyway. Don't fall asleep. With that head injury, you could go into a coma. I'll make some coffee. And some calls. Do you still have Allison's keys?"

"Yes."

"Good. You're moving into her apartment."

Chris found the makings and put coffee on. While it was brewing, using the phone on Michele's kitchen wall, he dialed information and asked for the number of LaSalle Academy in Manhattan. Michele, through whom Chris could get to both Labrutto and Rodriguez, assuming he could fashion some kind of a plan, needed to be nursed, fed her drugs, and – for want of a nicer word – imprisoned for the next few days. If John Farrell felt he needed to make amends for what he did to Chris twenty-seven years ago, then here was his chance.

6.

"Joseph?"

"Yes?"

"It's me, Jodi."

"Hi. What's up?"

"Someone else is looking for Woody."

"What?"

"Someone else is looking for Woody. I thought you should know."

"Who?"

"A guy named Rocco Stabile."

"How do you know?"

"Patrice called me. This guy Stabile stopped by the bar today."

"What did he say, exactly?"

"He wanted to know who Woody hung out with last night, and where."

"Did Patrice tell him about your girls?"

"No. She thought he was a cop. She said she hadn't seen Woody in a couple of weeks."

"Woody's dead, Jodi."

"Dead?"

"Killed by Stabile's people."

"What's going on?"

"Do you still have your place in Florida?"

"Yes."

"Get on a plane. Take Nicole and the other girl that was with Woody. I'll call you in a few days."

"I'm not going anywhere until I know what's going on."

"Woody did a hit. A mob connected hit. He killed two people. He was eliminated as a witness. Now they're wondering if he spilled his guts to somebody, to eliminate them, too. Are you following me?"

"Yes."

"Things will calm down, but you have to go away for a week or two."

"How do you know all this?"

"I talked to Woody, then I saw him get shot."

"Christ."

Joseph had arrived home, that is, at Marsha's twenty-first floor apartment overlooking the East River, taken ten milligrams of Valium, and fallen asleep on the plush sectional sofa in the living room. The buzzing of his cell phone had awakened him with a start. Now, his head clear, he was standing on the balcony, the phone to his ear, watching with one eye as the light from the setting sun turned Queens' industrial riverbank into a magic kingdom of shining smokestacks, geometrically shaded rooftops and glittering windows.

"Nicole can be a bitch," Jodi said. "What if she won't come?"

"Someone else may have seen her with Woody at the Royalton, or at the hotel. They'll kill anybody they think talked to him last night. Tell her that."

"Including you. Come with us."

"I can't. There's something I need to do. Maybe I'll fly down next week. We can play."

"I'm worried, Joseph."

"That's good. You'll be cautious. But it'll be fine. I have a plan."

Joseph did not have a plan. Plans did not play a prominent role in his life. The furthest ahead he thought was to the identities and hangouts of the people, usually women, he could borrow or scam money from. Occasionally, when desperate, he could be creative. He once staged an accident in which twelve street people in a van he was driving sustained whiplash injuries when he was rear-ended by a bus on Sixth Avenue. The lawyer he referred his passengers to gave him ten percent of each settlement, and he made an easy ten thousand dollars. But this was not an insurance scam he had on his hands now.

Before taking his Valium and falling into a dead sleep earlier, he had called Vinnie Rosamelia, who told him that the albino had ransacked Chris' apartment late last night, and that this morning, Rocco Stabile had stopped by asking for Chris. Earlier, from Lou Falco, he learned that Ed Dolan, knowing of the Scarpa-Chris Massi connection, was looking at Chris as a suspect in the Scarpa/ McRae murders. Dolan would soon discover, if he had not already, that Chris had visited Allison's apartment on Sunday, which would make his case against Chris that much stronger.

The hit on Woody by a DiGiglio soldier, the search of Chris' apartment – obviously for the stolen DVD – Rocco Stabile's inquiries, these all meant one thing: it was Junior Boy who was in the snuff film business, not Barsonetti. DiGiglio, proud of his reputation as an honorable, even noble, gangster, would kill anybody who could expose him: Scarpa, Allison, Woody, Chris. And Dolan – the psychotic cocksucker – now had compelling evidence connecting Chris to a double murder. DiGiglio or Dolan alone wanting Chris dead would be bad enough, but both of them at once pretty much guaranteed that his brother's life was over – unless Joseph could think of something, could actually come up with a plan that would save Chris' life. Standing on the balcony, his tailored gray slacks and dark blue silk shirt wrinkled from sleeping in them, gazing down at the river but not seeing it, Joseph smiled. No one took him seriously. He was a lackey, someone to be taken advantage of, or abused, to be tossed an occasional crumb in deference to his father. The last thing anyone saw him as was a threat.

Marsha was in Northern California, painting. She would not be back until Saturday. The bargain they had initially struck – she could have a fling with a sexy, dangerous thirty-two year old as long as she let him roam at will and financed his life style – had lately turned into something else. They liked each other. It would be hard to say which of them was more surprised by this turn of events, Marsha, the never married workaholic – her drug was her art – or Joseph, clean of heroin but daily edging closer to the abyss.

Marsha gave Joseph, who had never had a credit card, a thousand dollars a month, and paid his tab at two local restaurants. Searching through her desk for her checkbook, he thought of what she said when they got home from dinner with Chris and the kids on Saturday night: *He's a handsome guy, your brother, but you're handsomer, and a lot more fun. He's too serious. What cross is he carrying? His disbarment? That's probably a blessing. Still, I knew you had a brother, but I never knew how much you loved him until tonight. I saw it in those beautiful eyes of yours all night long.*

7.

Guy Labrutto had refused to say word one to the investigators sent by Ed Dolan to interview him, and the documents obtained in the search of his home revealed nothing incriminating. Corporate taxes were fully paid by West Coast Productions, his porn video company, and Labrutto paid the appropriate personal income tax on the substantial salary he took annually from the business. "Consultants fees" of close to two million dollars per year were paid to Claremont Enterprises, a New Jersey company that invoiced for services that included casting, script editing, talent development and marketing. This company was owned by the same two men, brothers named Alphonse and Achilles Cirillo, who owned and operated a strip club called RazzMaTazz on Route 46 in Garfield.

State records showed that Claremont was formed in 1992 by Thomas M. Stabile, Esquire, a known mob lawyer and, of course, Rocco's brother. Alphonse and Achilles, dumbfounded that the authorities would be interested in them for any reason, referred Dolan's investigators to Stabile, who politely refused to say anything unless and until he received a subpoena. The Cirillos, with their gold necklaces and onyx pinky rings, were no script editors, and were probably passing their "fees" on to Junior Boy via Tom Stabile, whose presence guaranteed that the don was involved. To make matters worse – excruciatingly worse

– forensics had just reported that the fingerprints found on the water bottle and glass taken from Labrutto's living room were a near match to Chris Massi's but inconclusive for courtroom purposes.

All of this information came to Dolan in a report he received on the Thursday afternoon following the murders. As he read it, a familiar mix of dread and anxiety began to drum its fingers in his gut. Of late, he had kept this old foe at bay with drugs: Paxil and Zoloft prescribed by a psychiatrist on Fifth Avenue who charged four hundred and fifty dollars for a fifty-minute session the sole purpose of which was to write a prescription. He was certain that a victory over Massi and DiGiglio would vanquish this enemy as well.

And he was close. Without having to work very hard, or do anything rash, meaning illegal, he was very close. He had the Massi-Scarpa connection, he had Chris' fingerprints in Allison McRae's apartment with the hooker's statement that she had let him in on Sunday. He had Labrutto's name and address in Scarpa's wallet, and he had the Labrutto-DiGiglio connection. But he was not close enough to indict anybody. He did not have enough on any individual suspect to leverage them into a traditional testimony-for-free-pass deal, and empaneling a grand jury was out of the question. Everyone would take the fifth amendment and he'd be worse off than when he started, having tipped his hand with nothing to show for it.

Dolan knew that the panic he was feeling came from his fear that this, his one, great opportunity to avenge his father's death, was slipping away from him, that never again would he have both Junior Boy and Massi within such tantalizingly easy reach. The efforts of the Christian Brothers at LaSalle Academy and of the Jesuits at

196 Sons and Princes

Fordham to instill in their students the simple premise of all morality – that the end never justifies the means – had had no effect on Ed Dolan. In fact, like all true believers, he saw his point of view as the morally correct one. He was perfectly justified in returning hurt for hurt, death for death. He had tried to terrorize Massi with a false indictment and a disbarment complaint grounded in lies, but he now saw the inherent softness of that approach. Indeed, Chris' acquittal at the trial could be viewed as evidence of Dolan's timidity. He would not let that happen again. All he needed was a better plan, a stronger will, and he would prevail. His faith in the tenets of his cult-of-one invigorated, lost for a second in his daydream, the ringing of his telephone jarred Ed Dolan forcefully back to reality.

Picking it up, and listening to his secretary, it was as if the machinery of the universe had been all along operating quietly but efficiently for the sole good of Ed Dolan Jr. Joseph Massi was at the front desk, asking to see him, and only him.

"What should I do?" his secretary asked.

"Bring him back," Dolan answered, "and then hold my calls."

Dolan had not seen Joseph Massi since the June day twenty-four years ago when he and Chris graduated from LaSalle. The younger Massi, a pretty, eight-year-old boy in a blue blazer and tie, with a mop of thick black hair and big, liquid eyes, had held his mother's hand the entire day. That he had turned out a junkie and a punk was common knowledge and a source of satisfaction to Dolan. Anything that hurt the Massi family made him happy. But beyond that, Joseph did not interest him. There would have been little or no gratification in destroying such a weakling. Better that he lived to torture his parents and his brother. Entering his office, Joseph, still pretty, in his summer-weight, finely spun dark blue suit, creamy turtleneck and braided Italian shoes, looked more like a Ralph Lauren model than a habitual heroin user.

"Joe Massi."

"Ed Dolan."

They faced each other in the sunlit room, Dolan at his oversized government-issue desk, Joseph settling in a worn faux leather chair with brass studs around the seat.

"You look good," Dolan said. "Have you quit using?"

"You haven't changed," Joseph replied.

"You want some kind of royal treatment? You're a junkie. State your business."

"I can help you with the Scarpa and McRae murders."

"How?"

Joseph drew a DVD in a jewel case from the pocket of his suit coat and put it, with one of his calling cards, on Dolan's desk. "That's a snuff film," he said. "The male lead is an albino who works for Guy Labrutto. Nick and Allison were killed because they found out about the film."

"I'm not impressed."

"Labrutto and Anthony DiGiglio are in the snuff film business. Junior Boy ordered the killing, Labrutto and the albino carried it out."

"How do you know this?"

"It's on the street."

"So I'll subpoena the street to testify before the grand jury, and the case will be all wrapped up tight."

"I can get Junior Boy on tape."

It had been obvious that Joseph, who was trying to remain calm and focused and not doing a bad job of it, was on a mission of some kind. But a kamikaze mission was the last thing Dolan expected, and the one thing guaranteed to get his full attention.

"How?"

"My nephew's fourteenth birthday is on Sunday. Junior Boy's having a party at his house. You wire me. I'll get him to talk about the snuff film and the murders."

"In return for which, you want what?"

"I want you to lay off Chris. You know he didn't kill anybody."

Dolan did not respond immediately. He picked up the DVD, read the title and flipped open the case, eying the shiny silver disk inside.

"Where's Chris now?" he asked.

"He took a vacation. I don't know where to."

"Where'd you get this?" Dolan asked, holding the DVD up and tilting it toward Joseph.

"Allison gave it to me. She stole it from Labrutto."

"How did you know her?"

"She was a friend of an old girlfriend."

"They fake these things," Doaln said, "to make them look violent when they're not."

"This is the real thing. Take a look at it when you get a chance."

"I will. If it's real, we'll talk some more."

"What about Chris?"

"If he didn't kill anybody, what does he have to worry about?"

"You. Your vendetta."

"And you thought only the Sicilians were good at that."

"What about Chris?"

"If I get Junior Boy, your brother can walk."

"I have one other condition."

"What's that?"

"If there's trouble in the house, or the wire goes dead, your people have to be ready."

"Junior Boy wouldn't do violence in his own house," Dolan said, "with his family there."

"He might. Your guys have to come in. I need your word on that."

"I couldn't protect you afterward."

"I'll run."

"Okay. If you go in, you'll have backup."

"I ran into an old friend of yours last week," Joseph said, getting to his feet.

"Who's that?"

"Johnny Logan, remember him?"

Dolan sat straighter in his chair and stared hard at Joseph. He did not respond.

"He's got a colostomy bag," Joseph continued. "The poor fuck. He gets some kind of government check. Isn't he a cousin of yours or something? I thought he was long dead, actually."

Dolan, remaining silent, eyed Joseph standing now behind his chair. Logan had survived his stomach wound and told the police that he had shot Dolan in a fight over money, Dolan having drawn first. What else could he say? If he had tried to finger Joe Black, the Velardo family would certainly have killed him. He went off to a five-to-fifteen-year prison sentence for manslaughter, and had not been heard from since.

The true story had spread quickly, however, from Logan's girlfriend at the time, Moira, and Andy O'Brien, who soon thereafter sold Valerio's and moved to Phoenix. Everyone in the Greenwich Village/Lower East Side/Mafia subculture knew what happened in Valerio's back room that February night, including, without doubt, Joseph

Massi, who was now, incredibly, reminding Ed Dolan of *who killed who* twenty-seven years ago, throwing it in his face.

But Dolan remained calm. Joseph would soon be dead. Either that or Dolan would have hard evidence of Junior Boy DiGiglio's involvement, along with Labrutto, in three murders: the snuff film victim, Nick Scarpa and Allison McRae. With that, he could make a deal with one of them, preferably Labrutto, for testimony implicating Massi. He could not lose his cool and scare off Joseph, his junkie stalking horse, no matter how much he wanted to throw him out the window. That Joseph could be the instrument of Chris' final fall was the sweetest of ironies, a gift from the gods.

"I don't know the guy," the prosecutor finally responded.

"He was asking about you."

"You need to get fixed, don't you, Joseph," Dolan said, ignoring this last remark, forcing a sympathetic smile. "I can see it in your eyes. Hold off. I need you clean. Keep Sunday morning open. If this film is the real thing, that's when you'll get wired, and we'll go over the plan. Don't go and O.D. on me in the meantime."

After Joseph left, Dolan sat and contemplated the various aspects of his windfall. The type of operation that Joseph Massi was suggesting, involving the wiring of a civilian with no law enforcement experience, required the approval of the head of the criminal division in Washington, the number three man in the Justice Department. The approval process took some time, and expedition was rare. For a true national emergency, it might be done in a day or two. And then, if it were known that the civilian was a heroin addict going into a houseful of innocent people, including women and children, the chances for approval would be virtually nil.

But Dolan wasn't worried about the approval process. He would bypass it. He would put a remote wire on Joseph's chest himself, a dud, and give him a voice-activated tape recorder to put in his pocket. He would tell him to arrive at a certain time, and instruct his surveillance team to leave when they saw him pull up. If DiGiglio did a strip search, Joseph was a dead man, but who would know or care? If he made it out alive, with Junior Boy incriminating himself on tape, it would be a home run.

He could deal with Joseph later, maybe set him up for a kill by DiGiglio's people as part of a truly outside-the-box plea deal. His only fear was that Joseph would lose heart and back out. Ed Dolan hadn't prayed in almost thirty years, and he wasn't about to start now. But, he readily acknowledged to himself that if he were to start again, his first request would be that Joseph Massi stay strong on his present course, that he walk into Anthony DiGiglio's Tudor mansion on Sunday afternoon wired for sound and ready to martyr himself for the only religion that really mattered, the only cause worth praying for: Ed Dolan's revenge.

8.

Despite its great success, Junior Boy DiGiglio was not content as his family entered the new millennium. He was sixty-six years old, and he had no heir. And there was no one in sight that fit the necessarily giant-sized bill. Frank's son had shown promise. Cautious, reserved, disciplined, and with an inner toughness like his dad, he had gone to college in California, where he met and married, had a child with Down Syndrome, and decided not to return East. Aldo's two sons, now in their early forties, were undisciplined, arrogant hotheads. Corrupted early by money and power, their antics were an embarrassment to the don – drunk and partying, they had recently crashed a boat into the dock at a marina at the shore – and a constant source of friction between him and his brother. Aldo had been the same way as a boy, but their father's steady, quiet anger had eventually scared him into manhood. Junior Boy did not expect the same thing to happen to his two nephews.

Without the right leader, the family would fall apart, succumb to the pressures of the American popular culture. Personal ambition and greed would prevail over loyalty and honor. The family would descend to the level of the Sopranos on television, where made men had sex in front of one another with strippers in the back rooms of bars, and where young women were beaten to death with golf clubs in parking lots for no reason. The fear of a such a future for the DiGiglios kept Junior Boy up many long nights in the winter and early spring of 2003.

With the botched double murder in Alpine, the don's brooding over succession to power quickly took a back seat to much more urgent concerns. The don had yet to speak to Labrutto face to face. First Rocco and then Aldo had met with him and extracted his story: Scarpa was forced by Mickey at gun point to drive to the cliff, with the now-dead Woody Smith following. Rodriguez was supposed to jump out, which would be Smith's cue to ram the car over the edge. At the lookout, Scarpa went wild inside the car. Mickey had to shoot him in order to get free. Chris Massi had shown up unexpectedly with Scarpa. He disappeared soon after Scarpa and the girl went out. Labrutto did not know where or why.

On the Sunday following the murders, Junior Boy sat at his massive desk in his study and went over this story one more time in his mind, deciding again that it was half truth and half lie, that it was a virtual certainty that Labrutto had betrayed him somehow. He would not lie to Aldo, and thus to the don, to cover up a venial sin. The true story would be revealed soon enough. Matt's birthday party was getting underway. Labrutto was there. Aldo had been instructed to bring him into the study at three o'clock. The surveillance van that had been appearing at irregular intervals at the curb near the entrance to the house's long driveway had arrived at noon. But Labrutto was a relative, and the party was good cover, and the house had been swept for listening devices early that morning. It was now two forty-five. The knock on the door was premature, but it was time to get to the bottom of this situation. He would learn the truth, if not today then very soon, and the process of protecting himself and the family would begin. If Labrutto had to go, so be it. Aldo would have to accept it, and his wife would never know the truth. The income Labrutto brought in would be missed, but the man would certainly not be. The world would be a better place without Labrutto and his misfit sidekick.

But it wasn't Guy Labrutto who Aldo led into the room. It was Joseph Massi, Chris' younger brother, Joe Black Massi's junkie son.

Aldo directed Joseph, beautifully dressed, his face pale, but otherwise handsome and immaculately groomed, to a leather chair facing the don. He placed a small cassette recorder, a remote mike with duct tape on it, and a DVD on the desk in front of Junior Boy. Then he went to stand behind Joseph. The French doors behind Junior Boy's desk gave onto a stone terrace littered with dozens of potted plants and flowers basking in the spring sunlight. Junior Boy rose and swung the doors shut. While the doors were open, a gentle breeze, along with noise from the party on the wide, flagstoned patios and lawns below, had drifted in to the don as he sat alone at his desk. Now the room was quiet and still. The don returned to his seat, and looked at Joseph and then at Aldo.

"He asked to see you," Aldo said. "I said sure and had Nicky search him."

Junior Boy stared down at the three items on his ornate, marquetry-embossed blotter, then back up at Joseph.

"Ed Dolan," Joseph said. "You know who I'm talking about?"

"Yes," Anthony replied. "I know who he is. What about him?"

"I think he killed my father, and now he wants to kill Chris, or put him in jail forever. I made a deal with him. I would talk to you with a wire on if he'd leave Chris alone.

There's backup outside. Now that the wire's been cut, they'll be in here any second. I did this for Chris, Junior Boy."

DiGiglio stared calmly at Joe Black Massi's second son, understanding, after hearing this incredible but obviously true statement, why the young man sitting across from him was so pale and on edge.

"The gray van left about a half hour ago," Aldo said, "and the grounds have been swept all day, including the woods."

"Talk to me about what?" Junior Boy asked.

"The murder of Nick Scarpa and Allison McRae."

"To implicate me?"

The don did not receive an answer. Young Joseph was a blood relative to his grandchildren, and had been to a dozen family parties. He had never been searched, and, apparently, did not know about Junior Boy's policy of searching everyone who asked for a private meeting. "Tell me what Dolan said. About me," Junior Boy said.

"He thinks you ordered the killings because Nick and Allison found out about the film. The one on your desk. 'Candy Meets Ron.' It's a snuff film."

"What's a snuff film?"

"A girl gets killed while having sex."

"A girl gets killed while having sex?"

"Yes, shot in the head. It's a thing some guys get off on."

Anthony shook his head. This was the kind of thing he had been brooding about all winter, America's insane appetite for sex and violence. What better way to combine the two than in a film such as Joseph Massi had described? He was angry now, although he didn't show it.

"What does it have to do with me?"

"Guy Labrutto made it. His albino friend stars in it. Dolan knows that you and Labrutto are in the porn video business together. He thinks this is one of your products. Chris took it from Labrutto's house on Monday, while the murders were taking place."

"How did Dolan get it?"

"I gave it to him."

"To set me up?"

"To save Chris. I didn't think you'd let Labrutto make a film like this. I assumed you'd be shocked and angry when I told you about it, that Dolan would come up empty."

"Does Chris know you're doing this?"

"No."

"Where is he now?"

"Junior Boy. They know I'm here. You have to let me go."

"We've been looking for him."

"Leave him alone. He doesn't know anything. This was all my doing."

"Do you have anything else to tell me?"

Joseph shook his head, slowly, and looked at his watch.

"No," he said, "I was trying to save Chris' life. It looks like Ed Dolan set me up. He wants you, too, Junior Boy. It's not just cops and robbers with him. He's possessed."

"Thanks for the warning," Junior Boy said, nodding, and then, looking up at Aldo, he said: "Make it neat and quick, and far away."

"You want him to talk some more?"

"No."

"Tell us where his brother is?"

"No. Go."

"Let's go," Aldo said, tapping Joseph on the shoulder and then, when he was on his feet, guiding him to the far rear corner of the room and down the stairway that led to the garage directly below them.

Far away was DiGiglio family shorthand for a hit in which the body was never found. In special cases, such as those involving the family's renegade drug dealers in the sixties, the body needed to be found, for the message that it sent. Otherwise, a body and its location were evidence, and there was no need to hand the police their first clues in a murder investigation.

Junior Boy was not without sympathy for Joseph Massi. He had made a play for his brother's life and would pay for it with his own. He had not fallen apart or begged. It was for those reasons that he ordered Aldo not to torture him to extract information regarding Chris' whereabouts. His death would be as painless and honorable as possible under the circumstances.

Chris and Joe Black were also on the don's mind when he gave those orders to Aldo. But he did not dwell on the Massi family very long. There was other business to attend to, like watching "Candy Meets Ron," which he did on the DVD player Teresa had given him last year, along with twenty-five or thirty of his favorite movies, as a Christmas present. When he was finished, he called Nicky Spags on his cell phone and asked him to bring Labrutto in.

"I just watched this," Junior Boy said when Labrutto was seated in front of him, holding up the DVD in its clear plastic case. "'Candy Meets Ron.'"

"Thank God it turned up," Labrutto replied. "You have to destroy it."

"Have you seen it?"

"Yes."

"Did you make it?"

"No. Mickey did, before he came to work for me. I told him to get rid of it. He said he would, but I know now he never did. How did you get it?"

Junior Boy stroked his chin with his thumb and forefinger and stared at Labrutto for a long moment before answering, keeping all emotion out of his eyes.

"Mickey's your albino friend?" he said, finally.

"Yes."

"Did you confront him?"

"Yes. He said it was a leftover copy."

"He wasn't trying to sell it?"

"He says no."

"Are there other copies?"

"No."

"Other films?"

"No."

"Why didn't you tell Aldo at first that Chris Massi was at your house on Monday?"

"I didn't know he would show up with Scarpa. He disappeared right after Nick and the girl went out. When I realized he took the film, I panicked. I thought he might bring it to the police. I tried to track him down to get the film back, but when I couldn't find him, I decided to tell Aldo. That's it, that's the truth. I panicked."

Labrutto seemed pleased with himself at the telling of this lie.

"And the thing on the cliff?" Junior Boy asked. "What happened?"

"Scarpa went nuts. It was botched. I'm sorry, Junior Boy."

"You know you need my permission to do a hit?"

"Yes, of course, but they were stealing. I thought you'd approve."

"If it looked like an accident, I'd never find out."

"Yes, that was the idea. I wanted to solve it easily and quickly, with no headaches for you or anybody else."

He was gaining confidence, this Labruttto. More pleased with himself by the minute.

"Did Massi say why he came along with Scarpa?"

"No, maybe they're old friends. I don't know."

"So you were stuck with him?"

"Right. I couldn't let him go out with Nick and the girl. I offered him a drink."

"Well, there's no harm done," Junior Boy said. "But I'm sending someone to live with you. You teach him the pornography business, he'll teach you the ways of the family. You bring in a lot of money for us, and I want it to stay that way. I can't have any more fiascoes like this one."

"You mean live with me at my house?"

"Yes. I'm told it's a big house."

"Fine. Good. Who will you be sending?"

"I'm not sure yet. Probably Rocco."

"When?"

"Today."

"I see."

Labrutto, the don knew, did *not* see. He was confused, no longer quite so pleased with himself, which is how Junior Boy wanted him to be. Was Rocco Stabile a blessing or a curse? Would he – Labrutto – soon be made a member of the family, or dead? Did the don believe him or not? He had no choice but to go along, to let Stabile, potentially his killer, into his home. To protest would be a sure sign of guilt, and, worse, to reject a gift offered by Junior Boy: the possibility of being asked to join the DiGiglio family, of becoming a made man.

"Who knows," Junior Boy said, watching Labrutto as he sat in obvious dismay, "maybe, we can come up with something for you to do for the family, something you can make your bones on. Let me think about it."

"Thank you, Junior Boy."

"One last thing," the don said, holding the DVD out toward Labrutto.

"Yes?"

"How do you break these things?"

"You want it destroyed?"

"Yes."

Labrutto took the DVD from the don's extended hand, removed it from its case, and, using his two hands, snapped it into several pieces. As he did this, Junior Boy watched, taking note of Labrutto's stubby, hairy hands. When he finished, the don smiled for the first time, but it was not a warm smile, not a smile meant to encourage confidence or a sense of security. Far from it.

9.

The next day, a week to the day from the murder of Nick and Allison, Chris went out early to buy coffee and a bagel at a bakery on Elizabeth Street around the corner from La Luna. He had gone out twice in the past few days, both times to see how Michele and John Farrell were doing, which was both good and bad. Though her physical injuries were beginning to heal, Michele, terrified by the memory of Mickey Rodriguez breaking her door down and repeatedly pounding her face and head with his fists, craved her heroin more than ever. This was not the time for a forced withdrawal, especially without the help of methadone, which Farrell could not get without a prescription.

When her small stash of dope ran out, Farrell went on the street and bought more, cooking and injecting it himself, trying to spread out the time between fixes as much as possible. He would wean her gradually, he said, but in a week or two, she would be strong enough to go out on her own, and how could he then prevent her from selling her body to get high? In addition, though there was a good deal of leeway in his *emeritus* status, he could not stay away from LaSalle indefinitely. On reflection, Chris realized, the scenario on Suffolk Street was mostly bad. Michele would soon be among the walking dead, and Farrell could be arrested for what he was doing, and, worse, tossed out of the Christian Brothers in disgrace after fifty years in the order.

On Friday night, Chris had had dinner with Joseph, Vinnie Rosamelia and Lou Falco in Lou's apartment. Although Joseph had a high tolerance for heroin, and could function almost normally under its influence, Chris could tell that he had started using again. He could spot the signs, where others might not, especially in his brother, who was fastidious about his appearance: the long sleeved shirt, the tiny pupils, the lack of interest in food, the slower speech patterns. In the past, Chris would immediately raise the issue, get in Joseph's face about it, but on Friday, he didn't. Even when they were alone at the end of the night saying goodbye, he let it go.

There was something else in Joseph's eyes besides the glaze of heroin, and something in his voice, as well. Chris had not been able to put his finger on it. Fear, bitterness, resignation? Something new and unusual was lurking beneath his brother's customary casual hipness. Chris, losing patience, and getting claustrophobic holed up in La Luna's back room, had announced his intention to leave Lou's the next day, Saturday, to find a more comfortable place to live, but Joseph had prevailed upon him to stay at least over the weekend.

Chris had not spoken to Joseph since, and, returning from the bakery, sipping his coffee in what passes for dawn's early light in New York, he made up his mind to immediately check into a decent hotel and call his brother. His share of the proceeds from the sale of his parents' house had arrived in his bank account, and so money was, for once, not an issue. He did not doubt the seriousness of the trouble he was in. He continued to assume that someone in the DiGiglio-Labrutto-Barsonetti triangle wanted him dead. He would be foolish to act on any other premise. But a week of inactivity was enough. It was time to be pro-active; precisely how, he did not know, but he would figure that out once he was settled someplace with some air and light, where the thinking would be easier, less oppressive.

He assumed that the Barsonetti proposal was now moot, and his reaction to this thought was one of disappointment. He looked back with something like nostalgia to the day – just a week ago – when the only problem on his plate was whether or not to become a hitman for the Mafia.

These were Chris' thoughts as he reached the corner of Elizabeth and Hester streets, where he stopped to take another sip of coffee. When he finished, bringing the Styrofoam container slowly away from his lips, his attention was drawn to a petite blonde woman confronting Lou Falco in front of La Luna. It was Marsha Davis, and she was shouting at Lou, who was trying to quiet her, holding his arms out in the classic "there's nothing I can do" configuration. Marsha, hugging a large tan envelope to her chest, tried to step around Lou, who blocked her way, the two of them moving in dance-like tandem for a few seconds, stopping abruptly when Chris approached.

"Chris," Marsha said, "tell this man who I am."

"What are you doing out?" Lou said to Chris.

"I go out every morning for coffee," Chris replied. "This is Marsha Davis, Joseph's girlfriend."

"We have to talk, Chris, please," Marsha said.

"Let's go inside," Lou said, dragging them both into the restaurant.

Lou locked the door behind them and then guided them to a table in the back corner, flicking on the lights – in wall sconces at intervals around the rectangular room

– along the way. The round table was set with a service for four over a white tablecloth. Chris sat in the corner, with Marsha opposite him and Lou to his right.

"What is it, Marsha?" Chris said. "You don't look good."

"When Joseph left yesterday morning, he gave me this envelope. He said if he hadn't returned by ten p.m. to give it to you." She handed Chris the envelope. "I was up all night. When he didn't come home, I took a cab down here."

Chris slit open the envelope with a butter knife and extracted its contents: a letter to him in Joseph's handwriting, three copies of "Candy Meets Ron" and three mini-cassette tapes in opaque plastic cases. Clipped to the letter was a check for a hundred thousand dollars and change payable to Joseph from the lawyer in Jersey who handled the sale of Rose and Joe Black's house. It was endorsed on the back by Joseph to the order of Christopher Massi.

Dear Chris, the letter said,

> If you are reading this, then I am dead. Don't waste your time trying to find me, thinking that I am alive. I'm not. Listen to the enclosed tape and you will understand what happened. I have been thinking lately about my life, and I finally realized the only person who ever really loved me was you. Mom hated pop and used me as a weapon. Pop had no room for a weakling son in his heart. You were a great athlete, then a big lawyer. You could have dismissed me from your life, but you never did.

I also realized that I was a junkie, which must sound funny since I've been a junkie for fifteen years, but not until this week did it hit me that I really am one, that I'll always have to inject heroin into my veins. I returned your love all these years by sticking a needle into my arm. I tried to make up for it by helping you in this situation you're in, but I failed. I have to give you some advice: Ed Dolan will not fight you clean, so don't fight him clean. Don't rely on the courts or the law. You are in a different kind of battle with him. I remember when you beat him up after pop killed his old man. You came home with your hands all bruised and bloody, and you were heartsick at what happened. You hated pop. But you were wrong to feel that way. Pop fought for his life, and now you have to fight for yours.

With love, your brother,
Joseph

When Chris looked up, Marsha was crying, and Lou was shaking his head.

"What is it?" Lou asked.

"Do you have a tape player for these?" Chris asked, pointing to the cassettes.

"It's upstairs," Lou replied. "I'll get it." He rose from the table and went into the kitchen, where there was a stairway that led to his apartment on the floor above.

Marsha was wiping her eyes with the napkin from her place setting. When she finished, Chris handed her the letter. She read it, and then said, softly, "I loved him, too."

Chris did not reply. He felt, irrationally, that by remaining silent, he was keeping Joseph alive. Lou returned with the tape player and inserted one of the cassettes, pressing the play button and adjusting the volume.

"Joseph Massi," they heard.

"Ed Dolan."

Pause.

"You look good. Have you quit using?"

Pause.

"You haven't changed."

"You want some kind of royal treatment? You're a junkie. State your business..."

They listened to the full conversation between Joseph and Dolan at Dolan's office, then inserted the other two tapes, which turned out to be copies of the first. Then Chris put the tapes, the DVDs and the letter back in the envelope.

"Can I borrow this?" he asked Lou, picking up the tape player.

"Yes."

Chris put it into the envelope, which he then clipped shut.

"Is he dead?" Marsha asked.

"Yes," Chris answered. "Ed Dolan is a federal prosecutor here in New York. He sent Joseph into Junior Boy's house wearing a wire. He probably figured if he got something on Junior Boy, fine; if the wire was discovered and Joseph killed, that would be fine, too. I was an assistant U.S. Attorney for five years. Dolan never would have gotten approval for that kind of an operation. There was never any backup. He didn't count on Joseph taping their conversation, though."

"And Junior Boy is some kind of a mobster?"

"Yes, the real life kind."

"How can you be sure?"

"That Joseph is dead?"

"Yes."

"I know Junior Boy. No one gets a private meeting with him without being searched first. Once the tape was found, he would have to kill Joseph. He could never let it get out that he let someone caught with a wire live. It would be a sign of weakness, an encouragement to others."

"I'm afraid he's right," Lou said.

"But what's to be done?" Marsha said. "Shouldn't we notify the police. Where's Joseph? Where's his...his body? We surely have to find his body and bury him."

Chris and Lou looked at each other. It would be a miracle, they knew, if Joseph's body were found.

"We'll have a service some day, Marsha," Lou said, "but it'll have to wait. For now, we don't want anyone to know what we know. Not the police, not your doorman, no one. Do you understand what I'm saying?"

"You're saying that both Dolan and DiGiglio would want to kill anyone who knows what we now know."

"That's it exactly."

"But why would this Dolan man do such a thing?"

"My father killed his father," Chris said, "gunned him down in a bar. He's hated me and my family ever since."

"The fucking bloody swine," Marsha said.

"Will you be all right, Marsha?" Chris said. "I'm sorry to be abrupt, but it's not safe here, and I have things to do."

"I'll get a cab."

"Do you have someone you can be with?" Lou asked.

"Yes, but I'd rather be alone."

Marsha rose, as did Chris and Lou. At the front of the room, sunlight was streaming through the restaurant's picture window, casting the words "La Luna" in shadow across the first row of tables. The mundane, as it is wont to do, had bumped up hard against the sublime. Another day, like millions of others before it, was beginning, but this one without Joseph Massi, a failure in many respects, but one who had managed to be a friend, a lover and a brother, respectively, to the three people who stood, brokenhearted, facing each other in the shadows at the back of the room. It was a morning each of them would remember vividly for the rest of their lives, especially Chris, who, in the time it took him to read Joseph's letter, had gained and lost a brother. It had fallen to him to be the last living member of his small family. A torrent of memories, of Rose, Joe Black and Joseph, both bitter and sweet, were pushing hard against his heart, but he held them back. He had to get away, to a place where he could grieve, and think, and plan his revenge.

Book III
Chris

1.

Chris had not planned on staying at Suffolk Street until he arrived and saw the state of things there. Brother Farrell, who had called him while he was packing a bag at La Luna, did not look well. There was something in Farrell's veined and lined face that was beyond weariness: the long inward look that a dying person begins to take when death becomes inevitable, something Chris did not know at the time. He only knew that Farrell needed a break. And it was obvious that Michele, nodding out on Allison's bed, in the same tee shirt, jeans and sandals she was wearing when he first met her just eight days ago, was not about to give him one. The consumptive look common to all deeply strung out addicts on her gaunt, sallow face, she lay there quietly enough, but her stillness was deceptive. Both Chris and Farrell knew that her facial tics and arm jerks were signs that her current high was coming to an end.

"I need to go out," Farrell said. "She'll need a fix soon, but I don't want to leave her. She's getting stronger and could go off on her own."

"When was the last one?"

"Four a.m."

"You've been going on the street?"

"Yes."

Farrell had never bought drugs before, and did not know that, with the advent of the reliable cell phone, cold street transactions were nearly a thing of the past. The ones that did go down were fraught with danger, involving, as they did, the bottom muck of the inner city drug culture: desperate junkies and crack heads with box cutters, as likely to be selling rat poison as heroin; transvestites hoping to score sex with a man; speed freaks with anger and energy to burn; hookers looking to lure a stranger with cash to a mugging in an abandoned building. Neither had he ever cooked heroin and shot it into a junkie's veins before. Finding one that wasn't collapsed, in a part of the body not covered with scabs and scar tissue, was not an easy or pleasant task.

"I'm sorry," Chris, who knew the street heroin and crack scene vicariously through Joseph's many entanglements with it over the years, said. "I shouldn't have asked you to do this. I wasn't thinking straight."

"She's starting to bitch," Farrell said, "because I've been buying lousy stuff, cut like crazy, rip-off stuff."

"Has anybody been here?"

"Someone came to fix the door to her apartment, but that's it. I watched through the peep hole."

"What kind of money have you spent?"

"Let's not talk money, Chris."

"I'll reimburse you."

"Reimburse me? Shall I go out and get receipts from the scum I bought from?"

"I never should have gotten you into this."

"I offered to help, if you'll recall. It's obvious you're in some kind of trouble. As to my money, I'm required to give it away, or have you forgotten that, too?"

"Brother Farrell, I do have a problem on my hands, but I can't leave this girl like this. Take a break, I'll watch her for a few days."

"Call me John. The *Brother* business isn't necessary, anymore."

"I couldn't do that."

"Our friend will be in lots of trouble if she misses just one fix," the cleric said. "Once I got back late from a buy. *Bang it in!* she said, *pump that fucking thing!*"

"I'm not fixing her," Chris said. "I'll take her through withdrawal. She's young, and her injuries are mostly healed."

"You mean force her?"

"Yes."

"Why?"

Chris shrugged. "I'm not sure, but I'm not going out and buying heroin, and I'm not leaving her alone."

"Do you know what to expect? It's not pretty."

"My brother...my brother's a junkie," Chris replied. "I've heard him talk about it. He went through it a dozen times. It's not complicated."

"Not for you."

Chris shook his head. "I've had enough of heroin. I don't even know what it looks like, but I've had enough of it for ten lifetimes. It won't kill her to go through withdrawal. I'm not letting her out to get fixed, but you have to leave. You've done enough. If I need you, I'll call you."

"Who is she to you?"

"I just met her a week ago."

"What's going on?"

"I can't tell you. I can tell you this: being around me can be dangerous to your health. You need to keep that in mind."

"I see. And act accordingly."

"Yes."

"When I finally sobered up," Farrell said, "I stopped running away from my friends. You know about pride and such, Chris. You wouldn't insult me now, would you?"

"No, I wouldn't. But it was an accident we were in that night, that's all it was. You don't owe me your life."

"I'll decide what I owe, and to whom."

"I'm sorry, Brother," said Chris said, seeing the grim line of the old man's mouth and the set of his jaw. "It hasn't been a good day."

Farrell took a breath and stared at Chris. He let the breath out, and, to Chris' relief, the moment pass.

"Can you get your hands on some Valium?" Farrell asked. "It'll help a bit. If you can get it down her."

"Probably."

"Don't overdo it. She'll only have to withdraw from the Valium, which could be worse."

"Anything else?'

"No," Farrell replied. "Like you said, it's not complicated. No heroin, and in three or four days, the worst will be over. Of course, they'll be long days. Call me if you need me. I'm not going anyplace."

Chris nodded.

"One more thing," Farrell said.

"I'm listening."

"You can pray. Pray that this poor girl doesn't suffer too badly, and that what suffering she does have will mean something, will redeem her of her sins, heal her broken spirit; otherwise, why are we here? What does all this mean, otherwise?"

2.

"You notice I haven't asked any questions. Like, *who is this woman, and what are you doing here?*"

"I noticed."

"Well? What the fuck is going on?"

After John Farrell left, Chris called Vinnie Rosamelia and asked him to bring over Valium, food to last three or four days, a hammer, some nails and clothesline rope. Vinnie arrived two hours later to find Michele twitching and sweating, begging Chris to let her go out on the street. They had persuaded her – with a promise that Vinnie would score her heroin – to swallow some Valium, twenty milligrams, a huge dose, but she had been threatening to throw herself into walls, and they were afraid she would open the wounds on her face.

As they spoke, sitting at the kitchen table, they could see her, lying on the sofa in the living room, an arm crooked over her forehead, twitching less, sweating less, the Valium beginning to dull her central nervous system. "Have you spoken to Lou Falco?" Chris asked, ignoring Vinnie's question for the moment.

"No. I was in the Hamptons," Vinnie answered. "I was walking in the door when you called."

"Joseph's dead."

Vincent, never at a loss for words, sat quietly as Chris related the events of the morning.

"Are you sure?" he asked, when Chris finished. "Maybe they're holding him someplace."

"You know better than that, Vin," Chris said. "Junior Boy would never let him live under those circumstances."

"I'm glad your mother's not alive."

"Me, too."

"With a junkie," Vinnie said, "you're always thinking about them dying."

"I know."

"But not like this, of course."

"It's not a bad thing," Chris said. "Better than finding him cyanotic, with a needle in his arm."

"How are you doing?"

"I'm coping."

Chris was both coping and watching himself coping at the same time. *Shock*, he thought, *early grief*, assessing himself, aware that he was living in a world parallel to but slightly behind the world of others, staying close to his dead brother for a while, until he could finally let him go.

"What now?" Vincent asked. "Who's this broad?"

"She's a friend of Allison McRae's," Chris said. "Labrutto was lining her up to star in his next snuff film. He sent the albino over here to terrorize her. I'm staying here until I can figure out what to do."

"She'll have the jones of all time when she comes down off of that Valium."

"I know."

"I can get her some dope."

"No, I'm cleaning her up."

"Come on."

"I can use your help."

"Chris, are you kidding? She's a junkie and a whore. She'll be sticking a needle in her arm within a week."

"That's up to her."

"She'll probably be dead of AIDS in six months. Let's buy her a couple bags of smack and get the fuck out of here."

"I'm doing this, Vin," Chris said. "Are you helping me or not?"

"Why?"

"Why?"

"Yes, why? Give me a reason."

"I never tried to save Joseph."

"Yes, you did."

"No, not really. There was a part of me that said, let him die."

"So this girl's a replacement junkie?"

"You could say that."

"It won't work, Chris."

Chris did not answer. He had no illusions about saving Michele, or the therapeutic value – for either of them – of forcing her through withdrawal. Watching himself again, it occurred to him that he was pushing his *bad* luck, a strange and inexplicable thing to do.

"What do you want me to do?" Vincent said.

Chris took an envelope from his pants pocket and slid it across the table.

"It's Allison's' rent notice," he said. "This is her apartment. Someone slipped it under the door this morning. Go next door and pay it, and also pay for apartment six; that's Michele's place. There's a check in there for twenty grand. Cash it. After you pay the rent, I want you to get me three or four cell phones registered to phony names."

"Anything else?"

"I need a Saturday night special, untraceable, and half a dozen porn videos featuring violence. A faux snuff film or two would be nice. Bring me the rest of the cash in fifties and hundreds."

"Anything else?"

"That's it for now."

"Whatever you're planning on doing, you better not be doing it alone."

Chris did not answer. He was looking over at Michele, who had turned onto her side. The features of her face were beginning to re-emerge as her bruises healed: straight nose, wide mouth, a strong brow softened by blonde eyebrows, a hint of freckles across her high cheekbones. Remembering her blue eyes, he thought it a face that might once have been pretty, even beautiful. Not now, though. She was snoring raspily, and her nose was running.

"I think her nose is broken," he said.

"That's not all that's broken on that girl."

"Are you staying around the city?"

"Yes."

"What about the weekend?"

"I'll stick around."

"Thanks."

"What's on your mind, Chris, exactly?"

"I'm not sure yet."

"You're not thinking of going after Junior Boy, are you?"

"It's Ed Dolan I want. I've had enough of him."

"Can I talk you out of this?"

"No."

"You'll have the whole justice department up your ass."

"Maybe. Will you help me?"

"Sure, I hate that motherfucker."

"I do too, Vincent. I do, too."

When Vinnie left, Chris picked up Michele and carried her into the tiny, ten-by-ten foot, windowless bedroom and laid her on the bed. No more than ninety pounds, she was like a frail, gangly child in his arms, her rib cage protruding and the bones of her back pressing hard against his hands.

He then brewed coffee. Sitting with it in the kitchen, he replayed the tape of Joseph's meeting with Dolan. He rewound it, then, using his cell phone, dialed the number of the U.S. Attorney in Foley Square, telling the receptionist and then a secretary that he was calling to give Mr. Dolan an anonymous tip in the Scarpa-McRae murder case. When Dolan picked up, he put the phone down on the table, placed Lou Falco's mini-cassette player next to it and pushed the play button. When it was finished, about twelve minutes later, he clicked the phone off. Then he called Teresa and asked her to arrange for a meeting between him and her father sometime over the coming weekend, giving her Vinnie Rosamelia's number, and asking her to call him with the time and place. When she reminded him that he was scheduled to see the kids on Saturday, he canceled, knowing that if Dolan was looking for him, his ex-wife's house would be an obvious place to stake out. Then, after nailing the front door shut, he pushed the sofa over against it and stretched out on it, hoping to sleep while Michele slept, knowing that once she woke up she would not sleep again until she was clean. Two hours later, he was awakened from a fitful sleep by Michele clawing at his shirt, screaming:

"Who the fuck are you?!"

"I'm Chris."

"What are you doing here? Get up. Let me out. Where's the priest?"

"He had to leave."

"Did you give me those pills?"

"Yes."

"I want more."

"Maybe later."

"Maybe later? Are you fucking crazy? Get up. I'm going out."

She circled the small apartment, found her bag in the kitchen and strode over to stand before Chris, who had sat up on the sofa. Her makeup had been washed off, probably by John Farrell. Taking out a small mirror, she began to apply lipstick, botching the job as both hands shook, out of control. A sheen of sweat covered her face, which was still discolored and lopsided from her bruises, under which her skin was a pale, almost translucent white. The roots of her once spiky but now perspiration-matted, white hair, Chris noticed, were not brown but a darker shade of blonde.

"Calm down," he said. "I'll give you some Valium later, but you're not going out. You're going through withdrawal."

Michele dropped her lipstick into her bag without drawing in the tip or replacing the top. Then she threw the bag at Chris' face and leaped at him, tearing at his hair and dragging her nails across his face, screaming, "Let me out of here, you fuck, you cocksucker. Let me out of here!"

Chris pinned her arms to her sides, and, rising, lifting her with him, carried her – kicking and screaming, trying to bite his face and neck – into the bedroom, throwing her in and slamming the door shut. Instantly, she was banging at the door, but he held his body against it until she collapsed to the floor inside, where he could hear her sobbing. Then he nailed the door shut, leaving the nail heads exposed so he could tear them out quickly, if necessary. He had put a jug of bottled water in there earlier and a basin she could use as a bedpan. If she started to get self-destructive, he would go in and tie her to the bed, but her sobs turned to whimpers, and then there was silence. He looked at his watch. It was two p.m., ten hours since Michele's last fix, a hit that was probably more sugar or powdered milk than heroin.

Fifteen minutes later, while he was reading one of Allison's screenplays – the adaptation of Steinbeck's East of Eden – he heard Michele retching in the bedroom. Afraid she would asphyxiate on her own vomit, he pulled the nails out of the door and went in. She was lying on her back on the bed, sweating profusely, her shirt covered in a viscous, greenish puke. When he approached her, she pulled her legs up and curled into the fetal position, holding her stomach with both hands.

"Where's the priest?" she asked, her face shiny with sweat, grimacing from the cramps in her stomach.

"I told you, he left."

"I need a fix. You have to help me. I'll die."

"No, you won't. People don't die from this. Have you been through it before?"

"No."

"How long have you been using?"

"I don't know. A year."

"I'm sure people have talked about it."

"I didn't listen."

"The most important thing is this: you may wish you were dead, but you won't die from withdrawal."

"How the fuck do you know?"

"My brother was a junkie."

Michele balled up even more, touching her forehead to her knees and groaning, then releasing a little.

"I have to go to the bathroom."

"I'll help you."

He took her by the shoulders and rolled her onto her back. She resisted at first, but he was much stronger. Tears were mixing with the perspiration on her face, which was now a ghastly pale green, her bruises like the marks of some unspeakable disease. In her once pretty blue eyes, now dilated to twice their size, Chris saw fear, fear and a despair so deep that it chilled him and filled his own eyes with tears.

"I shit myself," she said.

Scooping her up, he carried her into the bathroom, where he pulled off her clothes – soggy with puke and liquid feces – and put her in the shower, where he propped her up with one hand while soaping her with the other. He did this twice, then shampooed and rinsed her hair. He wrapped her in two towels, put her on the couch, then went and showered quickly himself, afterward pulling on fresh jeans and a tee shirt. When he returned to her, she was in a ball again, trembling, saying she was cold. He pulled the blanket off of the bed and put it over her, then lay down next to her and put his arms around her to try to warm her.

"How old are you, Michele?"

"Thirty."

"What's your last name?"

"Mathias."

"Do you want to get dressed?"

"Yes. I have to go out."

"I'm not letting you out."

"I can't believe this. Who are you?"

"I told you, Chris Massi, Allison's cousin."

"That albino freak killed her."

"He'll kill you, too. That's another reason why you can't go out. That's why we're in this apartment. It's safer."

This was probably not true. Rodriguez could have killed Michele, but didn't, a sign perhaps that Labrutto was acting without Junior Boy's or Jimmy Barson's knowledge or consent. Labrutto would want to be careful not to commit another unauthorized killing. If it was Mafia people who had hunted down Michele, they surely would have killed her. Also, Rodriguez had a chance to kill Chris on the day he pummeled Michele, but he didn't take it: more evidence that Labrutto was off the reservation. It seemed likely that Labrutto, Barsonetti and DiGiglio were acting, if not at cross purposes, with agendas hidden from each other. This was bad for Labrutto, who had no power, and good for Chris to know. Although he was certain that the stolen snuff film put him in a dangerous position, he felt he had some room to maneuver on the Labrutto/DiGiglio/Barsonetti front.

"You go out," Michele said. "I'll pay you. I'll do anything you want. You can be my pimp."

"Do you have money?"

"No."

"It's three o'clock. I'll give you some Valium tonight. There's nothing else I can do for you."

Michele's head had been covered by the blanket, which she now pulled away as she turned to face Chris. She was sweating again, and mucous was beginning to run from her eyes, which looked both empty and panicked at the same time.

"Why are you doing this?"

"I'm planning on killing some people, and while I'm doing that, I'm seeing you through withdrawal. Forcing you would be more accurate. You're free to start shooting up again as soon as it's over."

He had not planned on telling her this, but, when it came to expressing his thoughts of the last few hours, he could not see the point of lying. Michele continued to stare at Chris, the confusion in her eyes giving way for a mournful second to a bitter realism: this man, this stranger, was actually going to force her to withdraw cold turkey from heroin. Chris knew, from his many experiences with Joseph, that junkies hated reality. They pictured themselves withdrawing in a beautiful clinic in the mountains, sleeping through it while miracle drugs cleansed them intravenously. Michele's stomach would be cramping violently, all of her joints aching, even her fingers, the dim light in the apartment blinding her, and every nerve in her body was crying *heroin, heroin, heroin*. If she had the strength, she would, he knew, have killed him with pleasure, then gone out and mugged the first old lady or bum she came across for money to score. She could see the needle entering her arm or, better yet, a fresh vein in her groin.

"Why me?" she asked.

"You were available."

"You fuck."

"You're almost through the first day. Two more and the worst will be over."

"I can't do it. I can't."

"You have no choice," Chris said. "When you're clean, I'll walk out of here, and you can score and get high, do whatever you want."

"Don't fucking worry, I will."

Michele turned her head to the side and fell silent. Chris covered her with the blanket and began kneading her shoulders with his hands, wondering, as he did, what

Ed Dolan was doing and thinking and feeling at this very moment, and how Anthony DiGiglio would react to the idea of a meeting. If Chris was right, knowing his adversaries, his boyhood friend would over-react, unwittingly letting his guard down as he did. His former father-in-law's guard would go up, he would be cautious, but intrigued, and the stage would be set for Chris to do what he had to do.

3.

"What did Allison do when she first got here?" Chris asked.

"She waited tables. She was trying to enroll in acting classes," Michele replied.

"Did she mention her roommate in L.A. at all, Danielle Dimicco?"

"In the beginning, she did."

Chris and Michele were sitting at the small folding table in the apartment's cramped kitchen on the sixth morning after Joseph's death. Michele had gone through her withdrawal. Chris had made tea, and she had taken a few sips, but the rest was getting cold in the cup.

"Was she a junkie?"

"No. Labrutto got her hooked."

"Then he used her in porn movies."

"Right."

"And as a recruiter for his next snuff film."

"I guess so."

Chris had spoken to Danielle Dimicco three times in the last two weeks: to tell her that her friend Allison McRae was dead; to tell her that Joseph was dead, and to hear the results of the inquiries he had asked her to make regarding Allison's friend, Heather Jansen. Heather and Allison, it turned out, had met just before Allison left California for New York. Heather, like Allison, from the

Midwest, and like Allison, an orphan, had been kicking around Los Angeles for a couple of years trying to find a life. Pretty, vivacious, in her mid-twenties, she worked to put a roof over her head and to party. She had no known relatives and one or two friends at the temp agency that sent her out steadily on secretarial jobs before she stopped answering her phone in February. It was from these people that Danielle put together Heather's two sentence biography, which Chris titled, "The Perfect Snuff Film Victim."

Joe Black and Joseph had died violent deaths, but their faces remained in Chris' mind's eye as they had been in life, one handsome and strong, the other beautiful and weak. Nick Scarpa had literally gone down fighting. Chris had no trouble imagining the fire in his eyes as he grappled with Mickey in the car at the edge of the cliff. Allison McRae's senses had been blunted by heroin. It was Heather Jansen's face at the moment of her death that haunted Chris. It was for her as much as for anyone else that he was planning on becoming a multiple killer.

"I need to stay here a few more days," he said.

"Do I have a choice?"

"I'm asking you."

"Sure."

"You're free to do what you want," Chris said, "but I'd appreciate it if you'd wait until I left before starting to shoot up again. I paid your rent and the rent for this apartment for the month. I don't think you should move back to your apartment."

"Right now, I just want to sleep."

"There's one Valium left. It might help."

"Where is it?"

"In the bathroom."

"Who was here last night?"

"A friend."

At around midnight, while Michele was in the bedroom trying to sleep, Vinnie had stopped by with the movies and a bundle of cash, which Chris had wrapped in a dish towel and put in the back of the cabinet under the kitchen sink. Two days ago, his boyhood friend had delivered three untraceable cell phones. Two of these Chris had used to repeat his tape-playing call to Ed Dolan, on successive days. The third phone he was saving for a final call to Dolan.

Vinnie was due back soon with the gun and the remaining cash. When he was there last night, Vinnie told Chris that he had heard from Teresa, and that his meeting with Junior Boy was scheduled for tomorrow, a Sunday, at noon, at Benevento on Forty-Fourth Street. Teresa also asked Vincent to tell Chris to stay away from her house in North Caldwell as it had been under twenty-four hour surveillance since Monday, which Chris knew coincided with his first call to Dolan.

"You said something about killing some people," Michele said.

"When?"

"I don't remember. When you first got here."

"You were delirious."

Before answering, Michele's sunken eyes fixed on Chris's. For the first time since he met her, he saw something in them that was not put there by drugs or the need for drugs.

"Stay as long as you want," she said. "I'm not interested in going on the street."

For the moment, Chris was about to say, but he held back. That was the reply, ten times out of ten, he would have made to Joseph in similar circumstances.

"I'll get that Valium now," Michele said, and Chris watched as she rose and walked the few steps to the bathroom. Although the apartment, which had only two small windows, was very warm, she was wearing a bulky cardigan sweater, flannel pajama pants and thick socks.

While Michele was in the shower, John Farrell arrived. "I've been trying to call you," he said, once inside and seated in the living room,

"My phone is dead," Chris replied, "and so is Michele's." He had removed the batteries from both phones. He did not want messages accumulating that a third party might be able to access. Michele did not have a land-line phone in her apartment.

"How is she?"

"She's okay."

"Is that her I hear in the shower?"

"Yes."

"What do you plan to do with her now?"

"Nothing."

"Nothing? She'll be craving heroin badly."

"I plan on giving her some money. She can do what she wants with it."

"I can help her find a program."

"Fine."

"How long are you staying?"

"A few days. I'll call you when I leave."

Farrell looked slowly around, nodding slightly once or twice, as if noticing the apartment for the first time. Chris had kept it clean and neat, but there was no denying its meanness, its hopelessness.

"Whose place is this?" the cleric asked.

"A woman named Allison McRae, a friend of Michele's."

"Where is she?"

"She's dead."

"I see. What happened?"

"She was killed by the same people who beat up Michele."

"Allison McRae? Isn't she the one who went over the cliff?"

"That was her."

"I've been reading about it in the Daily News. How are you involved?"

Chris did not answer. He did not want to patronize Farrell, a man who had lived a long, hard, decent life, but neither did he want him to be an accessory to murder.

"I'll be dead soon, too," Farrell said. "Take it as a last request. I might even be able to help."

"Dead soon?"

"I was diagnosed with lung cancer a month ago. Advanced stage. They tell me I have six months, maybe two or three on my feet."

Chris stared hard at Farrell as he took this in. It could not have been easy for the old man to state plainly that he was going to die. It takes courage to live, and faith, but more courage and more faith to die, more of both than Chris felt he had at the moment.

"My brother's been killed, too," he said. "Ed Dolan set him up."

"Ed Dolan?"

"Yes. He's also looking to charge me with the murder of Allison McRae and the other person in the car, Nick Scarpa."

"So much death. Will there be more?"

Before Chris could answer, Michele came out of the bathroom, wearing the same sweater, this time with jeans and a pair of even thicker socks. She had shaved her head and stood smiling crookedly when she saw the two men.

"You're back," she said to Farrell.

"I am," he responded, rising to shake her hand. "Now that you're clean, I'll reintroduce myself. John Farrell."

"The priest," Michele said, taking in the frail old man before her, whose presence in his clerical black shirt and slacks and white clerical collar was somehow still commanding.

"No," Farrell said. "I'm a member of a religious order. The Christian Brothers. You can call me John. How are you feeling?"

"Cold. Scared."

"Craving dope?"

"Yes."

"It takes three to six months for it to stop."

"Three to six months?"

"Yes. The best way to do it is to go into a residential program."

"Can't I get methadone from the city?"

"You don't need it. You're already clean. I can help you get into a program."

"I'd rather work it out myself."

"You mean you'd rather go back on the street," Chris said.

"You'll be gone soon," Michele said, her face blank. "What do you care?"

"Yes," Farrell said, "what do you care?"

Chris shook his head, got up from the sofa and went to his overnight bag on a chair near the bookshelf. Reaching in, he took out a handful of twenty dollar bills.

"Here," he said to Michele, walking toward her and reaching out with the bills in his hand. "Go out now. Get it over with."

Michele stepped back as Chris advanced. They both stopped at the same time, facing each other a few feet apart. Chris threw the money on the floor.

"Take it," he said.

"Fuck you," Michele answered, and, turning, went into the bedroom, slamming the nail-scarred door behind her.

John Farrell, still standing, said quietly, "Let me help, Chris."

"You can take care of Michele when I'm gone," Chris answered. "I'll pay for her treatment."

"Of course."

"My brother was a junkie. Did you know that?"

"No."

"And my father was a hitman for a Mafia family. They're both dead now."

"There were rumors about Dolan's dad and your dad."

"They're true."

"You need to take your anger out on the right people." Farrell looked down at the twenty-dollar bills on the floor and over at the bedroom door as he said this.

"I plan on it."

In the afternoon, Vinnie Rosamelia stopped by with groceries and a small television, but no gun. Michele ate half of a tuna salad sandwich for lunch and then returned to the bedroom. She nodded when Chris introduced Vinnie, but was silent during the brief time it took for the three of them to eat. Vinnie had thought to buy the gun without using an intermediary because he did not want any witnesses who could connect it to him and thus to Chris, except for an anonymous street dealer. After a couple of aborted attempts, however, he realized that there was too much that could go wrong in a cold street buy. The seller could be a cop, the gun could be unsound or traceable to crimes under investigation, Vinnie could get ripped off or killed. He had, therefore, decided to trust his bartender, a savvy kid whose beautiful face and body belied his cunning and hard-earned ability to maneuver in the city's underworld, and was waiting for an answer. Joe Black's .44 Ruger was in Chris' overnight bag, but he needed two guns, both of which had to be disposed of immediately after they were used.

The television was Vinnie's idea, but, although he had been cooped up for two weeks, Chris had no interest in watching it. When Vinnie left, he brought it into the bedroom and put it on Michele's dresser while she glowered at him from the bed through the haze of her cigarette smoke. There is not much to do for a heroin addict going through withdrawal: sponge her down, bring her some water, clean up her puke and diarrhea, listen to her moan for endless, sleepless hours. In the past few days, to divert himself, Chris had managed to read most of the screenplays lined up on Allison McRae's little yellow book shelf. Her notes in a cramped but confidant script filled the margins. She was Kay in both Godfather movies, the teenage hooker in Taxi Driver, Bonnie Parker in Bonnie and Clyde, the world weary housekeeper who almost makes a man out of Paul Newman in Hud. Allison's intelligent, often poetic comments were just as interesting as the scripts – her legacy.

When he lay down on the sofa to sleep on Saturday night, Chris smiled as he stared up at the shadowy ceiling. He had forgotten completely about the things that had been so pressing on his mind and his heart in the

lifetime prior to the one he had just begun: his disbarment and so-called public disgrace, the devil's bargain that
Junior Boy had offered him, the anxiety about what to do
for a living. After reading Joseph's letter at La Luna, he
had stepped into a new world where there was no room
for such mundane worries. Such are the blessings of big
trouble: it puts little trouble in perspective. The dead paraded slowly across Chris' mind as he lay there: Joe Black,
Rose, Heather Jansen, Allison McRae, Nick Scarpa, Joseph. They reached out for Chris as they passed, mouth-
ing something he could not make out. Honor me? Don't
forget me? I love you? Exhausted, he fell asleep.

4.

On paper, Benevento was owned by Paul DeLuca, a legitimate restaurateur who owned two other successful restaurants in Manhattan, but it actually belonged to the DiGiglio family. The family owned, in similar arrangements, half a dozen other restaurants in and around the city, which Junior Boy used, on a randomly rotating basis, to hold special and regular meetings with his people and important colleagues. Benevento was in the shape of a long rectangle, with the bar in front on the left and a balcony seating area that overlooked the main dining room. The hallway in the back that led to the restrooms also led to the don's private dining room, which contained, along with his always-set dinner table, a sitting area with four comfortable chairs around a circular coffee table and a small bar off to the side, all resting on a beautiful Persian rug in muted maroon and gold tones. The don and his two brothers were seated at three of these chairs when Nicky Spags brought Chris into the room on Sunday at noon.

"He's clean," said Nick.

"Sit," Junior Boy said to Chris, indicating the empty chair across from him. "You can go," he said to Nicky. Chris sat and rested the small black bag he had with him on the floor next to his chair. Nicky Spags' face had registered only the mildest of professional curiosity when he saw the contents of the bag. Chris knew that it was not for Nicky to judge the transactions of his superiors, but to simply ferret out weapons and listening devices, and, with his massive bulk and unnerving smile, instill the fear of God in those admitted through him into the don's presence.

"Do you want a drink? Something to eat?" Junior Boy said to Chris.

"No, thanks."

"There's water there," DiGiglio said, pointing to the set-up on the coffee table: a bottle of Pellegrino, four cut-crystal glasses, a silver ice bucket and a small bowl of lemon wedges.

"I see it."

Moving slowly, deliberately, the don made himself a drink and sat back in his seat. He put the glass down on the end table next to him after taking a sip, then remained silent for a moment, the fingers of his right hand drumming softly on the arm of his plush chair.

"We've been looking for you," he said, finally.

"I thought you might be."

"And now you come to us."

Chris nodded: "Right."

"What's in the bag?" Aldo said. Fidgeting in his chair, he had barely waited for the don to speak first before blurting out this question.

"Hold on," Junior Boy said, holding his hand up in Aldo's direction, but keeping his eyes on his former son-in-law. Then to Chris:

"Your brother? Is that it?"

"No."

"Do you know what he did?"

"Yes."

"How?"

"He left me a letter."

Chris noticed the deepening concentration in Anthony's eyes as he said this. Had the old man believed that he had conspired in Joseph's near-demented scheme?

"He left you a letter. That's convenient," Aldo said. "We thought you sent him, that you masterminded his idiot fucking plan."

Chris stared over at the man who he knew could not control his two asshole sons, now in their forties. The fruit had not fallen far from the tree. It must have been Aldo who pushed the Chris-Joseph conspiracy theory, as an argument for eliminating Chris. Chris stared at Aldo for a second, but said nothing.

"He had to die." As the don said this, Chris saw Frank's head turn as he shifted his gaze from him to his older brother, surprised possibly by this open admission of murder.

Chris had changed his mind about the nature of Joseph's death. For years, he had lived with the thought that one day he'd receive a call telling him that his brother had been found dead in a gutter. At first, Joseph's execution-style murder had stood up well to this scenario. In an admittedly macabre way, it had more dignity. But watching Michele go through withdrawal this past week had given him a new insight into addiction, and a respect for its power to overwhelm the will. Joseph would have died peacefully from an overdose, at least compared to the terror that must have been pounding in his heart and brain when he was taken someplace dark and leafy and the barrel of a gun was placed against the back of his head. And he must have thought himself a fool as well to be so taken in by Ed Dolan. Could there be a worse death? *If he had to die, then so do you, Junior Boy,* Chris thought.

"I'm not here about him," he said out loud.

"Then what?" Junior Boy said.

"I have a proposition to make."

"Go ahead."

"I assume you realize that Joseph was set up by Ed Dolan. He figured if Joseph's wire was not discovered, he might get something on you. If it was, and Joseph was killed, who would know or care? He broke every rule in the U.S. Attorney's office, and made himself an accessory to murder. That's how badly he wants you, Junior Boy. He wants me, too. He pulled me in to talk about the Palisades thing. He's a renegade, and he won't stop until we're both dead or in jail. I can stop him."

"How?"

"Joseph taped his meeting with Dolan to arrange for the wire. I brought you a copy. It puts Joseph in your house, wearing a federal wire, on the day he disappeared, which is not good for you. It's also very bad for Dolan."

The DiGiglio brothers stared hard at Chris. They were not, he knew, used to being threatened, or told harsh facts, by anyone, let alone someone outside the family. The around-the-clock surveillance on Teresa's house must also be unsettling.

"It gets worse," Chris said. "Joseph gave Dolan a copy of the snuff film that I took from Labrutto's house. If he links it to the DiGiglio family, it's all over for you."

"How would he do that?" Anthony asked.

"He'll work the Palisades murders," Chris replied. "Someone will break: Labrutto, the albino. I'm guessing there was a helper. Someone would rather give you up and go into witness protection than get executed. Dolan will put the making of the snuff film on you. Whether you were behind making it or not is irrelevant to him. He'll charge you with the vicious killing of an innocent girl for profit. Even if you fight it and win, you'll lose. You'll be the *Snuff Film Don*. Dolan wants you, Junior Boy. Nailing you for the snuff film will make him a huge star, untouchable. And he wants me worse than he wants you."

"So you want us to kill Dolan?" Aldo said. "Is that it? A federal prosecutor?"

"No," Chris answered. "I'll kill him."

"*You'll* kill him?" Frank said, raising his eyebrows. "Just like that?"

"Yes."

"In return for what?"

"Two things," Chris said, directing his reply to Junior Boy. "I want my son to live with me for the next four years, and I want Labrutto and the albino to help me."

"Your son?" Aldo said. "What's he got to do with this?"

"Help you how?" the don asked.

"I'll set Dolan up," Chris said to Junior Boy, ignoring Aldo. "When I say come, I want Labrutto and his friend to come, immediately."

The set of Junior Boy's face – passive, unperturbed, alert – had remained unchanged from the moment Chris entered the room, but on hearing this answer, his eyes narrowed and he appeared to smile slightly. What he was thinking Chris could not tell. It might have been approval, it might have been respect, it might have been sudden insight into Chris' motives.

"How will you set him up?" Frank asked.

"I've been playing Joseph's tape to him on the phone. He's probably ready to crack. He'll meet me to get the tape."

"He'll meet you to kill you," Frank said.

"I'll take that chance."

"Who's Nick Scarpa to you?" Aldo asked.

Chris had attributed Aldo's confrontational attitude thus far to the bad blood between them going back to the incident with Aldo Jr. and Sal. He now guessed from this out-of-left-field question that the stocky, quick-to-anger DiGiglio brother had a special interest in Guy Labrutto, who he was worried Chris would kill to avenge Nick Scarpa's murder. In the Mafia culture, this meant one of two things: blood or money. It was virtually impossible to imagine that Aldo had a secret financial arrangement with Labrutto. Disloyalty was not in his nature. Which left blood. If Labrutto was somehow related to Aldo, then it would be that much more satisfying to Chris when he killed the chubby porn producer with the goatee and the supercilious attitude.

"Nothing," he replied. "A friend."

"You said you brought us a copy of the tape," Junior Boy said. "Where's the original?"

"In a safe place."

"What if Dolan refuses to meet? What happens to the original tape?"

"I won't use it against you, if that's what you're asking. But he'll meet me, to kill me. He's wanted me dead for twenty-five years."

"So you're telling us we have to trust you, put the family's fate in your hands?"

"I asked for this meeting," Chris replied, looking Anthony in the eye. "You could have me killed as soon as I walk out the door. The tape was intended to hurt Dolan, not the DiGiglio family. I'm sure Joseph tried to explain that to you. He was acting foolishly, but honorably. I won't turn the tape into something he never intended it for. I won't dishonor my dead brother."

"Then it's a deal," Junior Boy said, returning Chris' gaze and ignoring his brothers. "When do you want Matt?"

"Not until early September," Chris replied, "Just before school starts." As he said this, Chris reflected on the raw power the don would have to wield over Teresa in order to accomplish the transfer of custody of Matt. The fierceness of her resistance would make her ultimate defeat even more bitter, for it was a certainty that her father, having given his word to Chris, would prevail. Chris did not deny to himself the measure of satisfaction this thought gave him. Provided, of course, he lived until early September.

Junior Boy nodded his assent, and then readjusted himself in his chair and crossed his legs. Chris had watched him carefully, knowing how difficult, and important, it was to try to fathom his thinking. He took the don's ready assent to his proposal as clear evidence that the Dolan/snuff film problem had preempted all other family concerns. Jimmy Barsonetti, for example, would have a few more months of life. Except for the lone, indecipherable smile, his former father-in-law's eyes had remained expressionless, his demeanor calm. He had let Aldo vent but had not allowed him to push the meeting off course. For Junior Boy, the meeting was over, and Chris had no doubt that he was now thinking of the next several moves on the board.

"There's one other thing," Chris said, reaching into the black bag and placing its contents – the DVDs that Vinnie had bought for him, ten thousand dollars in cash secured by a rubber band and the Dolan cassette – on the coffee table. "I want Labrutto to bring these movies and the cash with him when he comes. The small one is the Dolan tape. That's for you."

"Are these snuff films?" Frank asked, picking up the DVDs and turning them over in his hands.

"No," Chris answered, "but they're nasty."

"So Dolan is killed in a deal that goes wrong," Aldo said.

"Something like that," Chris answered.

"Why can't you carry this?" Aldo asked, indicating the DVDs and the cash with a nod of his head.

"You want to do this hit yourself, Aldo?" Chris replied. "You're welcome to it."

"If you're playing both sides of the street, like your brother, you'll end up dead for sure," Aldo replied. "Like him."

There had been no attempt at revenge for Chris' assault on Sal and Aldo Jr., and the explanation for this came clear now. Aldo had wanted to seek it, but the don would not let him. The malice in Aldo's hooded eyes revealed another truth: it was Aldo who executed Joseph as a means of vicariously avenging the unforgotten insult to his sons. Chris would have bet his life on this.

"My brother died for me," Chris said. "I'm sure your sons would do the same for each other."

Aldo, his eyes flashing, was about to reply when Junior Boy, holding his hand up, said sharply to his brother, "That's enough," and then to Chris, "When will this happen?"

"A week, maybe two. No more than that."

"Here," Junior Boy said, handing Chris a piece of paper. "That's Rocco Stabile's cell phone number. Don't call him to chat. Call him when you want Labrutto and the albino. He'll make sure they go where you want them to."

Chris took the paper and nodded his assent.

"I have one more question," the don said.

"Yes?"

"Why did you accompany Scarpa to Labrutto's house?"

Somehow, Chris knew from the faces that stared back at him that Aldo and Frank still did not know about Junior Boy's offer regarding Barsonetti. What was it that seemed to be so important about sharing this secret with the don? Alone with Anthony, he might have answered truthfully, and, in that way, attempt to fathom the don's biggest secret, the secret to his power. He decided not to go there in the presence of Aldo and Frank, who he now realized had no power themselves. Junior Boy had it all. Without him, the family would cease to exist.

"Like I said," he answered. "He's a friend from the old neighborhood. I ran into him. It was a good chance to catch up."

Chris looked one last time from brother to brother to brother. He knew that the Palisades murders did not bother them. They could easily kill Labrutto and Mickey to cut off the trail of evidence that led from the botched killings to the family. But an obsessed Ed Dolan – with a Labrutto-made snuff film in his hand – could hurt them badly, and a DiGiglio hit on him was not an option. It would put the entire Justice Department on the warpath against the family. Now here comes Chris Massi offering to do it for them. The same Chris Massi whose brother they had just executed. The same Chris Massi who could devastate them if he decided to tell the authorities what he knew about the Dolan tape and the snuff film.

Aldo's anger at Chris was clouding his thinking. Frank, drone-like, with no dog in the succession fight, was content to follow Junior Boy's lead. Not that it would have escaped either of them that Labrutto and Mickey were meant to die along with Dolan. The don saw this, too, of course, but he saw much more. There was something in his eyes that could not be disguised by the matter-of-fact way he handled this meeting, a glint that spoke of both shrewd calculation and the cool reserve of a great king, which in effect he was.

I haven't fooled him, Chris thought. He knows I'm going to try to kill him to avenge my brother. It's almost as if he wants me to try. Labrutto and Dolan are throwaways somehow. *I'll accommodate you, Junior Boy, I promise. I'll kill Aldo and Frank, too, if they get in my way, but first things first.*

5.

"I think I found him, Ed."

"Good, where?"

"On Suffolk Street, the building that the McRae girl lived in."

"What's he doing there?"

"I don't know. The list of tenants turns up nothing, but I followed Rosamelia here twice, and the super told me that a gay guy with a goatee paid the rent on McRae's apartment and on a woman's named Michele Mathias."

"Who's she?"

"A local addict, a friend of the brother's, maybe."

In the pause that followed this statement, Ron Magnuson, sitting in his car on Suffolk Street, with a clear view of the front of number one-twelve, wondered what his boss was thinking. After ten years of working with him, Magnuson thought he had grown accustomed to Dolan's strange ways, but recently – just within the last week – the prosecutor's behavior had reached a new level of weirdness.

"Have you seen Massi?" Dolan asked.

"No."

"How long have you been there?"

"An hour. Rosamelia left a few minutes ago. Are you sure you don't want me to pick up Massi?"

"I'm sure."

"I can serve the order for the hair sample."

256 Sons and Princes

"That can wait."

"You want him followed if he comes out?"

"No. I just wanted to know where he was, in case we need him."

"He may not be in there."

"I think he is. Rosamelia's his good friend."

"I'll pack it in, then."

"Go ahead, and you might as well go to your seminar upstate. I can use Rick or Dean if I need something over the next few days."

Magnuson clicked off his cell phone, started his car, and sat for a moment as it idled and the gray dusk turned to night around him. It had been a long, and, in his opinion, wasted day. He had worked hard, not only to track down Chris Massi, but on the entire investigation into the double murder on the Palisades. And now it appeared that Ed Dolan, incredibly, was backing off. On reflection, the turning point occurred sometime last Monday afternoon, a week after the murders. Until then, Dolan had directed a very aggressive investigation. Antoinette Scarpa, in shock at the news of her husband's death only a few hours before, had been worked hard; Labrutto, Massi and Junior Boy DiGiglio hauled in and braced for more to come. Forensics had been all over Labrutto's house, and hair samples collected there were being matched to the McRae and Scarpa corpses, both still in the Bellevue morgue. A hair sample was wanted from Chris Massi, as well. He had moved from his Bedford Street apartment, but no doubt he would be found soon enough. Detectives were looking into Labrutto's story about his BMW sedan being in a body shop in Queens on the day of the murders. Others were tracking down the actors in the dozens of West

Coast Productions' porn flicks to see if anyone knew or remembered the McRae girl.

Magnuson had no doubt that Massi, Scarpa and McRae were in Labrutto's pretentious house in Alpine on the day of the murders, and he felt equally certain that either physical evidence or independent witnesses would confirm this. Arrests could then be made, and there was nothing like an arrest for first-degree murder to get someone to open up, perhaps point the finger further up the food chain. Magnuson had only a passing interest in Chris Massi. He had watched him for two weeks as, a year ago, he stood trial on Dolan's flimsy stock fraud charges. and, in his gut, did not believe the ex-lawyer was involved in the Scarpa/McRae murders. Labrutto on the other hand was a scumbag of the first order. It would be nice to nail him, and even nicer – an extraordinary coup – to make a case for murder against Anthony DiGiglio, probably the last and certainly the smartest and most elusive of the old school Mafia dons.

Last Monday – the day of Dolan's strange one-eighty – an intriguing NYPD report came across Magnuson's desk. A small-time drug dealer named Woody Smith had been gunned down, gangland-style, in front of his home in Bed-Stuy. A neighbor, though she claimed not to have seen or heard the killing, had been suspicious enough of a car parked outside her door for several hours that morning to take down its plate number, which traced to a lessee named Marsha Davis. Davis, in a brief interview, told detectives she leased the car for her boyfriend, one Joseph Massi. Distraught, looking ill, she claimed she had seen neither Massi nor the car in several days. Because the Smith murder had all the earmarks of a Mafia hit, the NYPD had reported it, along with its findings, to Ed

Dolan's task force. It struck Magnuson as too much of a coincidence that both Joseph and Chris Massi had been connected to Mafia hits occurring within a few days and a few miles of each other.

Magnuson did not know, and did not care to know, its genesis, but it had become clear in the last year or so that Dolan had a personal vendetta against the Massi family and Chris Massi in particular. Perhaps it had to do with another never-caught Mafia figure, the hitman, Joe Black Massi. It didn't matter. Magnuson had had a few vendettas himself over the years. In his business, personal motives to put criminals behind bars were not uncommon, and often fueled good work. When he brought the Smith report into Dolan to get authority to re-interview Marsha Davis and to start looking for Joseph Massi, he, therefore, expected the prosecutor to react not just positively but with near manic glee at having *both* Massi brothers in his sights. Instead, Dolan, his face drained of color, looking traumatized by something, waved him distractedly away and told him to come back in an hour. An hour later, some, but not all, of his color back, trying but not succeeding to make his request sound routine, Dolan told him to drop everything, including running down Joseph Massi, and find out where Chris Massi was staying; no more, no less: just his current address.

It had taken Magnuson a week to accomplish this task, a week in which he had done no other work, a week in which Ed Dolan kept to his office and called him two or three times a day for updates, a week of trailing and losing Vinnie Rosamelia in the city's sweltering heat. The detective had a life of his own, with two kids and a mother in a nursing home. He had gotten close enough to Ed Dolan over the years to know that no one got close to Ed Dolan.

Talented, driven, lonely, moody was how he described him to his wife and colleagues. Magnuson pulled out of his prime parking space – in front of a hydrant – and drove off.

He did not know about Dolan's deal with Joseph Massi, the snuff film or the anonymous telephone calls the prosecutor had been receiving. If he had, he would have seen his boss' current behavior for what it was: not a mood swing, but a descent into dementia.

●

Fifteen minutes after Magnuson left, Ed Dolan turned onto Suffolk Street and parked in the space the detective had vacated. In his suit jacket pocket was the standard-issue .38 caliber revolver that Dolan had reported stolen three years earlier, taking advantage of a legitimate break-in of his car one night while he was having dinner in Chinatown. On the seat beside him, in a faux-leather carrying case that looked like a point-and-shoot camera cover, was a cattle prod that he had found at a drug dealer's apartment a few months ago and surreptitiously pocketed. Powered by a single nine volt battery, it had been re-rigged to transmit thermal heat to its two metal prongs rather than electric impulses. Operated by a simple trigger, it was capable, Dolan had found, of burning through wood with not much in the way of pressure. A pair of FBI regulation-issue handcuffs and his cell phone were in the car's glove compartment. Number one-twelve was right across the street.

Eying the building, Dolan placed three twenty milli-gram tablets of Adderall, a dexedrine-based stimulant pre-scribed by one of his rotating psychiatrists, in his mouth and washed them down with the coffee resting in the cup holder on his console. Sixty milligrams would easily keep him awake through the night and probably for twenty-four hours. He had no doubt that Joseph Massi was dead and that Chris Massi was the person calling him to play the tape Joseph had so cleverly made. No doubt Chris thought he was being clever, too. His cleverness would soon have a deadly payoff, just as his brother's had, and Ed would be even with the Massis once and for all, their blood debt to the Dolans paid in full.

6.

While Ed Dolan was getting settled in his car, ready to wait the night out if necessary, Chris was sitting on the sofa in the living room of Allison McRae's miniature apartment. He had a direct view into the kitchen, where Michele was scooping vanilla ice cream into two blue bowls at the counter next to the refrigerator. Watching her lean into the oversized Häagen-Dazs container that was among the items Vinnie had brought over earlier, he saw her as a woman for the first time since he'd met her. Her head was covered with a fuzz of blonde hair not too much darker than the yellow-white ice cream. Below it, unweighted by heroin, her brow had cleared, and her eyes had been revealed to be an arresting gray-blue and very pretty. Her injuries had healed, but her fine-featured face, in profile, still seemed tender and vulnerable as she concentrated on the frozen bucket of ice cream, unaware that he was watching her. She was wearing the low-slung faded jeans and sleeveless cotton top that seemed to make up her entire wardrobe. Her body, food-starved until recently, was still rail thin, but somehow, full breasts and the outline of a round and pert rear end had appeared.

Femininity, which is not the same as sexiness, although sexiness is essential to it, is a matter of attitude as much as anything else. There was a certain pride in the way Michele carried the ice cream, one blue bowl in each hand poised in front of her, into the living room. Chris knew that women were innately and rightly proud to be attractive to men, but did not expect Michele's mental state to have progressed so far only four days post-withdrawal. Equally surprising was the fact that he was pleased to be the man she had decided to put herself on display for. This small surge of pride and femininity on Michele's part, and minor rush of feeling on Chris', came and went in a matter of a few seconds, but it is on such sudden and intuitive foundations that many relationships – good and bad – are built.

"When can I go back to my apartment?" Michele asked.

"I told you, never. You have to move. I'll give you some money."

They were facing each other in the living room, eating ice cream between sentences, Chris still on the sofa, Michele across from him on an old rattan chair, her back to the kitchen, her legs drawn up under her. They had eaten a mostly silent dinner together, which Chris had made, consisting of a tossed salad and macaroni and cheese from a box. Outside they could hear the sounds of the city as its night life began. The light from the kitchen spilled a few feet into the living room and mingled with the muted glare from the lamp on the end table next to Chris.

"Did Vinnie bring you a car?" Michele said. "I heard you talking about it."

"Yes, it's parked in the twenty-four hour garage on Delancey. I may have to leave quickly."

"How quickly?"

"I'm going out tomorrow morning. I should know more when I get back."

"I went to the woman's clinic today at St. Vincent's."

"You don't have to account for your day."

"I know, I'm free to do as I please."

"Right."

"They gave me some Buprenorphine."

"What's that for?"

"To reduce the craving."

"That's good."

"And some sleeping pills."

"Good."

"And they took blood, to test for AIDS and hepatitis."

"When do you find out?"

"They told me to come back next Monday."

Chris said nothing for a second, wondering how he would feel if he were waiting to find out if he had either, or both, of these diseases.

"Do you still feel like you were raped?" he asked.

Michele, awake, silent, had holed up in the bedroom for most of the last sixty-odd hours, drinking soda, chain smoking, occasionally nibbling indifferently at the odds and ends of the packaged food Vinnie had brought over on Saturday. She came out to shower – four times – and once this morning to go to the clinic, although she did not tell Chris her plans. Instead, she said, just before leaving, "I feel like I've been raped."

"You should be grateful," he had said.

"Why? Because you did such a wonderful and noble thing for me?"

"Because you're clean."

"And humiliated."

"That's a small price to pay."

"What do you know about prices? On your high horse."

Vinnie had knocked on the door then, and their first conversation since Saturday morning abruptly ended.

"No," Michele said now in answer to Chris' question. "Violated might be a better word."

"If you have AIDS then you can really feel sorry for yourself."

Michele, her ice cream finished, the bowl on the coffee table in front of her, gripped the arms of her chair when she heard this and leaned forward as if to reach across and rake her nails – painted a bright red that afternoon – over Chris' face. Chris, remembering his last clawing a week ago, ran the fingers of his right hand across his cheek bone, where the deepest of her frantic scratches had only recently healed.

"I don't feel sorry for myself," Michele said, easing slightly her grip on the chair.

"I think you do."

"I feel sorry for my son, who was killed in a fire that I started, and for my daughter, who was taken away from me. She lost her twin brother and her mother on the same day."

Chris had taken Michele's anger over the last few days as a positive thing. He had expected post-withdrawal apathy and listlessness, but instead, there was the ebb and flow not only of anger but of other real feelings to be seen in her eyes. A raw mix of embarrassment and humility, pride and fear that was evidence, perhaps, of the character so sadly missing in general in junkies, who had endless excuses for their inability to stay clean. In the same way, the tragedy that Michele had just recounted so succinctly did not overwhelm him with pity or even sympathy. If she could stop seeing it as an excuse, she might be able to live without heroin. It was her ticket into and out of addiction.

"When was this?" he asked.

"Last year. An eternity ago."

"Were you high at the time?"

"Yes. I was at a party across the street. I left a cigarette burning in the apartment."

"And your husband?"

"We weren't married. He left after the twins were born."

"Where are you from?"

"Right here, all my life on the Lower East Side – a loser who killed her son – a beautiful, innocent, five-year old boy."

Chris listened for a moment to the noises on the street below: people talking and laughing as they walked by, cars stopping, starting, now and again honking. A couple of hip restaurants had opened up around the corner on Clinton Street, drawing college kids and yuppies to mix with the native hookers and drug heads. They could find a lot of local color in this room, he thought, shaking his head slightly, collecting himself before answering.

"I'm angry at other people, Michele," he said. "Not you. I'm taking it out on you. I'm sorry."

"Who are you angry at?"

"My father, because he was a killer. My brother, because he was a junkie; my mother, for making him a junkie. Myself, for living a good life while they suffered. They're all dead now."

There were tears in Michele's eyes, and running down her face, which was otherwise still as she stared at Chris.

"I'm sorry," he said again, realizing what it must have taken to talk about her lost children.

"You can't die too, Chris," she said. "You can't. Please tell me you won't. I can't lose you, too."

The world, which had receded during their conversation, intruded before Chris could answer, in the form of yellow lights flashing at the apartment's lone front window. Chris got up to look out, and saw, five stories below, a city tow truck double-parked across the street, its strobe light breaking the darkness in jagged swirls. The driver, a stocky black guy with his sleeves rolled up and a Mets cap tilted back on his head, was leaning into the driver's side window of a car parked at the opposite curb. A light came on in the car, a black nondescript sedan, and then went off, and the driver backed away, tipped his cap and went back to his truck. His two-way radio squawked for a second as he tuned it in to report to his station.

"What is it?" Michele asked.

"Nothing, a tow truck."

Chris then walked the few steps to where Michele sat, and, standing behind her, put his hands on her shoulders, which were bare except for the thin straps of her blouse.

"I won't die if you won't," he said.

Michele reached up, took one of Chris' hands, and placed it against her cheek. Holding it there, she cried, and Chris could feel her tears mingling with her warm breath on his hand. Outside, the strobe lights abruptly stopped, and the truck could be heard driving off. Michele pressed Chris' hand to her face as her sobbing – broken and child-like – subsided, and the room became silent. The world receded again, but they both knew that soon – tonight, tomorrow, soon – a cry would be heard in the night, or a fix offered, or a gun taken up, and it would return with a vengeance.

7.

The next morning, Chris was up early and had finished his coffee and was ready to leave by seven-thirty. On Sunday, after his meeting with the DiGiglio brothers, he had stopped by LaSalle Academy to ask John Farrell if he would be willing to lure Ed Dolan to a meeting at which Chris would kill him. As plainly as he could, he told Farrell that killing Dolan was not just a matter of avenging Joseph, but of stopping the prosecutor before he either killed Chris or brought him to his knees via a phony murder charge. Twenty-five years of bad blood and hate had to end here and now, and only by using a trusted intermediary would Chris have any reasonable chance of success.

Sitting in a pew at the back of the school's simple, boy-proof chapel, his hands folded in his lap, occasionally glancing up at the altar, the old man nodded when Chris finished, and said, *Do you know The Maze? It's the fortress prison in Long Kesh, outside Belfast, where the English lock away convicted IRA members. My brother Frank died there last year. He helped blow up a convoy of English soldiers in 1971. Combatants are fair game, Chris. I doubt I'll burn in hell for helping you kill this madman. If I do, I'll meet Frank and we can have a laugh. The hatred and bad blood between the Irish and the English, by the way, go back six hundred years.*

They planned to meet at eight this morning, in the chapel again, to discuss the details. As Chris was washing and putting away his coffee cup and spoon – an old habit – Michele appeared in the kitchen rubbing the sleep from her eyes.

"I slept," she said. "The sleeping pill must have knocked me out."

"That's good."

"It's just another drug."

"Don't beat yourself up. You need to sleep."

"Where are you going?"

"To see John Farrell."

"Are you coming back?"

"Yes, of course."

"I never asked you about your brother."

"We'll talk about it tonight."

"You have beautiful eyes."

"You do too."

Michele, barefoot, wearing a short tee shirt and yellow bikini panties, with her arms folded across her chest, smiled on hearing this, at first tentatively, as if she had forgotten how, and then fully, revealing even white teeth and a light in her eyes that Chris guessed had not shined for a long time.

"How tall are you?" he asked, assessing her from her feet to the vee of her crotch to the planed surface of her too-thin but lovely stomach to the top of her nearly bald head.

"Five-seven, taller in heels."

"Are you going out today?"

"Yes."

"Do you have money?"

"I still have all those twenties you threw at me."

"Why don't you pick up something for dinner?"

"I will."

Chris turned to leave, but before he reached the door, Michele called his name, and he turned around.

"Yes?" he said.

"Nothing. Be careful."

"I will."

●

When Chris left, Michele stood staring at the door. *What if I get addicted to you, Chris, instead of heroin? What if I fall in love with you – a man from a world as different from mine as the Earth is from the moon – and you break my heart, you laugh at me, or reject me because I sold my body, or fuck me and leave me, then what do I do?* These thoughts propelled her to the front window, where, looking down she saw Chris a moment later emerge from the building and stop for a second at the bottom of the front steps to look at his watch. When he looked up, a blond man, his eyes blazing like a martyred saint's, was approaching him rapidly from the opposite side of the street. Chris took a step back, but the crazy blond man, pointing a gun, was on him in a heartbeat, and sticking the gun hard into Chris' side. Then, stabbing at Chris with the gun, he was leading him by the arm back across the street to the passenger side of a black car covered in dust and grime. First Chris and then the blond man entered the car through the passenger door, and Michele could clearly see Chris' face in profile as he situated himself in the driver's seat, and, after an exchange of words, buckle his seat belt, then slowly edge out of the tight parking space and drive away.

Michele, standing rigid at the window, was so stunned by what she saw, it took her brain a few seconds to register that it was real. When this happened, she pulled on her jeans, raced down the five flights of stairs to the street and ran at full speed on the sidewalk toward East Broadway, the direction Chris and the blond man had taken. But the black car, when she got to the corner and looked frantically north and south, was nowhere to be seen amid the river of traffic that courses all day long on the city's main avenues.

Standing in the morning sun, oblivious to the pedestrians flowing by, she was seized by the same feeling of helplessness and despair that a year ago had gripped her outside her apartment on Henry Street as she watched firefighters smash windows and spray tons of water on the burning cauldron that was consuming her son. Turning back, she wished, as she had on that night, that she were dead, and decided that as soon as she got back to the apartment she would find a way to kill herself. About halfway back, near Grand Street, she was stopped and surrounded by four Asian teenagers, one of whom, a girl with orange spiked hair and several face rings, Michele had apparently knocked to the ground on her fruitless chase after the black car.

"You crazy fucking bitch," this girl said. "Are you crazy? Are you fucking crazy? We should cut you, bitch. Where's your money? Where's your stash?"

"Where's your money, bitch?" said another, a boy no more than sixteen, with tattoos up and down both arms. "You owe us."

Michele, breathing heavily, adrenalin racing through her veins where once there was blood, leaped on the orange-haired girl, grabbed her by the throat and ran her against a nearby brick wall. The girl, the back of her head opened up and bleeding, slumped to the sidewalk. The others, stunned, took a tentative step or two toward Michele, but without stopping to catch her breath, she ran at the boy with the tattoos and, closing with him, began clawing his face with her nails, digging in hard and with a fierceness and a feeling of satisfaction she had not before this confrontation known existed. The boy broke free, and he and the other two bolted, leaving the orange-haired girl moaning on the ground and Michele standing there in her bare feet ready to kill anyone who came near her. No one did. Indeed, if any of the dozen or so people walking along Suffolk Street had seen anything like a fight they were not acting like it, and so Michele, collecting herself, hurried back to the apartment.

When she got there, she was no longer interested in killing herself. She had found and charged her cell phone the day before, and now she turned it on and put it on the kitchen table. Then she washed her hands, face and feet, put on an old pair of running shoes she found in Allison's closet and sat facing the phone. She did not know Vinnie Rosamelia's last name or how to get in touch with him, or John Farrell. Her parents lived in Queens, and would refuse to talk to her, thinking she wanted money. Her only friend in the neighborhood had been Allison McRae. The police were out of the question. She knew instinctively that Chris was in trouble beyond their reach, and besides, why would they believe an emaciated whore with tracks up and down both arms?

She had come to Suffolk Street to die, believing that the God she knew as a child had long ago forsaken her. Clean of heroin only four days, absurdly in love with a man she barely knew and well beyond her station in life, her will to live returned with the force of a river breaking through a dam. With it came the ancient language of prayer, forgotten words that appear without effort in our hearts in times of crisis. She prayed that someone would call or stop by, and that Chris would somehow endure whatever it was the man with the blazing eyes had in store for him.

8.

As Michele began praying, Chris was driving the black sedan through the Holland Tunnel. Ed Dolan, turned in his seat, was aiming his .38 revolver at Chris' rib cage.

"How did you find me?" Chris asked.

"Your friend Vincent went once too often to Suffolk Street."

"Where are we going?"

"When you get out of the tunnel, get on the Turnpike going north."

"And then where?"

"A nice place where we can talk."

"Let's talk now."

"You want to try to talk yourself out of this predicament, is that it, Chris?"

"Why not? What do you want from me?"

"I want the tape you've been playing for me all week long."

"Let's turn around, then. It's at the apartment. I'll get it for you."

"No, Chris, there's more to it than that."

"If you kill me, there's a copy in a safe place. It'll come out."

Chris was bluffing, looking for leverage, but he could see from the deranged look in Dolan's eyes, and the dried spittle around his mouth, that his one-time friend was very close to becoming untethered from the world of reason.

"That's one of the things we'll talk about. There's a service area up ahead. *Vince Lombardi*. See it?"

"Yes."

They had just entered the New Jersey Turnpike, which was swollen with rush hour traffic. On either side of the eight-lane, mega-highway, stood reed-filled marshland – the New Jersey Meadowlands – a small brown and yellow ocean, stagnant under the sun's hot eye, rimmed by the Manhattan skyline to the east and the fringes of North Jersey's flinty old factory towns to the west.

"Pull in and go all the way to the back, past where the trucks park. There's a dirt road back there."

Chris made his way through the service area, past the busy car parking lot, past a herd of behemoth tractor trailers, past the Dempsey dumpsters, to a desolate area where the blacktop was crumbling and the marshland confronted him like a wall. Directed to the left by Dolan, who intermittently jabbed him with the barrel of his gun, Chris edged along this wall of reeds until he found and entered the narrow dirt road, and followed it into the marshes. Someone, probably a hundred years before, had found the hard ground and beaten a snaking, now long forgotten path through the wetlands. The feathery tops of the reeds and bulrushes on either side reached delicately toward a very pretty blue sky, but they were so thick and high and still that, driving carefully through them, Chris realized that civilization was behind them, and that dead bodies, left here to mingle with the garbage, whether fifty feet or a mile from a road or a parking lot, could go undetected for eternity.

The road ended at a cul-de-sac on which sat a weathered plank shack, no more than fifteen-by-fifteen feet square, with a sagging pitched roof and sunlight gleaming through chinks on all sides. Behind it was a pond formed by the elbow of a stream that had been dammed up by garbage at both ends. Rusted metal drums and a dozen charred tires were strewn along the far bank. The rotting carcass of a once white heron was floating on the viscous petroleum-like scum that covered the pond's surface. The sun, rising to the east over Manhattan, beat down on this scene of desolation without mercy.

"Park there," Dolan said, nodding toward a bare patch of ground to the right of the shack.

Chris did as he was told. As he was turning the car off, he watched out of the corner of his eye as his boyhood friend took what looked like a camera in a leather case out of his jacket pocket. Using his left hand – the gun was still in his right hand pointing at Chris' stomach – the prosecutor unsnapped the leather case and drew the cattle prod out. In an instant, Dolan was jabbing the prod's metal ends into Chris' right arm, up near the shoulder. Reflexively, Chris struck out at the prosecutor, shoving him in the chest, but the prod had done its work, burning two holes through the sleeve of his navy blue polo shirt, and hissing though his skin and muscle before the force of his shove forced Dolan to pull it away. The smell of his burning flesh reached his nostrils at the same time as the pain reached his brain. Although he was in shock, he managed to take another backhanded swing at Dolan with his burnt arm, but the prosecutor easily warded it off with his gun hand, and then quickly opened the car door and got out, dragging Chris with him by the front of his shirt.

Outside, he pushed Chris through the stifling heat into the cabin, where he forced him into a battered chrome chair next to a table made of two saw horses and three planks. Chris, nauseous, about to pass out, slumped forward, hoping to get some blood back into his brain. Dolan let him stay that way for a second, then pulled him up by his collar and gazed with demented pleasure at Chris, who stared back through eyes cloudy with pain.

"That was in case you were thinking of trying something," Dolan said, placing the prod on the table and taking the handcuffs out his pocket. "Put your hands behind your back."

Chris complied, and Dolan snapped the cuffs onto Chris' wrists. He threw the key onto the table, then resumed his one-sided conversation. "If I poke that thing in your heart, you're dead, massive heart attack; in your balls, instant sterilization, not to mention the pain. Are you following me? I want the original tape and any copies you have. If you hold one back and try to hurt me with it, then this is what I'll do: I'll hunt down your children and I'll torture and kill them. I won't go to jail behind the tape, Chris. It's too ambiguous. And if I do, it won't be forever. When I get out, your kids are dead. Then they can put me away again, or maybe I'll kill myself, or maybe I won't get caught. I'm free as a bird right now, and I've been a bad boy."

"The tape's at the apartment," Chris said. "Let's go get it."

"No. It's too dangerous. Your friend Vinnie might be there. Anything can happen. Whose apartment is it? Your junkie girlfriend's? Michele Mathias? Is that her name?"

"Yes."

"Is she home?"

"I don't know, maybe."

"Does she have a car?"

"Yes."

"Do you have a phone?"

"In my front pocket."

Dolan fished the phone out of Chris' jeans and flipped it open, keeping the .38 pointed at his chest with his other hand.

"What's the number?"

"It's programmed. Push Speed Dial, then one."

Dolan pushed the two buttons on the phone, then placed it against the side of Chris' face.

"Tell her to bring the tape here. Something came up. You need it right away. She'll be happy to do you the favor. She'll give you great sex tonight, her hero."

After half of a ring, Michele picked up.

"Michele," Chris said into the phone, "it's me, Chris. I need you to do me a favor."

"Where are you?"

"In Jersey."

"I saw that guy take you away."

"Okay. Fine."

"What do you want me to do?"

"There's a plastic bag under the sink. The car keys are in it, and the garage ticket, and some other stuff, some tapes. I need you to bring everything to me."

"Where?"

"Write this down."

He gave her the directions, which were pretty simple, and as soon as he was finished, Dolan yanked the phone away and threw it on the table. Picking up the cattle prod, he stood behind Chris and brushed the prongs lightly over the top of his head.

"When she pulls up," he said, "I'll be standing behind you with the gun to your head. That should disabuse her of any funny ideas."

The shack's front door had long since been removed, and the two of them were facing the rectangular open space where it once stood. Outside, they could see the marshes sitting stonily still in the day's yellow heat, and, in the silence around them, they could hear the rumbling and whooshing of traffic on the New Jersey Turnpike. In twenty minutes or so, they would hear Michele's car as it came down the dirt road and then see it as it rounded the last bend on its approach to the shack.

"There's a copy of the tape in a safe deposit box." Chris said. "If I die, my executor will give it to the police."

"Then I'll go after your kids, like I said. But this isn't really about the tape, Chris. It's about us, you and me."

"All these years of hate, and for what? I didn't kill your father. I couldn't control what Joe Black did. I was fifteen years old."

"A cocky fifteen."

"You must have hated me before the killing."

"A little."

Chris' arm was starting to get red and swollen, and to ooze something like pus, and the pain where the prongs of the cattle prod had come close to bone was coming in stronger and stronger waves. He was talking only to avoid thinking about it.

"Don't hurt the girl, Ed. She hasn't done anything to you."

"So solicitous. Maybe I'll poke her in the pussy with my cattle prod. No more orgasms for Michele."

"Christ."

"How are your legs, by the way? What a career you could have had. The third fastest high school miler ever."

"They're fine."

"I think now's a good time to tell you: I broke those legs."

"What?"

"Sure. Your accident. I cut the brake lines on Brother Farrell's car. The poor fuck helped me out by having his usual few beers."

Chris' head slumped to his chest, the pain getting the better of him. Dolan stepped around to face him, and, lifting his face up by the chin, said, "Did you hear me? I broke your legs, and now your arm is a mess, and before I'm done, I'll maim you some more."

Although the pain in Chris' arm had if anything gotten worse since the initial burning, he was coming out of shock and finding that some of his natural reserve of strength was returning. He would have spit in Dolan's face, but his mouth was too dry to generate any saliva, which was just as well, because it was obvious that Dolan needed little or no excuse to use the cattle prod again. The look in the prosecutor's eyes was the look of a fanatic consumed by his cause. He was enraptured by his hate, and the only way Chris could think of to survive minute by minute was to continue talking, his words like lashes that Dolan hated and loved and somehow desperately needed.

●

Michele, driving the Jeep Cherokee that Vinnie had bought for Chris just two days before, found the dirt road easily enough, but after traveling only fifty feet or so on it, she drove down a gully to her right directly into the high reeds and stopped after about twenty feet. Getting out and

looking around, she saw that the car was completely con-
cealed from the road, as she had hoped it would be. In her
hand was a plastic bag containing two mini-cassettes and
Joe Black Massi's .44 Ruger with a clip inserted and the
safety off. Sticking to the marshes, she followed the con-
tour of the dirt road until she was at the right side of the
shack, which she could clearly see through the reeds only
twenty feet away. In front was the black car driven by the
blond madman.

Taking the gun, a compact canon, from the bag, and
holding it in front of her with both hands, Michele made
her way silently to the shack. Once there, trying to breathe
without sound, she squatted and looked through a chink
to where the blond fanatic was standing in front of a
slumping and very pale Chris, pointing a gun at his head.
Kneeling on all fours, she crept to the front, peeked her
head in the opening and found them in the same position.
Without thinking, she brought herself to one knee in the
doorway, aimed the Ruger at the blond man's back and
pulled the trigger. The gun's powerful kick flung her hand
upward as she fired, causing her to miss high, knocking
her onto her back at the same time. Dolan, his eyes bulg-
ing, whirled when he heard the blast of the .44 and fired
point blank at the doorway, missing Michele, who was lying prone on the ground.

Dolan, seeing Michele scrambling to get to her feet,
was taking careful aim at her when Chris leaped at him,
dragging the chair with him, head-butting the prosecutor
into the door post, the chair slipping away from him from
behind on impact. Keeping his balance, Chris then lunged
again, aiming his head at the slumping Dolan's face, catch-
ing him on the bridge of his nose. Dolan crumpled to the
floor, moaning, blood pouring down the sides of his nose

and into his mouth. In an instant, Michele was over him pointing the Ruger at his head.

"Don't kill him," Chris shouted. "Pick up his gun. It's right there. Keep your gun on him."

Doing as she was told, Michele backed up slowly and retrieved Dolan's .38 from the floor.

"Unlock these handcuffs," Chris said. "The key's on the table."

Chris was facing Dolan, who had managed to get himself to a sitting position against the wall next to the doorway. Michele put the .38 in the belt of her jeans, then, keeping the Ruger on the prosecutor, found the key and unlocked the cuffs.

"Give me the Ruger," Chris said, and Michele handed it to him.

Dolan was still dazed, but his eyes, rimmed with blood, were open and focusing on Chris, and his hands were braced on the floor on either side of him, as if he was preparing to pounce. Without hesitation, Chris covered the few feet between him and Dolan and swung the barrel of the .44 into the side of the prosecutor's face, absorbing with great satisfaction the unmistakable sound and feel of the crunch of bone breaking on impact.

Michele, Dolan's revolver in her hand, walked over to stand beside Chris. Breathing heavily, they stared down at Dolan, who had slumped to his side on the floor, out cold.

"Who is he?" Michele asked.

"I'll explain later. First, we have work to do."

Then, noticing Chris' arm for the first time, Michele said, "What happened? Did he burn you? I thought I smelled something burning."

"He did," Chris answered, "but we can't talk now. Help me get him in the chair."

Michele set the chair upright, then helped Chris pull and push the inert Dolan onto it.

"Put his hands behind his back, through the slats of the chair, then cuff them," Chris said. "Give me the revolver."

Michele handed him the .38 and set about her task. While she was doing this, Chris picked up his cell phone and the cattle prod from the table and went outside. In Dolan's car he found the cattle prod's leather cover, which he slipped over it, and, in the glove compartment, Dolan's cell phone. He threw the prod into the oily pond and watched it sink. Then, using Dolan's phone, he dialed Rocco Stabile's number.

"Rocco," he said when Stabile answered. "It's me, Chris."

"Hello."

"It's time for your two guys to make their bones."

"Where are you?"

Chris gave him directions to the shack, then added, "I won't be here."

"What about the other guy?"

"They'll find it easy to close the deal."

"It's not closed yet?"

"No, I saved the last part for them."

"You still want them to bring this other shit."

"Yes. They just have to spread it around."

"They're on their way."

Chris put the phone back into the glove box after clicking it off, then went into the shack to check on Dolan, who was still out cold, his hands intertwined through the back of the chair and cuffed tightly together. Picking up the key, making sure he had both guns, Chris took a last look around the shack, then led Michele into the high reeds to wait.

Twenty minutes later, a black BMW pulled up and parked behind Dolan's sedan. Labrutto and Rodriguez emerged from it with silencer-tipped guns drawn and, from opposite sides, slowly approached the open doorway. Labrutto peeked in, smiled and entered, motioning Rodriguez to follow. The sound of two muted shots could be heard, followed immediately by a thud and some indistinct conversation. As the porn/snuff film producer and the albino were returning, side-by-side, to their car, Chris stepped out from the reeds and shot them both with Dolan's gun, aiming and firmly but calmly squeezing the trigger the way Joe Black had taught him almost thirty years ago.

Labrutto, shot in the head, was killed instantly. Mickey, hit in the arm, was reaching wildly for his gun when Chris approached him and shot him at close range in the chest. This was followed almost immediately by another shot from another gun, this one hitting Rodriguez in the stomach. Chris had told Michele to stay in the reeds, but, turning, he saw she was standing behind him to his right, breathing softly, with the Ruger still aimed straight at Rodriguez.

"You can put the gun down," Chris said. "He's dead."

Only when Chris spoke did Michele tear her eyes away from the albino, whose lifeless body lay on its side, blood from all three wounds oozing onto the dusty hardpan.

"What now?" she asked.

"The bodies go in the shack."

After this was accomplished, Chris unlocked Dolan's handcuffs and threw him to the ground. He had been shot twice in the head. His brains were sticking to the back wall of the shack. The faux snuff films and numerous fifty and hundred dollar bills were scattered around the floor. Chris wiped his prints off of Dolan's .38 with his shirt and placed the small gun into the prosecutor's limp hand, pressing his fingers around the barrel and leaving it in plain sight on the floor next to the body. Using his shirttail, he delicately drew Labrutto's and Mickey's guns from their belts and placed them on the ground near their bodies.

Outside, he threw the handcuffs, the key and the Ruger into the pond, then yanked out some reeds and brushed away his and Michele's footprints from the hard-pan around the cabin and at the edge of the pond. They then entered the marsh and followed the road back to the Cherokee. Chris' arm was on fire and getting to be useless. He might lose it, but Dolan was dead, and Nick Scarpa, Allison McRae and Heather Jansen had been avenged. Only Joseph's score needed to be settled, but he could kill Anthony DiGiglio with his left arm, or no arms, if he had to.

9.

"That's the next thing you have to quit," John Farrell said to Michele, who was having her second pre-dinner cigarette. "Take it from me."

"One thing at a time," Michele answered. She was relaxed and happy – or as close to those two states as she felt she could get given the recent events of her life – and did not want to think about breaking another habit. She did not know that Farrell, a smoker for fifty years, was dying of lung cancer, although it had not escaped her that something was wrong. The white-haired cleric's usually lively eyes seemed dull, his civilian clothes were hanging loose and there was a slight but noticeable effort that preceded his speech and movement. Her heart went out to this gentle old man who had been unstintingly helpful and kind to both her and Chris these past few weeks. It occurred to her to ask after him in a pointed way, but something stopped her, possibly her fear that the truth would be more than she could handle at the moment.

She and Chris were sitting on the couch, facing Farrell in the rattan chair. They were drinking scotch from a bottle of eighteen-year-old Glenlivet, a gift from Farrell, who had a glass of club soda in front of him. The noise in the kitchen stopped and they looked up to see Vinnie carrying in a bottle of chilled champagne and four fluted glasses. He popped the cork expertly and poured each of them a glassful, then raised his glass, and said,

"To Karen Pierce."

"To Allison," Michele said.

"To Nick," Chris said. "And Joseph."

"Here, here," Farrell said.

They touched glasses all around and drank.

On their return to Suffolk Street from the Meadowlands, Chris had used the last of his throw-away cell phones to call the New Jersey State Police to report hearing shots while changing a tire at the back of the Vince Lombardi Service Area on the Turnpike. That night, the TV news was full of the bizarre triple slaying in the Meadowlands. The next morning, the Post's front page headline, run over a black-and-white photograph of the blood-stained bodies surrounded by hundred dollar bills on the floor of the hut, said, *Shack Attack! G-Man, Two Others Dead.*

Two days later, it was reported in all three of the city's major dailies that a search of Assistant U.S. Attorney Ed Dolan's Upper East Side apartment was said by a reliable government source to have turned up a real snuff film, as opposed to the pretend versions found strewn around the shack. The same source also told reporters that a year ago the shack in the Meadowlands had been used as a lookout by FBI agents responding to a tip that a mob murder was about to go down. The tip had never materialized, but Dolan's team had been notified of the operation, and it was believed that the career prosecutor had visited the site.

The media frenzy that followed lasted several weeks and had Karen Pierce, the U.S. Attorney for the Southern District of New York, recently transferred from Washington, on the defensive from her first day on the job. Articles recounting Dolan's career were run, all of which mentioned the fact that he was said to be recently working on what he believed was a connection between the Scarpa/McRae murders and organized crime. One or two stories referred to the DiGiglio crime family as his target, although each noted that no evidence connecting the DiGiglios to the Palisades murders had ever been produced publicly.

The consensus was that the deaths of Guy Labrutto – a known maker of pornographic videos – and his associate, Mickey Rodriguez, had made proving such a connection extremely difficult, if not impossible. No mention was made of Chris Massi. Yesterday, Pierce had issued a press release, carried in this morning's papers, announcing that the Scarpa/McRae investigation had been closed on the theory that the likely killers – Labrutto and Rodriguez – were dead,; that Ed Dolan's task force had been dissolved and would be reorganized in Washington, and that Dolan's personal and professional activities going back at least five years would be thoroughly scrutinized by her office.

When he finished drinking, Chris looked over at John Farrell, who was slumping in his chair but smiling. The temporary flush of excitement on his cheeks was a sad reminder of the old Brother Farrell, the one whose face was permanently pink, before cancer drew the shades on his eyes and turned his visage pallid and gray. The old man had made Chris promise not to tell anyone that he was dying, and Chris had thus far complied. He had held his breath while Vinnie was popping the champagne, hoping that his toast would not be to life or health, as it might logically have been, given that Michele had kicked her habit and Chris' arm had healed well – and that they were both alive.

"I feel cheated, in a way," Farrell said.

"Maybe you'll get another chance," Chris replied.

"What does that mean?" Vinnie said.

"I talked to Teresa this morning," Chris said. "She says her father wants to talk to me."

"Does he know where you are?"

"No, no one does."

"Maybe that's all he wants to do, talk."

"I don't think so."

"Why not?"

"I can connect him to the snuff film, and to Joseph's death. What would you do?"

"You're the father of his grandchildren," Vinnie said. "You got Dolan off his back. He can't be thinking of killing you."

"I can't take the chance."

"What about Aldo and Frank? They'll come after you."

"Let's not talk about it tonight," Chris said. "Tonight, let's just eat and drink and be happy that we're alive."

It had taken two weeks for Chris' wounds to heal. Deep, but not to the bone, they had been cleansed and coated with silver nitrate solution on a regular basis. The silver nitrate, along with sterile dressings and anti-inflammatory medication, were spirited by John Farrell from the infirmary at LaSalle. Demerol for pain was provided by Vinnie, who also brought over and installed an air conditioner that provided Chris with much needed relief from the increasing summer heat.

Michele did the nursing. While she did, Chris told her about his connection to the Scarpa and McRae murders, the story of Joseph's life and death and the latest version of his own life story, including his misbegotten relationship with Ed Dolan, his brief running career and the car accident that ended it. By the middle of the third week, Chris was able to move his arm with a minimum of pain and discomfort. Michele's AIDS and hepatitis tests had come back negative. To celebrate their health, and the welcome announcement from Karen Pierce's office, they invited Farrell and Vinnie for dinner.

"Yes, don Massi," Vinnie said, with mock solemnity, raising his glass. "Tonight, the war stops for a few hours. Tonight, we celebrate your health and your victories."

"To the first gay consigliere," Chris said, smiling and raising his glass as well.

By ten o'clock, Farrell and Vinnie had gone, the dishes were done, and Chris and Michele were sitting in the living room sipping coffee. Michele was smoking. Her cigarettes, Marlboro reds, were on the coffee table between them. Chris, sitting Indian-style on the floor, facing Michele on the couch, picked up the pack, took one out and lit it.

"I didn't know you smoked," Michele said.

"I have one every ten years or so."

They smoked and listened to the sounds of the street below and the city beyond.

"Would you like some music?" Michele asked.

"Sure."

Michele rose and went into the kitchen, where she turned on the transistor radio that was on the counter. It was already tuned to a jazz station that Chris liked. As she returned to the sofa, the husky sound of Ben Webster's saxophone came drifting after her.

"There's no danger now," Chris said, when she was seated. "You can go back to your apartment whenever you're ready."

"What brings that up?"

"You've brought a lot of things over from your place. The radio, for instance."

"I thought you'd like the music while you were laid up."

"I did and everything else you did for me."

"Do you want me go?"

"No."

"Are you sure?"

"Yes."

"Then I'll stay. What are your plans?"

Chris took a hit from his cigarette and laid it in the ceramic ashtray they were sharing. He had started smoking in law school, eventually enjoying most the unfiltered Camel and a drink that were his reward at the end of a long day of work. When Tess, then six, questioned the smell of his apartment, he quit. That had been ten years ago. Through the smoke rising in lazy spirals from the ashtray, he saw images of Michele: flung on her back by the kick of Joe Black's Ruger, standing over the dead and bleeding body of Mickey Rodriguez, the gun still pointed at his crotch, the hot sun pounding down on them and searing the tableau forever onto his brain.

"We might as well move to your apartment," he replied. "I'm pretty sure I'm safe down here."

"Safe from what?"

"From being bothered while I figure out what to do."

"I don't think your ex-father-in-law plans on killing you."

"What makes you say that?"

"The way you described him. I think he's a lot like you, and I don't think it's a killing you'd do."

Chris was not surprised at this insight from Michele. Once her head had cleared, she had proven to be intelligent and remarkably adept at getting beneath the surface of things. He did not respond immediately. He was planning on killing Junior Boy, whether Michele's analogy was correct or not. He would kill Aldo and Frank, too, if he could get them all together. They would all know at once then that it was Joseph's life they were paying for with theirs.

"Look at it this way," he said finally. "The don would avenge the death of a brother. Therefore, I would, too."

"But not tonight."

"No," Chris answered, smiling. "Tonight, I'm staying right here."

Michele's hair was now about an inch long, and she had done something to it. Parted and styled, it looked like the edgy kind of hairdo any hip young downtown babe might have. The bruises on her face had healed completely, and she was wearing lipstick and strategically applied makeup that accentuated her classic features. The effect of her dual struggles – to stay clean and to cope with the unforgiving memory of what she had done to her children – had stamped these features with a dignity that only such suffering can impart. The courage she had shown in firing Joe Black's Ruger at Ed Dolan's back was, Chris knew, nothing compared to the courage it would take for her to stay on her new path. Love was a mystery to Chris, as it is to all of us, but respect was not. Respect he understood.

"Do you like me Chris?" Michele asked.

"Yes, you know I do."

"I wish I could say I don't remember my days on the street, but I do."

"Crime and punishment," Chris answered.

"What does that mean?"

"You thought you were punishing yourself for what you did to your son, but you weren't. You were avoiding it.

Now that you're clean, and able to feel again, you can start paying whatever price it is you really have to pay."

"Who decides that?"

"You do."

Michele crushed out her cigarette and remained silent for a second. The shadow that was never far from her face crossed over it. Watching her in the lamplight, Chris admitted to himself that he had meddled in her life for reasons having to do with his own pain and frustration. He winced at the selfishness and the hubris of such behavior. Still, here she was, clean, healthy, alive to the sexy tips of her fingers and toes.

"Do you like me enough to kiss me?" Michele asked.

For his answer, Chris got up, went to the couch and sat next to Michele. Taking her face in his hands, he looked at her and saw that the shadow had passed from her eyes, in whose depths he could see the same mix of need and desire that were surely in his. He continued to hold her face as they kissed, and she kept her hands at her sides. Their lips touched gently at first, making it seem to Chris that they were suspended in space, that they could hang there, connected this way, forever. The pressure built, and then their tongues met, and with a gasp, Michele was in Chris' arms, holding him tightly as her mouth found his neck and cheeks and eyes. Pulling apart for a second, they smiled dumbly at each other, having each had their first taste in a long time of life's sweetest drug.

They got out of their clothes, stopping to touch and kiss along the way, in no hurry at first to end their high. Soon, however, the blood was pounding in Chris' head as forcefully as it was in his erect, rock-hard penis, and, laying Michele on her back, he entered her with a stabbing pleasure that – stopping, motionless for a long second or two – he allowed to flood his brain. Beginning slowly, as she raised her hips to draw him in deeper, Chris let his senses take over until they found the rhythm that is as old as the universe yet somehow unique to each couple, and that with surprising swiftness brought them both to orgasm. Stunned, they lay facing each other on the couch, the air conditioner humming steadily in the background, while from the radio came the voice of a DJ pitching a jazz cruise around Manhattan. Toward the end, Chris had opened his eyes to see Michele looking up at him and smiling. This memory stayed with him as he rolled them so that they were lying side by side, facing each other, still joined at hip and crotch. It was a smile that humbled him, such was its pure joy at being loved.

"I'm having a smoke," Michele said.

"Go for it."

"Do you want one?"

"No, I'll have my next one in 2013."

Michele grabbed her cigarettes and went first into the bathroom, then the bedroom. When she came out, she was wearing one of Chris' polo shirts, a white one with a blue collar. Chris had slipped on the khaki walking shorts he had been wearing, and was lying on the couch, his head propped on a pillow, listening to the radio. Michele lit a cigarette and sat at his feet, smoking, stroking his ankles with her free hand.

"It must have been hard for you," she said, "when you realized you couldn't run anymore."

"It was a bad day."

"Or two."

"Or two."

"I feel something right here."

"There's a plate in there with screws in it."

She had been caressing the faded vertical scar on his right leg where the surgeon had entered to recompose his shattered tibia.

"Is the other leg the same?"

"No, that was a simple fracture. It was the right leg that did me in. The engine crushed it."

"Did you have a lawsuit?"

"My father didn't believe in lawsuits. He thought they were a form of charity."

"Did you ever run again?"

"I tried to run the following year, but I re-broke the right leg. That's why there's a permanent pin in it."

"My son's name was Christopher."

Chris had sat up and reorganized himself into a semi-lotus position facing Michele, whose hand he now took and studied, gathering his thoughts for the turn their conversation had taken.

"Named after whom?"

"No one. I just liked the name."

In the Southern Italian culture, the first son is named after the paternal grandfather. Chris, still staring at Michele's small, lovely, almost childlike hand, caressing it gently, recalled the day in June of 1989 when he told his parents he was naming his new son Matthew. Rose had put her hand to her brow and gone to the kitchen sink. Joe Black, flinty, absorbed this blow with dignity, but Chris could see the briefest flicker of sadness, and even pain, appear and disappear in his father's dark eyes. It was a day he wished he had back again. Lifting his eyes to meet Michele's, he said, "Where is he buried?"

"In Queens, near my parents."

"And your daughter?"

"She's alive, Chris."

"No, I mean what's her name?"

"Grace."

Christopher and Grace, he thought, simple, lovely, symbolic names. "That's a pretty name," he said out loud. "Have you thought about visiting her?"

"That's not possible."

"I think you're wrong."

"I don't want to see her."

"Why didn't your parents take her?"

"They're old. My father has MS."

Michele's cigarette had burned down to the filter. Removing her hand from Chris', she crushed it out and lit another one.

"I could help you," he said.

"Help me do what?"

"Get a lawyer, find her, start the process. I doubt they terminated your parental rights."

"What does that mean?"

"It means you're still her mother. You could see her, get her back eventually. You'd have to stay clean, and you probably only have this one shot."

"I plan on staying clean."

"Then you have to do it. She needs you."

Chris could see by the stricken look on Michele's face that, though she had raised the subject of her children, she had not expected it to lead so quickly and so directly to the issue of choice and personal responsibility. He had not planned on this unhappy coda to their love making, but momentum and timing were everything when it came to taking action in life, and the longer Michele waited to confront this issue the more likely it was that she never would.

"She needs to forget me."

"That's the point," Chris replied. "She'll never forget you. She'll long for her real mom for the rest of her life. Think about it. How can you go forward and leave her behind?"

"What if they won't let me see her?"

"Then at least you know you tried."

Michele threw her head back, and sucked on her cigarette, reminding Chris of the day they first met on the front steps of the building, a lifetime ago. She blew the smoke out and said, "I was happy for a few minutes."

"I'm sorry."

"It's not your fault."

"Will you think about it?"

"Yes, I'll think about it. What else would I think about?"

"How much you love making love with me."

Michele smiled at this and, putting out her cigarette, crept into Chris' arms.

"How much time do we have?" she said, her head on his chest.

Chris knew what she meant. To her, it was not possible that their time as lovers would be anything more than a brief interlude. Defeat was the leitmotif of her life, in the very air she breathed. And him? Why had he closed his heart to love? Why always so cool and distant? Because his legs were broken as a boy? Because Teresa loved power and prestige more than she loved him? His had not been the first unhappy childhood, the first disillusioned heart. Had his pride been a false refuge after all? Surprised and confused at the surge of feeling in his heart he was unaware at the moment that these questions were also answers.

"Enough, I hope," he replied.

"I don't think it will ever be enough," Michele replied, raising her head and pressing her lips to Chris', and then, while kissing him, she said softly, "but let's not waste any of it."

10.

Two days later, Chris was standing on the concrete esplanade that overlooks the east end of Bryant Park. On the sunken lawn below and on the park's perimeter walkway, people in ones and twos and small groups were everywhere enjoying the temperate early July day, walking, reading, playing chess, eating an early lunch, sitting quietly on the numerous slatted folding chairs that dotted the green landscape. The tall plane trees that surround the lawn, with their handsome, dappled trunks, were reaching for the sunlight that was just now breaking through clouds that had brought a brief morning shower.

Among those sitting quietly, his hands in the pockets of his baggy shorts, his black hair falling with studied casualness across his forehead, was Matt Massi, in the precise location near the Forty-Second Street entrance that Chris had designated as their meeting spot. As Chris watched, his son reached into one of the cargo pockets of his shorts and took out a pair sunglasses – silver-rimmed with cobalt blue lenses – and slipped them on. He had showed up at the African Queen at ten o'clock asking for his father. Vinnie had called Chris, and the meeting had been arranged.

Chris studied Matt for a second before heading over to him, trying to read his body language. His slouching posture was more subdued than relaxed, and the disdainful curl usually to be seen on his beautiful lips was for once missing. Chris knew his son. Before he turned into a sneering princeling, he had been an unpretentious, happy boy, but one who took pains, like many boys – sometimes successfully, sometimes not – to conceal his emotions. What Matt was feeling, he did his best to prevent the world from seeing. Watching him, it struck Chris that the cool facade his son had affected of late served more than one purpose. In the last two years, their relationship had been a one-way affair, with Chris doing all of the reaching out. Now here they were at Matt's request. Whatever the reason – and Chris was fairly certain that the boy would not have gone to all this trouble unless something important was on his mind – it was good to see his mask down and some of the raw stuff of the old Matt on display.

"Hello," Chris said, sitting in a folding chair across from and at a slight angle to Matt, who had sat up straight and taken his hands out of his pockets when he saw his father approaching. "Those are nice glasses."

"Thanks."

"Can I see them?"

Matt slid the sunglasses off of his face and handed them to Chris, who studied them for a second before slipping them into the front pocket of his shirt.

"Are they too cool or something?" Matt asked.

"We're in the shade here," Chris replied. "What's up?"

"What's up? What's up with you?" said Matt. "We haven't seen you in a month."

"I've been working. I told your mother that, and Tess."

"Working on what?"

"Research, private investigating."

"Did you move from Vinnie's?"

"Yes."

"Where?"

"I can't tell you that."

"Why?"

"It's the case I'm working on. The client doesn't want anyone to be able to find me."

"Do you have a new cell phone number?"

"Yes, but I can't give it to you."

"When were you planning on seeing us?"

"When the case is over. In a few weeks."

In the more than ten years since his divorce, Chris had not gone more than two weeks without seeing Tess and Matt. In the last two years, his record had been spotty, but Matt, preoccupied with his illusions of gangster grandeur, seemed hardly to notice. Suddenly he was asking questions, demanding, in effect, Chris' attention. What the genesis of this change was Chris could not fathom, but he was sure it wasn't because he missed his father. Why would he miss the one adult in his life who derided his Mafia conceit?

"Do you like it? The stuff you're doing?" the boy asked.

"No, I don't," Chris answered, "I've got one last thing to do, then I'm done with it."

"Then what will you do?"

"I don't know. Something will come to me."

"Ed Dolan died."

"I know. I saw it in the paper."

Chris looked into his son's eyes as he said this. In them, he saw not just the boy's simple satisfaction that the man who had tried to ruin his father's life was dead, but something else as well, something that spoke of calculation, of counting up a series of facts.

"I'm taking the exam for LaSalle next week," Matt said.

"Good."

"You're not surprised?"

"No."

"Do you still want me to?"

"Of course."

"Mommy took me to see LaSalle."

"What did you think?"

"It's okay."

"Real kids go there. It's not Upper Montclair."

"No, but that's okay."

"How is your mother taking this?"

"Not well. How are you taking it?"

"Is that what this is about?" Chris said. "I've been busy. You guys were supposed to be going to the shore. I'm getting the apartment back soon. I fully expect you to go to LaSalle in September and live with me there."

Matt looked down at the ground, then up at Chris, who knew that some kind of moment of truth had arrived, but he could not guess what it might be.

"What is it, Matt?"

"Where's Uncle Joseph?"

"Uncle Joseph?"

"Yes."

"I don't know."

"He was at my party."

"I know."

"He said he'd call me to go to a Yankee game."

"You know the story with him, Matt."

"I saw him leave the party. I was having a smoke in the back room of the garage. There's a small window there. He came down the stairs from Grandpa's study with Uncle Aldo and Nicky Spags. Nicky had Uncle Joseph's arm behind his back and a gun to his head."

Chris took this in, gazing as he did, into Matt's fine, dark eyes.

"Did anyone else see this?" he asked.

"No. I was alone."

In Matt's eyes, there was both fear and determination, neither a facade, both starkly real, the same mix of emotions Chris remembered feeling on the day he said to Joe Black, *what happened with Ed's father?* The message that Chris' eyes conveyed to his father was the same as the one Matt's were conveying to him today: *Tell me the truth. Don't lie to me. I can cross this threshold and survive, but I need to know the truth.* It was this sudden willingness to accept the hard things of life that had set Chris on the road to manhood, and now the same thing was happening to – and inside of – his son.

"He was wearing a hidden tape recorder," Chris said, "a wire. They found it on him. He's dead."

"So grandpa...?"

"Yes. He ordered it."

"Uncle Joseph?"

"Yes."

Matt's hands were resting on his thighs. He lifted one toward his face, but abruptly brought it down. He was crying. Chris let him cry for a few seconds, then took the sunglasses out of his pocket and handed them to his son. Matt wiped his eyes with his knuckles, then put them on.

"He loved you, Matt."

At this Matt broke down, and Chris moved his chair next to him and put his arm around his shoulder.

"Cry," he said, feeling the boyness in Matt's bony arm as he pulled him closer. He sat there and held his son, listening to his crying, until it slowed and stopped.

"I hate grandpa. I hate his fucking guts."

"In his world, he did what was right."

"How could that be?"

"Nicky Spags found the wire. He was doing his job. It was either kill him or kill Joseph."

"Kill Nicky?"

"If he let Joseph live, then he would have exposed a weakness to an underling. He could not let Nick live under those circumstances. But if he killed Nick, it would be for no good reason, it would violate your grandfather's rule against senseless violence. There was a good reason for killing Joseph. I would have done the same thing."

"You don't want me to hate grandpa, yet he killed your brother."

"I don't want you to let your emotions rule you."

"Why not? I do hate him."

"Think about the danger. If you let him know how you feel, he'd want to know why. You don't want him to know what you know."

"He wouldn't hurt me."

"What if Aldo found out? Can you trust him? He wants one of his sons to be the don."

"I won't let them know."

"I think that's a good idea."

"How do you know about Uncle Joseph?" Matt asked. "Were you in on it together?"

"No, he left me a letter."

"Why did he do it?"

"He thought he was helping me."

"How?"

"You don't need to know that now. Someday, maybe, but not now."

Matt took the sunglasses off and again wiped his eyes with his hands. There would be no challenge to this last answer, no desire to see and hear more of the new and intense world his father had so bluntly and graphically put on display. The opportunity had arisen to show the boy the true face of the Mafia and Chris had taken it. *That face, Matt, is hard and remorseless. It will kill your beloved uncle, your best friend's father, it will kill you if you break the rules. Once you commit to it, you either live by those rules or die by them.*

"What now?" Matt said, putting the glasses into his cargo pocket, his eyes red but dry.

"What do you mean *what now?*"

"I don't know. It just seems like...like it can't be left at this."

Matt's reaction thus far to Joseph's execution had been typical of any young boy thrust into the same position, but this answer, loaded as it was with the notions of revenge and honor, was not so typical. If Joe Black's blood was coursing through his son's veins, Chris needed to know it, because it was blood that was proud and strong and not afraid to kill, blood – as Chris had recently learned – that could not be denied, only disciplined.

"There's nothing to be done," Chris said. "Try to put it out of your mind."

Matt shook his head and said, "That won't be easy, Dad. The look on his face..."

The look on his face, Chris thought. I guess it was a look you were meant to see, Matt, and I wasn't.

"Does your mother know about Joseph?" Chris asked out loud.

"No, but she's worried."

"Why do you say that?"

"She and Uncle Joseph are always talking on the phone. She couldn't reach him. I think she went into the city to the apartment where he was living. When she came home, she locked herself in her bedroom. Since then, she's been different, moody."

"What about Tess? Does she know?"

"I didn't tell her, but she knows something's up. She's worried about Mom, and you."

"She's not to know."

"I know."

"Why?"

"Why what?"

"Why isn't she to know?"

"Because you say so."

"Because she would be in danger if she did. Do you understand what I'm saying?"

Matt sat up straighter in his chair, as if physically shouldering the responsibility of protecting his sister. This small gesture was both gratifying and painful for Chris to watch, so much did it signal of his son's new state: his prior foolishness acknowledged, his childhood over, his place in a Mafia family weighted with secrets and hidden dangers.

"Yes," the boy answered.

"Where is she now?"

"She's home. She said she'd take the train in if you wanted her to."

"Good. Call her. We'll go up to Josie's for lunch. She loves that place."

"Where should I tell her to meet us?"

"At the fountain in front of the Plaza. When you see her, just act normal. I don't want her to have the faintest clue as to what's happened. If she asks about Joseph, I'll tell her he took a trip someplace. Do you understand?"

"Yes, I do."

"Good. Make the call, then we'll take a walk. I have to see a lawyer over on Fifth Avenue. Tess won't be here for an hour at least."

11.

Two weeks later, Chris and Michele were in the Cherokee heading east on the Long Island Expressway. Chris had retained a lawyer, a woman named Barbara Lopez, a former colleague of his at the U.S. Attorney's office who years before left to start what was now one of the most successful family law practices in Manhattan. Barbara had quickly learned that Grace Mathias, now six, was living in a foster home in Glen Cove on Long Island, under an emergency court order that was typical in cases of egregious parental neglect. The order, a copy of which Chris gave to Michele, was renewable every six months on application from Child Welfare Services. It did not terminate Michele's parental rights and specifically permitted her to petition the court at any time "for good cause" for the return of custody of Grace to her.

Barbara Lopez' advice had been succinct: "She's in a foster home with five other kids. Some people make their living that way. The law favors the natural mother, but she has to be clean and she has to act soon, otherwise, Child Welfare will argue that the kid has bonded with the foster parents, has school ties, etc. It would help if she had a job and was in a court-sanctioned treatment program, where they can monitor her urine. If she's willing to do all this, she can get her daughter back."

"I can get you a job," Chris said, "but it's more for me than for you."

"What does that mean?"

"It's at a restaurant where Junior Boy sometimes has dinner. I need to gain entry. That's where you come in."

Michele remained silent. They had come to the beginning of one of the major construction projects that seem to be endlessly underway on the Expressway and were now in stop-and-go traffic. Unnerved by the thought of facing Grace, of seeing fear and loathing in her daughter's eyes, she had resisted Chris' attempts to persuade her to act immediately regarding custody. Even though Chris had offered to pay all expenses, including lawyers' fees and the cost of a good rehab program, she had refused to budge. Last night, torn between two fears—of losing Chris and of facing her daughter—she had agreed to go with him to Glen Cove.

"Why don't I just bring a gun to work and kill him for you?" she said, and then added, when Chris did not answer immediately, "I'm kidding, of course."

"I was thinking maybe you could plant a gun someplace," Chris said, "but when he has dinner there, they close the place to the public, and I'm sure they search it thoroughly and sweep it for bugs."

"So what can I do?"

"Vinnie knows the owner. He can get you hired. You have to make an impression of a key. I'll show you how. Then you have to let me know when Junior Boy books the place. That's all."

"Will they let me have Grace back if I'm an accessory to murder?"

"You're already an accessory to three murders."

"They weren't premeditated, which means I'm still a good mother."

"Michele, will you help me or not?"

"Yes, I'll help you. I'm good at waiting tables. And helping you kill people."

"Are you nervous about seeing the lawyer?"

"Yes. I'm doing it for you."

"So you've said."

The traffic was beginning to un-jam, and Chris concentrated for a moment on getting into a lane that was moving better than the others. He had lowered the windows while they were stuck in traffic and turned off the air conditioner. When they were up to speed again, he did the reverse, and the noises of the busy highway were blocked out.

In the quiet of the moving car, he thought about their last exchange. Michele's feelings for him were tangled up with her post-withdrawal anxiety and her fear of failing again as a mother. But when was love not tangled up with other feelings? If things happened for a reason, then why wouldn't life's biggest thing – falling in love – happen for the most important of reasons? By admitting her need for him, wasn't Michele simply admitting she needed his love – his particular love – to heal the wounds of a lifetime? And where was the person walking the earth who did not have a lifetime worth of wounds?

"I don't want us to end," Michele said, breaking into these thoughts.

"We won't."

"Do you mean that?"

"Think about it. Think about what we've been through. We're glued together by all that."

"What about Grace?"

"What about her?"

"Why would you want her in your life?"

"Because she's your daughter. Because she belongs to you."

"I'm not sure if I want her in my life. Why can't you accept that?"

Because if I accept that, then I'm not sure I want you, Chris thought. Out loud he said, "There's something you should know. There's no lawyer in Glen Cove. I'm taking you to see Grace. She's in a summer school program. Recess is at eleven-thirty. I was going to spring this on you, force you to look at her through the fence, but now you have a choice. We can turn around if you want."

"Fuck," was Michele's answer.

"I thought it would be easier for you this way."

"What kind of summer program?"

"I'm not sure. Barbara Lopez is trying to get the records."

"Is she slow?"

"I don't know. It might just be a way for the foster parents to get free day care. We can turn around if you want to."

"If we turn around, you'll hate me."

"I won't hate you," *but I'll lose respect for you, which in my world is worse*, Chris thought, and, looking at Michele as she stared straight ahead, the set of her face grim, he knew she was thinking the same thing.

"Why are you doing this to me, Chris?"

"I told you, you were available to be rescued. I like to finish what I start. Of course I didn't plan on falling on love with you."

"Love that involves rescue doesn't last."

"Who said that?"

"I did."

They were silent for a while, thinking their separate thoughts as the car passed another exit on the highway.

"I'm worried you'll get killed," Michele said.

"That's a possibility."

"Where's the restaurant?"

"It's on Canal Street over by the river."

"What's your plan?"

"The restroom is in a storeroom in the back. There's a door in the storeroom that goes out to an alley, a small street actually, which Vinnie says is big enough for a car. It leads to the back of some tenements. I'll go in that door and wait for Junior Boy to use the bathroom."

"That's the key you want."

"Yes."

"You'll just walk down the alley?"

"No. The place will be guarded. I'll have to figure something out."

"What if DiGiglio doesn't go back?"

"He will. I'll wait."

"And stay with me?"

"Yes."

More silence.

"Are we turning around?" Chris said. "We're almost at the exit."

"No," Michele replied. "There's no fighting this."

Glen Cove, once a vital commercial and retail hub servicing Gold Coast communities like Lattingtown and Locust Valley, had, by 2003, lost whatever individual character it once had to the suburban sprawl that had swept from west to east across Long Island like a plague since the end of the Second World War. Its downtown was bleak and quiet and strangely inaccessible, and the surrounding neighborhoods were a jarring mix of lovely old homesteads and cookie-cutter tract housing.

Chris, who had been here the week before, showed Michele the small ranch – one of fifty or so of the same size, shape and style – where Grace lived, and then drove to the nearby Cole School, a retro red brick affair tucked into a sagging, crowded neighborhood that looked more like parts of Brooklyn than suburban Long Island. On one side of the school was a small parking lot, on the other an unimpressive asphalt-covered playground surrounded by a chain-link fence. The building, as they circled it looking for a parking space, seemed too quiet as it sat baking in the late morning sun, and Chris hoped he had not chosen a holiday of some sort.

He parked on a side street. As they were walking toward the perimeter of the playground, a bell clanged, and a moment later, thirty or so children poured out of the school's side door, held open by a tall, angular black woman carrying a clipboard and a brown paper bag. Michele took hold of Chris' arm as she scanned this noisy crowd, and he felt her stiffen at the sight of two little girls, one blonde, one brunette, who were among the last to emerge. These two stopped and talked for a moment, and then the blonde ran off toward the group of wooden picnic tables where most of the kids were settling in to their lunch. The brunette turned and went back into the building.

"Is that her?" Chris asked, looking toward the blonde, who had found a seat on an empty bench.

"No," Michele answered. "She's the dark one."

Chris felt the pressure on his arm increase.

"Where did she go?" Michele asked in a soft, barely audible voice.

"I don't know," Chris answered. "She'll come out again."

A moment later, she did, this time carrying the lunch box she had apparently forgotten. When she emerged into the bright daylight, she stopped for a second and looked toward Chris and Michele, shading her eyes with her free hand.

"We're too far away," Chris said, feeling Michele's nails digging into his biceps. "She can't recognize you."

And then Grace was in motion again, running toward the picnic tables, where she joined the blonde girl on the seat saved for her.

"She has a friend," Michele said, releasing her death grip on Chris' arm.

"It looks that way."

The kids quickly ate their lunches and then dispersed to various areas of the schoolyard, leaving the teacher, her back to Chris and Michele, alone at a picnic table, flipping through the papers on her clipboard while slowly eating a sandwich. Grace and her friend ran to an aluminum sliding board where the blonde girl joined the line of kids waiting their turn. Grace sat on the ground nearby and watched her classmates climb the ladder and rush down the slide, some at daredevil angles, some in twos, squeezing together stomach to back. Their shouts and laughter drifted on the hot air to Chris and Michele.

"Why isn't she playing?" Michele asked, but before Chris could answer, the blonde spilled off the end of the slide, ran to Grace and, pulling her up by her hands, ran with her to the end of the line. In a few seconds, they were at the top of the ladder and then flying down together, their hair streaming behind them. Jumping up, they returned quickly to the end of the line. After their third tandem slide, they walked together holding hands to a nearby bench, where they sat and talked, sometimes putting their heads together the way little girls do. At the lunch area, the teacher was getting up, straightening out benches and looking at her watch.

"We should go," Chris said, taking Michele by the arm, "someone will see us and think we're up to no good."

In the car, Michele rolled down her window to take a last look at Grace, who, along with the rest of the class, was grabbing her lunch box and lining up to return inside.

"I could move out here," she said, her eyes still on her daughter. "She can keep her friend."

"It would probably be a good idea if you were living here when Barbara Lopez files her petition with the court."

"Would you come and visit me?"

"Of course."

Michele watched intently until Grace was in the building, then turned in her seat to face Chris and said, "I'll take that waitressing job first."

"You don't have to. You could move now if you want. I'll find another way to get in."

"No," Michele said. "We're a team."

"An unlikely team, but you're right."

Chris started the car and was about to pull away from the curb, when Michele put her hand on his arm to stop him.

"Chris," she said.

"Yes."

She was silent for a second, lightly caressing the puckered scars remaining from Chris' burn wounds, as if attempting to divine in them the future or, at least, the combination of words that would correctly express her thoughts.

"Do your wounds still hurt?"

"Yes," he replied, thinking of Joe Black and Rose and Joseph, of all of the hurt that family can pile on as it burns its way across the years from one generation to the next. "And I need you to help me heal them."

12.

Chris picked his cell phone up in the middle of its first ring.

"They've arrived," Vinnie Rosamelia said at the other end.

"Good. Who's on the corner?"

"It looks like the same guy."

"Not Nicky or Joe Pace?"

"No."

"We're leaving."

Chris snapped the phone shut, then turned to John Farrell, who was sitting on the couch, and said, "Are you ready?"

"Yes, I'm ready"

"Then let's go, before the car gets towed."

Chris locked the door to Michele's apartment – they had moved into it six weeks ago, on their return from their trip to Long Island – and he and the old man headed down the stairs and across the street to the ten-year-old blue Chevy sedan that belonged to LaSalle Academy and that Farrell had borrowed for the evening. A week earlier, Michele had moved to Glen Cove. She had done her job: worked for five weeks at Sorrento, the restaurant on Canal Street, made an impression of the key to the back door using her makeup case, which Vinnie had lined with clay, told of Junior Boy's first visit, and then of the second one, scheduled for tonight.

On the night of the first visit, Chris and Vinnie had driven by to check out the security arrangements, which were simple enough: Nicky Spags and Joe Pace at the front door and a slender but obviously hardened and experienced soldier at the corner of the alley. Yesterday, with Farrell in civilian clothes, he and Chris had made a dry run. Tonight, in his clerical garb, Farrell was a priest who had been called to give the last rites to a parishioner living in one of the tenements at the end of the alley.

On the back seat of the Chevy, there was a folded canvass tarp, several gallon cans of house paint, trays, brushes and other tools of the painter's trade. Chris lay down on the floor and Farrell covered him with the tarp. The Saturday night special – a .22 caliber Beretta – that Vinnie had purchased for him, was tucked into the waist of Chris' jeans. On its barrel was a silencer fashioned from a cardboard toilet paper tube and duct tape. The drive to Canal Street, through a light, misty rain, took fifteen minutes. To Chris, it seemed endless, fifteen minutes in the dark on the floor of a moving car being more than enough time to confront his fears and to review his life.

His nuclear family – as outside-the-box as any in history – paraded across his mind's eye. It hurt him to think that of them; it was only Joseph he knew at all and only because Joseph had given his life for him and then penetrated his heart from the grave with his letter. By his children, he hoped he had done well and tried to think only of the love and concern on their faces when he saw them last six weeks ago. As to women, there were only two, Teresa and Michele. Teresa was a surprise, but in the dark, Chris understood that his passion for Michele must have run along the same long forgotten channels through which he and Teresa had connected twenty years ago. It was with great relief, and a strange sense of freedom, that Chris heard John Farrell say, after the longest journey of his life, "The restaurant's just up ahead, I see our man."

●

To John Farrell, whose cancer had spread to his brain, the ride was all too brief. He had refused chemotherapy and been told the week before by his physician to expect to die in "two or three weeks, maybe four." He had missed out in helping Chris do away with Ed Dolan, and this hurt even more when Chris told him about Dolan cutting the brake line on his car on that long ago but vividly remembered night twenty-seven years past. Tonight, he felt redeemed, his belief in God resurrected. On the verge of death, he wanted nothing more than to live fully until his strength was gone, and what better way to do that than to play a key role in the execution of a plot to murder a Mafia don? Since he had been given his fatal diagnosis of inoperable lung cancer, only three short months ago, John Farrell had thought long and hard about how he wanted to die, and now the universe, in the form of Chris Massi, comes along and hands him a choice: lay on his back and say the rosary for a month or two, his senses dulled by morphine, or walk onto the stage in a modern and very real passion play. He had swiftly chosen the latter. As he negotiated his way carefully across Lower Manhattan, the hazy glare of the headlights from on-coming vehicles penetrated his skull through his eyes like a knife. He had recently succumbed to the dire need for codeine tablets to ease his pain, spreading the dosages out to the last possible unbearable second. Today, he had not taken any, and yet the pain had somehow subsided. He knew that later, or tomorrow, it would return with a vengeance and so drove slowly. Nevertheless, he drew nearer each minute to his destination and, when almost there, was forced to say, in a voice that sounded too loud and too strong to be his own, "The restaurant's just ahead, I see our man."

In the ten or twelve times that Junior Boy and his top people had had dinner at Sorrento, no one had ever driven in or out of the small, unnamed street that was only fifty feet from the restaurant's entrance on Canal. Still, Phil Purcell, the trusted soldier who had so professionally executed Woody Smith, had no reason to doubt the frail old priest in the battered Chevrolet when he stopped him to ask him his business. For his part, John Farrell had no trouble acting the innocuous old man, hoping only that the pounding in his chest could not be heard and that his words were not as shaky as they sounded.

Halfway down the alley, the car was shrouded in complete darkness. At the end, Farrell parked diagonally to a group of overflowing garbage cans and, as planned, got out and went up the rickety steps of the tenement straight ahead. Perched on the landing, in deep shadow, he peered toward the street until he was certain the guard was not looking his way, then lit a cigarette and quickly threw it down and stamped it out, his signal to Chris that all was clear.

Chris, his jeans and black shirt matching the darkness, emerged slowly from the car, staying on his knees at first to get his bearings and adjust his eyes to the misty night. At the corner, about a hundred feet away, he could see a man in a dark trench coat, holding an umbrella, standing motionless in the rain with his back to the alley. Hugging the brick wall to his right – like someone escaping from prison in a B movie – he was about halfway to Sorrento's back door when Nicky Spags, his profile painfully clear in the cone of the street light on the corner, joined the man in the trench coat and, offering him a cigarette, tried several times to light it for him under the umbrella. When this could not be done, the two men turned and headed down the alley toward Chris, who put his hand to the handle of the Beretta and pressed his back closer to the wall. Nick and the tall soldier stopped after a few steps, and this time they managed to light the cigarette. Nick lit one for himself, and the two men stood and chatted for a minute, which seemed like an hour to Chris. When Nick left, the guard resumed his position on the corner, and swiftly, Chris made it to the door, where, using the key Vinnie had had made from Michele's clay impression – taking one last look at the guard – he unlocked the deadbolt and slipped inside.

Once inside, Chris put the key back into his pocket, returned the deadbolt to its locked position and surveyed his surroundings. They were as he expected them to be from Michele's description. He was in a small room with a cement floor and a high exposed ceiling from which swung a lone fluorescent fixture, not on. There was a stack of boxes about four feet high and several feet long to his left. Restaurant supplies filled the rough wooden shelves that lined the sheet-rocked but unfinished walls. The bathroom door was to his right. The door to the restaurant was straight ahead. It was closed, but light from the outer hall seeped weakly into the storeroom around its perimeter, which enabled Chris to get his bearings. He crouched behind the wall of cardboard boxes, moving one slightly so that he could see through them to the entry door. Then he checked his watch and sat Indian style to wait.

Over the next hour, several men came in to use the john, including Aldo and Rocco Stabile. Aldo had flicked on the overhead light when he entered, using the wall switch to his right, and no one bothered to turn it off. The don entered a few minutes later. While he was peeing, Chris rose and, moving quickly, carried two of the cardboard boxes – one of cans of peeled tomatoes, the other of gallon tins of olive oil – and stacked them against the door. He was standing outside the bathroom, the Beretta in his right hand, the safety off, aimed at the door, when Junior Boy emerged, smoothing the lapels of his conservatively cut, banker-gray suit. There was no mistaking the unguarded weariness on the don's lined and craggy face in the instant before he looked up and saw a gun pointed at him; nor the total comprehension and quiet command that shone immediately in his eyes when he saw who was holding that gun.

"I've been expecting you to turn up," Junior Boy said, his tone conversational, as if they were resuming a prior dialogue.

"You have to answer for Joseph, Junior Boy."

"I understand how you feel, but you're making a mistake."

"Where's his body?"

"On some property we own in the Catskills. I sent a priest up there a couple of weeks ago to give him a proper burial."

"You're kidding."

"No, I'm not. I didn't kill your brother, Chris. He killed himself. Suicide by Mafia, you could call it."

"He thought Dolan would save him."

"Maybe. He was cursed, your brother. It fell to him to pay Joe Black's cosmic debts. I had to kill him, you know that."

"Just as you know I have to kill you."

"No, that I don't know. Kill me for some other reason, but not to avenge Joseph."

"I don't have another reason."

"Then you can't pull that trigger. It would be a senseless murder. You'd be in the gutter with the rest of the scum."

I could easily kill this old man, Chris thought, and escape into the night. No one would ever know it was me. But why? To be able to kill – with or without mercy – is one thing. But to kill without honor, what does that make me?

"If it's any consolation," the don said, "your brother died like a man."

"The same way you'll die if I pull this trigger."

"Yes, exactly."

They're all gone, Chris thought, Joe Black, Rose, Joseph, abruptly, in the middle of lives they couldn't finish. Why is that? Why didn't I get the chance to say goodbye to any of them?

"Would you have killed me?" Chris asked.

"You didn't threaten me or my family."

"Yes, but what if I had?"

The two men, nearly the same height, stared at each other. A spark of recognition, of understanding, flashed quickly across Chris' mind. He thought he saw the same spark come and go in the old man's eyes. *Anthony DiGiglio had never had a son.*

"I would not have harmed you," the don answered, finally.

Chris eased his finger off of the Beretta's trigger, flicked the safety on with his thumb and lowered his hand.

"There's been enough bloodshed," he said.

"No, Chris, don't fool yourself. Don't spare me for humanitarian reasons. They're the worst and most evil of all reasons not to kill. Think of Dolan and Labrutto and Rodriguez. If you had spared them, they would have gone on to wreak more havoc."

"I have to go. Someone will realize you're taking too long."

"One last thing."

"What?"

"Succeed me as the head of the family."

"What?"

"I'm offering you my job, with my blessing, which guarantees your acceptance."

"You're not serious."

"I've never been more serious. Have you thought about what you'll do with your life? Even if you could, would you go back to lawyering after what you've done? It seems trite, doesn't it? You know the Mafia culture, our culture. You were raised in it. You can kill, and you can think. In fact, you're a brilliant thinker. And you're brave. How else to explain your presence in this room, with a gun pointed at me, the great don, with a dozen of my loyal retainers – all killers – just on the other side of that door?"

Before Chris could answer, there was loud knocking on the storeroom door, and Aldo DiGiglio said, in a raised voice, "June, are you okay?"

"Yes," Junior Boy answered. "Come in."

The door was stopped at first by the boxes, but Aldo shoved his shoulder against it, which forced the boxes back, knocking the one on top to the floor. This seemed to startle Aldo, who burst into the room with his gun drawn.

"You were taking too long," he said, surveying the scene before him, pointing his gun at Chris' chest. "I heard voices."

"It's okay," the don replied. "Put your gun away. I'm having a conversation."

"June...," Aldo said, his eyes on Chris' gun.

"I invited him here," Junior Boy said. "He brought the gun to protect himself. You can go. Tell Rocco to bring Phil and Nicky and Joe Pace back here."

Aldo, incredulous, did not move at first, but then he saw the look on his older brother's face, a look that chilled him tonight as it had whenever he had the misfortune to be exposed to it over the last sixty-odd years.

"Is the grave marked?" Chris asked, when Aldo was gone.

"We can't do that, Chris, you know that. But I can have someone lead you to it."

"What about Barsonetti?"

"I've been waiting to have this conversation."

Chris nodded.

"If you accept my offer," Junior Boy said, "you can order it. If not, I'll take care of it."

"Aldo hates me."

"He's retiring, too. He doesn't know it yet, but he is. Frank, too."

"Matt's coming with me, regardless."

"No one will stand in the way of that, whatever you decide."

"How long have you been thinking about this proposal?"

"Since you showed up at Benevento and played your hand."

"Did you know I'd come after you?"

"I thought you would."

"What if I just pulled the trigger?"

"Then I'd be dead, and you'd have a different life ahead of you. But you didn't."

"No, I didn't."

There was a knock on the door, and Junior Boy said, "Wait."

And then to Chris he said, "You can go. Think about what I said."

"I'll think about it," Chris answered, and then he turned and left. Outside the rain was coming down harder, soaking Chris through to the skin as he ran the fifty feet or so to the car. Inside, in the driver's seat, John Farrell was slumped against the steering wheel, dead.

EPILOGUE
Stone Ridge, New York, September 7, 2003

"Thanks, Rocco, you can wait in the car."

Chris and Matt watched the husky Rocco Stabile turn and walk, with surprising grace, even daintiness, back along the rough, overgrown forest path that they had followed to their destination. When he disappeared in the thick woods, Chris looked down at the spot Rocco had pointed out and then, beyond the tree line, out over the verdant valley below to the rolling brown and green hills in the distance. His hip younger brother left Manhattan only to travel to other cities, usually Las Vegas or Miami Beach, but he would spend eternity overlooking a bucolic valley dotted with cows and haystacks. Chris could only smile at the irony and hoped Joseph was smiling, too.

"Help me carry some rocks over," Chris said. "There's a stone wall over there."

A half hour later, working slowly in the late summer heat, they had laid six rocks of varying sizes and shapes in the form of a very crude cross on the grave. Matt sat on the biggest one to rest when they were done, while Chris surveyed their work, which in a week or two, would look more like a random group of rocks than anything else.

"It'll have to do," Chris said.

Matt remained silent. Two days ago, he had moved into his Chris' apartment in Tribeca. The next day, a Saturday, Tess had come in and they had gone out and gotten him some things for his room and some new clothes. Chris had made it clear that from today on, after their visit to Joseph's grave, there would be no more talk of the Mafia or the DiGiglio family. All signs of Matt's previous attitude had vanished and were replaced by a steady and serious demeanor in which Chris saw much of himself as a boy. Last night, his son, with only the vaguest idea of what it took to be a runner, had announced that he would be trying out for the freshman cross-country team when he started at LaSalle on Wednesday.

"Go on back to the car, Matt," Chris said. "I'd like a few minutes alone here."

Matt got up and, turning to Chris, said, "Dad?"

"Yes?"

"I think we should call Marsha."

"We can't bring her here."

"I know, but we should call her."

"Sure, we'll call her this week."

When Matt was out of sight, Chris sat on the big rock and, picking up some pebbles, began sifting them through his hands. Among the mail that Vinnie Rosamelia had brought over to his apartment on Friday was a letter from Karen Pierce, informing Chris that an investigation into Ed Dolan's case files had revealed serious improprieties in his handling of *U.S. V. Massi* and in the role Dolan played in Chris' disbarment proceedings. She invited him to come to her office, with his lawyer, to discuss the action that needed to be taken to get Chris' license restored and – "to the extent possible in an imperfect world" – his name cleared.

A week before, he and Michele had attended John Farrell's funeral at a Christian Brothers retreat house near Troy, New York. Michele was working for a catering company in Glen Cove, living in two rooms above their kitchen and going to rehab meetings three nights a week. After the funeral, they had driven back to Manhattan to Barbara Lopez' office where Michele signed the petition Barbara would file with the court for the return of custody of Grace. Three days ago, Chris had driven to Belleville, New Jersey, where he had given Antoinette Scarpa a check for twenty-five thousand dollars, and, crying, she had found and handed him the half-dozen letters Joe Black had written to her then-nineteen-year-old husband during his first stretch in prison. Chris had forgotten about those letters in the turmoil of his recent life. They now lay on his dresser, waiting to be read.

"I wish I had thought to protect you, Joseph," Chris said, getting to his feet. "If I had, you might be alive today, but I thought only of criticizing you. I won't make the same mistake with Matt. He did not choose his parents. Whatever I have to do to keep him safe, I'll do it. In your name."

Then Chris rolled the pebbles in his hand one last time, threw them on the grave, turned, and headed back to the waiting car.

Dear Reader,

The three novels that I call The Tristate Trilogy (*A World I Never Made*, *Blood of My Brother* and *Sons and Princes*) are connected not by characters or sequential plots, but by theme: the existential struggle against the demons, internal and external, that assail the human heart.

In *A World I Never Made*, though they didn't know it at the time, their own bitterness was as much an adversary to Pat and Megan Nolan as the terrorists that pursued them.

Jay Cassio and Isabel Perez in *Blood of My Brother*, were forced to fight not just the professional killers of a Mexican drug cartel, but the despair that threatened to kill their spirits.

And it was Chris Massi's pride in *Sons and Princes* that caused his world to shatter. He thought he had beaten the odds: of having a hit man for a father, a junkie for a brother, a Mafia princess for an ex-wife. But he hadn't. Humbled, he chose to fight back, and there, his story, his path to redemption, begins.

In the short stories I wrote to accompany *A World I Never Made* and *Blood of My Brother*, my intention was to explore not internal struggle, but the forces at work that shape the adult heart, the staging ground so to speak for the battle to come. The past as prelude.

The first of these, together in a small volume called *Anyone Can Die*, published in February, 2011, reach into the past, to incidents in the lives of the central characters of *A World I Never Made*.

I did the same in the trio of stories I wrote to accompany *Blood of My Brother*, collected in a volume entitled, *The Man In The Black Suit*, which will be released in June, 2011.

As I look ahead to the writing of the novella that will accompany *Sons and Princes*, it does not escape me that Chris Massi's future may be more interesting to readers, and more fun to write about, than his past.

James LePore
South Salem